W9-ATT-172

Table of Contents

Forever You

Denny drove us to the restaurant, where we met Peyton and Henry for dinner. They were already sitting down in a booth when we arrived. The waitress showed us to our seats, and Ellery stood there, looking at the booth.

"What's wrong?" I asked.

"There's no way I'm going to fit in there." She frowned.

Ellery was big, and she looked like she was going to give birth any day.

"Elle, I'm sorry. I should have requested a table. I don't want you squishing my goddaughter." Peyton laughed.

I called the waitress over and told her we needed a table. She accommodated us immediately. We sat down, and I asked Ellery if she was okay. She looked at me as we both started laughing about her not being able to fit in the booth.

"I better lose all this weight," she said.

"We'll go to the gym together, and I'll hire you a personal trainer," I said.

Peyton grabbed Henry's hand and told us they had an announcement. She held out her left hand and showed off her exquisite engagement ring. Ellery wanted to jump up and hug her, but she couldn't.

"Peyton, it's gorgeous! Congratulations!" she exclaimed.

I got up from my seat, kissed Peyton on the cheek, and shook Henry's hand. "Congratulations to both of you, and may you have a wonderful life together," I toasted as we all held up our glasses of wine, with the exception of Ellery; she had water. Ellery turned to me and gave me a look as if she was trying to figure something out.

"You knew, didn't you?" she asked.

"Knew what?"

"You knew Henry was going to ask Peyton to marry him, and you didn't tell me." She glared.

I smiled and that was enough to let her know that I knew. "Of course I knew. Who do you think went with him to pick out the ring?" I laughed.

"Wow, Connor, how could you not tell me?"

"Maybe because it was a surprise, and I know you. You would've called Peyton and told her about the ring."

"No, I wouldn't have," she said.

"Yes, you would've, and then you would've told her to act surprised," I said as I kissed her cheek.

Peyton looked at Ellery. "He's right; you probably would've," she said.

"I know, I would've," she said as she rolled her eyes.

The waitress brought our meals to the table. I looked over at Ellery, but she wasn't eating like she normally did. She was picking at her chicken. "You okay, baby?" I asked.

"I'm fine, honey. I'm just not very hungry." She smiled as she turned to me.

Henry and I talked about sports as Peyton and Ellery threw around some ideas for the wedding. We had a nice dinner, and we were in the company of great friends. I couldn't ask for a better evening. I ordered us another round of drinks and dessert for everyone. The waitress had been flirting with me and Henry all night. She brought the desserts to the table and brushed up against me with her breasts.

"Excuse me," Peyton said. "I saw what you just did, and don't think I haven't noticed what you've been doing all night. That man right there, that you just boob-brushed, is married with a baby on the way, and this man right here is my fiancé. If his wife wasn't about to give birth, she would have kicked your ass by now. So back off our men, and go find someone who isn't already taken." The waitress glared at her and then looked at Ellery.

"Yeah, what she said," Ellery spat.

The waitress turned and walked away in a huff. Henry took Peyton's hand and started laughing. Ellery put her hand on my leg under the table and squeezed it. I looked over at her as she stared at me.

"Connor, my water just broke; it's time," she said.

Chapter 1

Ellery

Connor stared at me as if he didn't understand what I'd just told him.

"What did you say?" he asked.

"My water broke, Connor. The baby's coming. We need to get to the hospital," I said as slowly as I could.

He jumped up out of his chair and helped me out of mine as he looked at Henry and Peyton.

"Her water broke. It's time!" he exclaimed.

Peyton quickly got up from her seat and ran over to me, while Henry remained calm.

"OMG! It's time! Henry, what do we do?" Peyton asked in a panic.

"Everyone relax," he said. "Ellery, are you having any pain yet?"

"No, not yet."

"Okay, good. Let's get in my car, and we'll get you over to the hospital." Henry smiled.

Connor put his arm around me as he guided me out of the restaurant. Before we made it to Henry's car, I abruptly stopped and doubled over in pain.

"HOLY SHIT!" I screamed.

Connor stopped with me and put his hands on my stomach.

"It's okay, baby. Breathe in and out, like we learned in our class."

I nodded my head and did what Connor said as the pain started to subside. Henry and Peyton told us to wait while they pulled the car up. When Henry drove up to the curb, Connor opened the door for me, and I slid in the back seat. He shut the door and walked around to the other side. Connor climbed in, sat beside me, and pulled out his phone to call Denny. After he hung up, he reached over and pulled me into him.

"I can't believe our daughter is coming," he said as he kissed my head.

I buried my face into Connor's neck as another contraction started. The pain was unbearable; it was worse than my cancer treatments, and I didn't think that could be possible. Connor held my hand and kept telling me to breathe. I swore I was going to lose it if he said it one more time. Peyton kept turning around and looking at me from the front seat.

"Are you all right, Elle?"

"Do I look like I'm all right, Peyton?" I said with gritted teeth.

It seemed like it took forever to get to the hospital. Once we arrived at the ER, Henry got a wheelchair, and Connor helped me from the car. I had only had a couple of contractions, and I was already wishing this was over. Connor wheeled me inside, and Henry led us up to the Labor and Delivery unit. Stopping at the unit desk, Henry gave them my name as the clerk showed us to my room. She handed me a cloth gown and said a nurse would be in shortly.

I changed into the cloth gown that was all too familiar to me. Connor helped me as Peyton and Henry stepped out of the room. I could feel another contraction coming, and I bit my bottom lip as tears started to fill my eyes. A nurse walked into the room and looked at me and Connor. It was Nurse Bailey. She looked at me with a smile as she walked over and patted my hand.

"It's good to see you again, sweetie." She smiled. She turned and looked at Connor. "Are you still the friend?" she asked.

Connor grinned, as he replied, "No; I'm the husband."

Nurse Bailey smiled and nodded her head. "Very good. I'm glad to see things worked out for the two of you. I knew they would."

She turned back to me as she hooked me up to the fetal monitor. "Look at you! You're having a baby." She smiled.

I tried to smile back, but another contraction was starting. I bit down on my bottom lip as Connor grabbed my hand. Peyton and Henry walked back into the room, and Peyton rushed to my side.

"I paged your doctor, Ellery, but I haven't heard anything yet," Henry said.

"Who's your doctor, sweetie?" Nurse Bailey asked.

"Dr. Keller!" I yelled through the pain.

"Dr. Keller had a family emergency yesterday and had to leave town for a few days. His partner, Dr. Reed, is taking care of his patients. I'll go call him," she said as she patted my hand and left the room.

The contraction ended, and I felt like I could breathe again. Connor sat on the edge of the bed and softly kissed my lips.

"I love you," he whispered.

"I love you too," I whispered back.

Henry walked over and explained to us how the fetal

monitor worked. He showed us at which point a contraction was starting, when it was at its peak, and when it was ending. Connor looked intrigued as he studied it. Peyton and Henry left the room to grab some coffee and to bring me back some ice chips.

"Can you believe Nurse Bailey is my nurse?"

"No, baby, I can't believe it. But I'm glad she is."

"Me too." I smiled.

"Look at our daughter's heartbeat," Connor said as he pointed to the number on the fetal monitor.

I smiled as I looked over at it and another contraction began. I grabbed Connor's arm and dug my nails into his skin. Did I feel bad? No, the pain of my nails is nothing compared to the pain of childbirth.

"Breathe, baby." He smiled at me as he stroked my forehead.

Peyton and Henry walked into the room with a cup of ice chips. She took one out and started rubbing it across my lips.

"Maybe this will help you feel better," she said.

"The only thing that's going to help me feel better is getting this baby out of me!"

Nurse Bailey walked in and said she needed to examine me. Henry and Peyton stepped out of the room again while Connor sat on the edge of the bed next to me, holding my hand. She explained that she needed to see how much I was dilated. When she finished, she looked at me and pursed her lips.

"Hmm, you're only dilated to one centimeter. You said your water broke while you were at the restaurant, correct?"

"Yes, I was sitting down at the restaurant when it broke," I replied.

Nurse Bailey looked directly at Connor. "You didn't by chance have sex today, did you?"

I looked at Connor, and he looked at me. "This is your fault!" I said.

"My fault? You're the one who invited me to take a shower with you before we left for the restaurant."

"Just relax, Ellery. Everything will be fine. I don't want you to worry," she said as she walked out of the room.

* * * *

A few hours passed, and I wasn't any further along. The contractions were getting worse, and Nurse Bailey stepped out of the room to call Dr. Reed. Henry was keeping a close eye on the fetal monitor, as was Connor.

I was lying on my side, and Connor wiped my forehead with a cool cloth. A contraction had just ended. I let out a deep breath and closed my eyes. I felt Connor kiss me softly on the forehead as he pushed back my hair.

"Get ready, Elle. Here comes another contraction," he said as he stared at the monitor.

"Why do you have to tell me, Connor?!" I yelled.

"I want you to be prepared so you can start your breathing. I don't want you to be caught off-guard."

Every bit of me wanted to kill him at that moment. The pain with each contraction was intensifying, and I felt like my body was trying to rip itself in two. As always, he was right and another contraction came.

"Breathe, Elle. Come on, baby; deep breaths."

"Connor, I think you better lay off; she's getting pissed," Peyton said.

I started screaming in pain. I promised myself that I wasn't going to be one of *those* women, but at that moment, I didn't care. I didn't care who heard me, and I didn't care what they thought. Connor was still telling me to breathe, and that was the straw that broke the camel's back.

"Tell me to breathe one more time, and I swear I'll castrate you, Connor Black!" I screamed.

I heard Peyton burst into laughter, and Connor looked at me.

"Wow, Elle. That was uncalled for," he said.

"No! What's uncalled for is you making me feel worse than I already do. I don't want to know when another contraction is coming! I don't want you to tell me to breathe! I know you're trying to help me, but all I need from you, babe, is silence."

Connor stared at me and took my face in his hands. "I'm sorry, baby. I didn't mean—"

"I know you didn't, Connor. It just hurts so bad, and I want it to be over," I said as I interrupted him.

"I know you do, and I can't wait to see our daughter. She's going to be beautiful, just like her mother." He smiled.

A tear fell from the corner of my eye and down my cheek as another contraction started; the worse one yet. I looked over at Henry.

"Please, Henry, give me an epidural. Please, I'm begging you."

"Ellery, I can't. You're not dilated yet. I'm sorry," he said as he shook his head.

I wanted to die. This baby was tearing me apart inside, and something didn't feel right. Nurse Bailey walked in and told Henry that Dr. Reed asked her to call him when I was dilated to five centimeters. Connor sighed, got up from the bed, and walked over to Henry.

"How much longer is she going to be like this?" he asked.

"Every woman is different, Connor. It's hard to tell. She's not even dilated to three yet. This could go on for another twenty-four hours."

"WHAT!" I exclaimed.

Peyton took my hand and started rubbing it softly. "Don't worry, Elle. We're here to help you through this."

Connor turned and looked at me. He tilted his head and gave me a small smile as he walked over and sat on the edge of the bed. "If I could have this baby for you, I would. I hate seeing you in so much pain," he said as he grabbed my hand and brought it to his lips.

"I love you, Connor," I whispered as I closed my eyes and braced myself for the next contraction.

"I love you, Ellery."

Chapter 2

Connor

Seeing Ellery in pain like that was killing me. My heart ached for her with every scream she let out and every tear that fell from her eyes. I called my mom, dad, and Cassidy to let them know that Ellery had gone into labor. They stopped in the room for a few minutes to talk to her and then took seats out in the waiting room. Ellery and I had discussed that we didn't want anyone else in the room during the delivery. Peyton had a hard time with our decision at first, but then understood. As Peyton and Ellery talked in between contractions, Henry asked me to step out into the hall.

"I don't want you to worry, but Ellery isn't dilating like she should be. I'm getting concerned because her water broke, and I don't want to risk an infection setting in. I think we need to let her get up and do some walking around to try and get her dilated."

"You tell me not to worry, but you're worried about an infection," I said.

"I'll call Dr. Reed and ask him what he advises," he said as he put his hand on my shoulder. "I'm watching her and the baby very carefully."

"Thanks for keeping me posted, Henry." I sighed as I walked back into the room.

Ellery was lying on her side, panting and trying to breathe through another contraction as she squeezed Peyton's hand. I walked over to her, sat on the edge of the bed, and grabbed her other hand.

"Ellery, look at me. I need you to focus on me, not the pain."

She nodded her head and looked at me as her pain continued to spin out of control.

"Our daughter is killing me, Connor. She's going to *KILL* me!" she screamed as the contraction came to an end.

Ellery closed her eyes. I took the cloth from the table and gently wiped her forehead with it.

"It's okay, baby. I'm here with you, and I'll get you through this. We've been through so much, and this is nothing."

Her eyes flew open as if Satan himself took over. "Nothing! Did you just say this is nothing?!" she yelled at me.

"Baby, you know what I mean."

"Uh oh, I think someone's in deep shit. If I were you, I'd get the hell out of here, and run as fast as you can." Peyton laughed.

I couldn't say anything right. Everything I said was wrong and just pissed Ellery off. I got up from the bed and pulled my phone from my pocket. After I had an idea that might help keep Ellery calm, I called up Claire and asked her if she could bring Ellery's classical music CD and the small painting of the baby cuddled up in the moon amongst the stars. I would stand in the doorway of the nursery, late at night, and watch Ellery as she stared at that painting while rubbing her belly. One night, I asked her about it.

"This is the fifth night you've been in here staring at that painting." I smiled as I walked into the nursery and placed my hands on her shoulders.

She reached her hand up and placed her hand on top of mine. "I feel serene when I look at it. I'm not quite sure why, but I do. So, whenever I start to feel nervous or anxious, I come in here, and it calms me down."

As I hung up with Claire, I walked over to Ellery and kissed her on the forehead.

"Claire is on her way with something that I think will help you relax."

She looked at me and tried to smile, but another contraction was starting. I sat down on the edge of the bed and let her squeeze my hand as tightly as she needed to. I was in awe of this beautiful woman that I called my wife and what she was going through to give me a child. When the contraction ended, she brought my hand up to her lips and kissed it softly.

"I'm sorry, babe. I know I'm hurting you," she said.

I gripped her face lightly with my hands. "You're not hurting me, Ellery. I love you, and I love what you're doing for us. You do what you need to in order to get through your contractions. I'm here for you, baby." I smiled.

Chapter 3

Ellery

I lay there and stared into my husband's eyes as he tried so hard to make me comfortable. Peyton was sitting in the chair next to the bed and she looked exhausted.

"Why don't you go find Henry and grab something to eat?"

"I don't want to leave you. You're going to need me." She smiled as she took my hand.

Connor looked over at her. "Peyton, I love you, but I'm her husband and the only person she needs right now."

Peyton knitted her eyebrows at him. "I suppose you're right, but I want to be here for her."

"You are here for her, and I appreciate it, but you really should take a break," Connor said.

"You and Henry should go have sex in one of the rooms," I said as I gave her hand a squeeze.

A smile brightened her face. "That's a great idea, Elle, but don't go and have that baby until I get back!" she exclaimed.

As Peyton walked out of the room, Claire walked in. Another contraction had started just as she set my favorite painting on the chair next to me.

"Oh God!" I started to scream.

As Connor looked over at me, he instantly grabbed my

hand, and I bit down on my bottom lip.

"Look at the painting, baby. Focus on the painting, not the pain."

"I can't, Connor. The pain is too horrible. I can't concentrate on anything but the pain!" I screamed.

Claire grabbed the cloth from the stand and wiped my forehead. "I remember the pain, Ellery. Just remember what the end result of that pain is." She smiled as she pressed her lips to my forehead.

As I smiled at her and slowly closed my eyes, Connor got up and walked her out of the room. I heard him in the hallway, thanking her for bringing the CD and the painting. Nurse Bailey came back into the room and told me she had to check me again to see how far I was dilated. She sighed after she finished checking me, and Connor walked back into the room.

"Any progress?" he asked.

"No. She hasn't dilated at all. I need to call the doctor. I'll be right back."

I looked at Connor as he leaned over and kissed my head. "I'm scared something's wrong," I said.

"Don't be scared. Everything's going to be fine. I just think our daughter's stubborn. She's starting to remind me of someone." He smiled as he ran his hand down my cheek.

Just as I was beginning to relax, another contraction started. Connor looked at the fetal monitor.

"How can you be having another contraction already? It's only been a few seconds since the last one."

The pain was different this time. It was more intense and radiated throughout my entire back. The pressure was so bad that I had to push.

"Connor, I have to push. I have to!" I screamed.

"No, Ellery. I don't think you can do that yet."

He held onto my hand as the sweat dripped from my face, and I screamed in pain. Henry, Peyton, and Nurse Bailey ran into the room. As I looked at Nurse Bailey, Peyton came over and took a hold of my other hand.

"I have to push. I have to. Please help me," I begged as the tears streamed down my face.

"Ellery, you can't push," Nurse Bailey said as she looked at Henry.

Suddenly, the monitor started beeping and all eyes went to it. Henry stood there and shook his head.

"Her blood pressure's dropping and so is the baby's heart rate. We need to get this baby out now!"

"I called Dr. Reed and he said he's on his way, but he said it'll take at least thirty to forty-five minutes for him to reach the hospital," Nurse Baily said.

"I don't give a shit how long it's going to take him. Go make sure an operating room is available, and page an anesthesiologist, STAT!"

The voices around the room were getting deeper and slower. The room started to spin as Henry clasped my shoulders.

"Ellery, stay with me," he said.

I wanted to give up. I couldn't do this anymore, and I couldn't stand the pain. My body was tired, and I could feel myself slowly drifting away. Suddenly, I heard Connor's voice.

"Baby, don't you dare give up. You better not give up on me. We've come too far, and we fought too hard to have our life together, and you will not give up! Do you understand me!" he yelled.

Suddenly, a group of people came running into the room and transferred me to another bed. I looked at Connor as I opened my eyes and the tears began to fall.

"I'm sorry. I'm so sorry. I love you," I whispered.

Another doctor came from behind and put a mask over my face. "I need you to take in a deep breath, Ellery. This will help you to relax."

With the mask on my face, I looked over at Peyton and saw that she was crying. They started to wheel me out of the room, but I wouldn't let go of Connor's hand.

"Don't worry, baby, I'll be right there. I promise you that I'll be there with you."

Chapter 4

Connor

I followed them out of the room and stood there as they wheeled Ellery down the hall. I was scared shitless and worried. If something happened to them, I didn't know what I'd do. I would never forget the look on Ellery's face as they wheeled her away from me.

"I'm going to make sure that Ellery and the baby are fine," Henry said as he put his hand on my shoulder. "Get changed and I'll see you in operating room."

I nodded my head as Ellery disappeared from my sight. Nurse Bailey handed me a pair of light blue scrubs and told me to change in the bathroom.

"She's going to be all right, Mr. Black. Now hurry up and put those on." She smiled.

As I walked into the bathroom to change, Peyton went to the waiting room and sat with my family. I quickly changed, and when I opened the bathroom door, Nurse Bailey was standing there, holding a mask in her hand.

"You need to put this on before we go into the room. It's for the baby's safety."

As I took the mask from her, she led me down the hallway to the operating room where Ellery was. She told me to wait outside the double doors while she went to make sure they were ready. A few moments later, she walked through the doors and motioned for me to follow her. When she led me into the sterile room, Ellery turned her head and looked at me. Immediately, she held out her hand. I smiled as I walked over to her, gently took her hand, and sat on the stool next to her.

"Hi." I smiled.

"Hi back," she whispered.

"Okay, Ellery, let's have this baby," Henry said as he started making the incision.

As she stared into my eyes, I leaned over and lightly rubbed her forehead with my thumb.

"I remember the first time I stared into your beautiful eyes." I smiled.

"In your kitchen, after you accused me of breaking your rule." She smiled back.

"Yeah, but I'll never forget the feeling that overtook me the moment you turned around and looked at me."

"I thought you were an ass," she whispered.

"I know you did, and I was, but you changed me, Ellery. You swooped in, broke all my rules, and completely turned my life around."

Suddenly, the cries of a baby jolted us back into reality. Ellery and I looked at Henry as he held our daughter up. "Congratulations, Mom and Dad." He smiled.

She was screaming as she moved her little arms and legs around. Henry handed her to the nurse, who took her over and cleaned her up.

"You did so good, baby. I'm so proud of you," I whispered as I kissed her.

"You look very sexy in that mask and those scrubs." She

smiled.

"Well, that was random." I smiled back.

I got up and walked over to where my daughter was being cleaned up. The nurse wrapped her in a pink blanket and handed her to me. I was incredibly nervous to hold her, but it was what I'd been dreaming of since the day Ellery told me she was pregnant.

"Ellery, I'm going to start stitching you up now and, when I'm done, then you can hold your baby," Henry said.

"Thank you, Henry, for everything." She smiled.

As I walked over to Ellery's side, she held out her hand. I sat down on the stool and brought our daughter closer to her so she could touch her. At this point, she had stopped crying, and she could barely keep her eyes open. She wrapped her delicate little hand around Ellery's finger. I watched as a tear fell from her eye.

"She's so beautiful, Connor," Ellery said.

"Of course she is. She's your daughter."

Ellery reached her hand up and softly stroked my cheek. I'd never felt this kind of feeling before. I loved Ellery so much that my entire existence revolved around her. I didn't think it was possible to love her or anyone else even more. Looking down at my baby girl, seeing the love of my life in this child, and knowing that we both created this miracle, made my love grow even more for both of them.

"I want to talk to you about something," I said as I looked at her.

"What is it?" she asked.

"I know we talked about a couple of different names for her, but I think we should name her after your mom, Julia."

Ellery stared at me for a moment as tears sprang to her

eyes. "I love it, Connor."

"I think she should have a name that's a part of all of us. I would like to name her Julia Rose Black."

Chapter 5

Ellery

"I love that name." I smiled. "Julia Rose Black is a beautiful name, and I think it fits her perfectly."

Connor leaned over and kissed my lips. Seeing him sitting there and holding Julia was one of the happiest moments of my life. Anyone who looked at him could see and feel the love he had for that child.

"All stitched up, Ellery," Henry said. "If you want, you can hold Julia now."

Connor looked at me and smiled as he put Julia in my arms.

"Are you feeling okay?" Connor asked.

"I'm feeling great." I smiled as I kissed Julia's forehead.

Henry cleaned up and walked over to me and Connor. "Congratulations, you two," he said as he kissed my head and shook Connor's hand.

The nurse wheeled me out of the operating room and back into my room. I couldn't believe that our daughter was here. It seemed like only yesterday that I found out I was pregnant. Once I was back in the room and settled in bed, Connor left to go tell our family and friends that Julia had arrived. As she was sleeping in my arms, Peyton walked into the room and instantly covered her mouth with her hands.

"Ellery, she's beautiful," she said as she walked over and

kissed Julia on the head.

"Isn't she? I just can't believe she's here." I smiled.

Connor walked into the room with his mom, dad, Cassidy, and Denny following behind.

"Let me see my beautiful granddaughter," Jenny said with a tear in her eye.

As much as I didn't want to let Julia go, I handed her over to Connor's mom. Denny walked over and sat on the edge of the bed. He took my hand and gently kissed it.

"You and Connor have made one beautiful little girl." He smiled. "I never thought I'd see the day that Connor would become a father."

"To be honest with you, I never thought I would see this day myself," I said as I looked down.

"Well, you fought, you won, and now you've been rewarded. I can't think of two other people who deserve this more than you and Connor."

"Thank you," I whispered. "I love you, Denny."

"I love you too, Elle." He smiled as he kissed me on the forehead.

When Nurse Bailey walked into the room, she announced that it was time for everyone to leave. She took Julia from Jenny and handed her to me, as it was time for my lesson in breastfeeding.

* * * *

I walked through the elevator doors to the penthouse. It felt good to be home. The past couple of days in the hospital were uncomfortable and starting to drive me crazy. Connor followed behind me with Julia, and Claire and Denny emerged from the kitchen.

"Welcome home, Ellery," Claire said as she gave me a light hug.

"Thank you, Claire."

The aroma of apple pie filled the air of the penthouse and it smelled wonderful. "Are you making apple pie?" I asked her.

"Yes, I am, and just for you." She smiled.

Connor looked at me and then at Claire. "What about me?" he asked.

"You can have some too, Connor," she replied.

Connor asked Denny if he could hold the car seat while he helped me up the stairs.

"Come on, baby. Do you want me to carry you?"

"No, I can walk. But thank you for offering." I smiled at him.

"You know what that smile does to me, Elle."

He took my hand and helped me up the stairs. We reached the bedroom, and I immediately lay down on the bed.

"I've missed this bed."

Denny brought Julia up to the room and set the car seat down on the floor. "Welcome home, you three." He smiled and then walked out of the room.

As Connor climbed on the bed and lay next to me, we both stared at Julia, who was sound asleep.

"She's perfect, like you," he whispered as he softly kissed my neck.

I smiled and closed my eyes as his lips traveled to the edge of my ear.

"I can't wait to make love to you," I whispered. "Especially now that I'm not pregnant anymore."

"I loved making love to you while you were pregnant."

Suddenly, Julia started to cry. We looked at each other and smiled. Connor got up and carefully took her from her car seat. I took off my shirt as he gently handed her to me and she latched onto my breast.

"There's nothing more beautiful than seeing you feed our daughter," he said as he sat down on the bed next to me and kissed me on the lips.

This was my family—the three of us—and I didn't want anything more.

Chapter 6

Connor

Six weeks later

Life was getting back to normal, as much as it could, with a baby in the house. Ellery had trouble breast-feeding after the first week, so we ended up bottle-feeding Julia, which made it easier for me to help out with the feedings. I tried to hire a nanny, but Ellery wanted nothing to do with it and said that she didn't want a stranger raising our child. I worked from home as much as I could, but I had reached a point when I had to start going into the office.

I was sitting at my desk, going over some paperwork, when a text message came through from Ellery.

"You better be home early tonight. I just left the doctor's office, and I've been cleared to have sex! You better be ready, Mr. Black, because tonight's the night!"

Just reading that made me hard. I'd been craving her, and I couldn't wait to be inside her again.

"I'll be home, don't you worry about it. By the way, I'm already hard." I quickly replied.

"Good. You better make sure you stay that way."

As I looked over at my computer, I saw that it was six o'clock. I needed to hurry up and finish going over some papers so I could get home to my wife and daughter. I called the florist and had them deliver two dozen roses to the office so I could bring them home to Ellery. Once the flowers arrived, I was finished for the day. I grabbed my things and headed out the door. Denny was waiting for me like usual in the front. When I opened the door, I threw my briefcase on the seat and climbed in.

"Beautiful flowers, Connor. You shouldn't have." He smiled.

"Tonight's the night, Denny. I get to have sex with my wife again!"

"Congratulations, Connor. Is someone looking after Julia while the two of you celebrate?"

"No, I don't think so. Why?" I asked.

"Good luck with that." He smirked.

I sighed because I honestly didn't know what he meant. As I got out of the limo, I told Denny I'd see him tomorrow. The elevator doors opened and all I could smell was Chinese food. I walked into the kitchen and saw Ellery taking the cartons out of the bag while Julia was awake and sitting in her bouncy seat. When I walked over to Ellery and handed her the flowers, I kissed her firmly on the lips. Julia started to whine.

"They're beautiful, Connor. Thank you."

"You're welcome, baby." I smiled.

"She's probably hungry again," Ellery said as she looked over at Julia.

"I'll feed her." I smiled. I walked over and took her out of her bouncy seat. The minute I held her, she stopped.

"I think she missed her daddy today." Ellery smiled as she set the food on the table.

I sat down at the table with her and attempted to eat. The

minute I picked up my fork, Julia started to scream. Ellery got up and warmed a bottle for her. She went to take her from me, but I wouldn't give her up.

"Let me feed her, Elle. You go and eat. You've been with her all day."

"But you worked all day. I can feed her so you can eat your dinner."

"No, now give me the bottle, and let me feed my daughter." I smiled at her.

"Okay." She smiled back as she handed me the bottle.

When I put the bottle in Julia's mouth, she instantly started to drink it. As I looked over at Ellery, she glanced at me and ran the tip of her tongue across her lips. She was so beautiful, but she looked so tired.

"Baby, you're getting me hard, and I'm holding our daughter."

"Oops. Sorry." She smiled. "Don't forget to burp her."

I took the bottle from Julia's mouth and set it on the table. When I put her over my shoulder and patted her back, she let out a big burp and then started crying for more. Ellery got up from her chair and took her from me.

"It's my turn now. I don't want you eating cold food," she said as she kissed me.

I took the food from the carton and began eating. The only thing I wanted was to get this dinner over with so I could make love to Ellery. When Julia finished eating, Ellery finished her dinner. I got up from the table and cleaned up while she took the baby upstairs to change her into her pajamas. Once I was done, I grabbed a bottle of wine and two glasses and took them up to our bedroom. When I walked in, I found Ellery and Julia passed out on the bed. I looked down at my cock, which was semi-hard. Just knowing we were finally going to have sex aroused me. As I sighed, I set the bottle of wine on the dresser. I walked over to the bed and carefully picked up Julia. She stirred, opened her eyes, and closed them again. I carried her to her room and laid her down in the crib. As I walked back to the bedroom, I changed into my pajama bottoms, climbed into bed, and wrapped my arms around Ellery.

"Sleep well, my love," I whispered to her.

* * * *

Startled out of a sound sleep, I rolled over, gave Ellery a kiss, and told her to go back to sleep. She was exhausted, and it was my turn to take care of Julia. Her cries echoed through the baby monitor as I got out of bed and headed towards her bedroom. I turned on the lamp and walked over to her crib. As I looked down at her, she looked up at me and stopped crying. After I leaned over and picked her up, I sat down in the rocking chair. I sat and stared at her as she moved her little hands around, cooing and kicking her legs within the blanket in which she was wrapped.

"You have no idea how much you and your mommy have changed my life," I whispered as I softly ran my hand across her cheek and slowly rocked back and forth. "I have so many plans for us. I can't wait to take you to the park and to the beach. I'm going to teach you how to skate, how to ride a bike, and how to swim. You'll always know how much Daddy loves you because you'll hear and feel it every day. You've already rocked my world, baby girl, and I love you so much."

Julia closed her eyes and folded her little hands. I looked up and saw Ellery standing in the doorway, smiling, as a single tear fell down her cheek. As I got up from chair and gently put Julia back in her crib, I walked over to Ellery and wiped her tear away. She wrapped her arms around me and held me tight. As I bent down and picked her up, she brushed her lips against mine. I carried her to the bedroom and laid her on the bed.

"I'm so sorry I fell asleep," she said.

"Don't be, baby. You're tired, and you need all the rest you can get," I whispered as my lips traveled to her neck.

"Make love to me, Connor."

I took down one strap of her nightgown and softly kissed her exposed breast. The soft groan that came from the back of her throat excited me even more. It had been too long, and I was going to make up for lost time. As I took down the other strap from her shoulder, I sat up in front of her and pulled her nightgown off, exposing her entire body. She looked at me and smiled when I shed my pajama bottoms. My tongue made circles around her belly button as I softly kissed the incision from her C-section. While my mouth was devouring every inch of her torso, my hands were fondling her breasts, taking her puckered nipples between my fingers. As she threw her head back and moaned, Ellery moved her fingers swiftly through my hair. I grabbed the string of her panties as she slightly lifted her hips and took them down. My finger lightly traced the inside of her thigh, all the way up to her clit. I moved myself up to her lips and forcefully kissed her when I felt the wetness and arousal from her.

"I don't want to hurt you, baby. It's been a long time."

"I'm fine. I need you so bad, Connor. I need to feel you inside me."

I dipped one finger deep inside her and then another. Her moans grew louder as she moved her hips up and down, begging my fingers to pleasure her. I climbed on top of her with my fingers moving in and out, rubbing her clit and bringing her to orgasm. Her body shuddered and shook as she released her warm pleasure all over me.

"That's my girl." I smiled. "Oh, how I've missed doing this to you."

We stared into each other's eyes as she whispered, "I want you to look at me as you make love to me."

I placed myself inside her while I stared into her beautiful blue eyes. As I pushed myself further inside, the corners of her mouth turned up. Her arms were wrapped around me when I slowly moved in and out of her.

"You feel so good, baby. God, I've missed being inside you and feeling you like this."

She brought her legs up and wrapped them around me as I picked up my pace and moved in and out of her at a steady speed. Our breathing was rapid and our hearts were racing. As I stared into her eyes with each thrust, she stared back, smiling and running her finger across my lips. I could feel her spasms around my cock as she was getting ready to come.

"Ellery," I moaned as I couldn't hold back anymore.

"Connor," she wailed as I poured myself into her.

Her body tightened as she threw her head back and came. My lips forcefully locked with hers, and I didn't want to stop. I finally broke our kiss and looked at her. She was smiling at me as I collapsed on top of her. Our breathing was shallow, and our heart rates were beating at the same speed.

"God, how I've missed having sex with you," Ellery said breathlessly.

I kissed her neck before rolling off of her. "I've missed it too, baby. You felt so good," I said as I ran the back of my hand across her cheek.

Suddenly, little sounds came through the monitor. Ellery

and I looked at the monitor on the dresser. Julia was stirring in her crib. A soft cry came from her and we looked at each other.

"Don't worry; I'll get her if she continues to cry." I smiled as I ran my finger across her jaw line.

"It's okay; I'll get her. You just worked very hard." Ellery smiled back.

We lay there in each other's arms, staring at the monitor and waiting for Julia to wake up. She didn't. As I reached my hand down in between Ellery's legs, I whispered, "Are you ready for round two?"

Chapter 7

Ellery

As I awoke, I reached over to put my arm around Connor, but his side of the bed was empty. I sat up and looked around. I didn't hear the shower running and Julia wasn't in her crib. I put my robe on and walked down the stairs to the kitchen. Connor was sitting at the table with Julia in his arms, feeding her a bottle.

"Good morning, baby." He smiled as he looked up at me.

"Good morning," I said as I walked over and gave him and Julia a kiss. "Why didn't you wake me? I would've gotten her."

"You looked so peaceful sleeping, and I was already awake when she woke up."

I poured a cup of coffee and sat down in the chair next to him. He looked so sexy in his black suit, and I wanted to take him upstairs and devour him before he had to leave for the office.

"Is something special going on today? You hardly ever wear a suit to the office."

"I have to go to court today. I told you last week," he said as he looked at me.

"Shit, Ashlyn and the trial. I completely forgot. I'm sorry."

"It's okay. You just had a baby and you're still trying to

adjust. Don't worry about it," he said as he put Julia over his shoulder to burp her.

Denny walked into the kitchen and headed straight to the coffee pot.

"Good morning." He smiled as he looked at us.

"Good morning, Denny." I smiled in return.

As Connor was burping Julia, she decided to spit up all down the back of his suit coat. I jumped up as he looked at me.

"Seriously?" he said.

I tried so hard to contain my laughter, as did Denny, but we both couldn't hold it anymore. I took Julia from Connor and held her while Denny handed him a towel.

"Don't you know by now that you shouldn't feed a baby while wearing a suit?" Denny asked.

"I guess I do now," Connor said as he walked out of the kitchen and up the stairs to change.

Claire came into the kitchen, and I handed Julia to her. I walked upstairs and into the bedroom where Connor was pulling out another suit from the closet. I stood there with a smirk on my face.

"What's that look for?" he asked.

"I just think it's funny; that's all."

"You think it's funny that our daughter spit up all over my five-thousand-dollar suit?"

"I do, and you don't need a five-thousand-dollar suit anyway. That's a ridiculous amount of money to spend. No one is going to know it costs that much, and you look just as sexy in a five- hundred-dollar suit."

Connor pursed his lips together and put the suit he pulled

out back in the closet. As he started walking slowly towards me, I knew the look on his face, and I knew I was in trouble. When he approached me, I put up my hands to prevent him from coming any closer. He grabbed my hands and threw me on the bed.

"You know how much I love it when you babble on like that." He smiled.

"Please, Connor, whatever you do, don't tickle me," I begged.

Suddenly, we heard Denny's voice from downstairs. "Connor, let's go. You're already late."

Connor kissed me on the lips. "You're lucky, Mrs. Black. But make no mistake; we *will* continue this tonight."

"I'll be ready." I winked.

Connor let go of my hands and walked back to the closet and pulled out his suit. I went back to the kitchen and took Julia from Claire. Shortly after changing his suit, Connor came down, grabbed his briefcase, and we walked him to the elevator.

"Bye, my beautiful little girl." Connor smiled as he kissed Julia on her head. "And goodbye to you, my beautiful wife," he said as he kissed me on the lips.

"Bye, babe. Good luck and call me."

He gave me a small smile before the elevator doors closed. I took Julia upstairs to change her diaper. Since I couldn't stop thinking about the trial, I was pissed that Connor wasn't talking to me about it. I wanted to be there for him, but since Julia had been born, I hadn't had time to think about anything else but her, and I was exhausted all the time. I changed Julia's diaper and carried her downstairs to find my phone. As I grabbed it off the kitchen counter, I dialed Peyton.

"Hello, bestie. Did you and Connor have amazing sex last night?" she asked.

"Good morning, Peyton, and yes, we did have amazing sex, but that's not why I'm calling."

"Oh, I thought you'd want to talk about it," she said with a disappointed tone.

"Are you busy today?" I asked her.

"I just have a few errands to run. Why?"

"Connor is at the courthouse because the trial is starting today, and I really want to be there for him."

"Did he ask you to go?"

"No, and he wouldn't either. You know how he is. I just wanted to know if you could watch Julia for a few hours?"

"Of course I'll watch that beautiful goddaughter of mine!" she squealed.

"Thank you, Peyton. I appreciate it."

"No problem. I'll be over in about thirty minutes."

As I was putting Julia in her bouncy seat, Denny walked into the kitchen. "I'm glad you're back. I need you to drive me to the courthouse," I said as I looked at him.

"Elle, I don't think that's a good idea. You shouldn't go there."

"It's not a matter of if I should or shouldn't. I want to, and I want to be there for my husband."

"I understand that, but I don't think Connor wants you there."

I rolled my eyes. "Don't you know me by now?"

"Yes. Just let me know when you're ready." He sighed.

I smiled as I walked over and kissed him on the cheek.

"Thank you, Denny."

"You know he'll probably yell at me for doing this," he said.

"Don't worry about it. If he says anything, I'll take care of him." I smiled.

I asked Denny if he could keep an eye on Julia while I went to get ready. As I was putting on my black skirt, Peyton came strolling into the bedroom, holding her.

"Are you sure you want to do this, Elle?" she asked.

"Of course I'm sure."

"You know that bitch is crazy, and you haven't seen her since you punched her out."

"I know I haven't and that's why it's time."

I put on my black heels, handed Peyton the diaper bag, and kissed Julia goodbye. "Everything you need is in here. If you're going to take her with you on errands, then you'll need the stroller and it's in the hallway by the elevator."

"Don't worry, Mom. I've got this!" She smiled.

"Denny, I'm ready to leave," I said as I grabbed by purse and we stepped onto the elevator.

Chapter 8

Connor

I sat outside the courtroom, waiting for the trial to begin. I hadn't seen Ashlyn since that day at the gym.

"Don't worry, Connor," Phil said. "She'll get what she deserves."

"Let's just hope the jury finds her guilty."

As we walked into the courtroom and sat down, I looked over and saw Ellery walking towards me. I instantly stood up.

"Ellery, what are you doing here?" I asked.

"I wanted to be here for you, Connor."

"Baby, I'm sorry, but I don't want you here. I don't want you involved in this."

"It's too late for that, Connor. I'm your wife, and whatever you're involved in, involves me. Now if you don't want me here, that's too fucking bad, because I'm here to support you whether you want me to or not. So deal with it, buddy!" she exclaimed through gritted teeth.

I sighed as I looked at her, shook my head, and sat down. She said hello to Phil and then sat down next to me.

"Where's Julia?"

"Peyton is watching her," she replied.

The lawyers walked into the courtroom and took their seats

up front. The guard opened the door off to the side and escorted Ashlyn into the room.

"Remind me to tell her how becoming that orange jumpsuit is on her and those chain accessories are to die for," Ellery whispered.

"You are to stay away from her," I warned.

Ashlyn looked directly at me as she entered the courtroom, and then looked directly at Ellery. I put my hand on her thigh because I was nervous she was going to get pissed and start something. Ellery could have quite a temper. She put her hand on mine and looked over at me.

"Relax, Connor."

I took in a deep breath as the judge entered the courtroom. Ashlyn's attorney stood up and asked the judge for a postponement due to her change of plea.

"Your honor, my client is pleading not guilty by reason of insanity due to the mental distress she was put under by Mr. Connor Black."

As I gasped, Ellery turned and looked at me. Her eyes were wide and angry. I couldn't believe what I'd just heard. My heart started racing.

"Is this true?" the judge asked as he looked at Ashlyn.

"Yes, it is, your Honor," she said as she nodded her head.

"Fine. The trial is postponed until one week from today," he said as he got up from his seat and went into his chambers.

As the guard walked Ashlyn out of the courtroom, she looked over at me and blew me a kiss. When Ellery went to get up, I grabbed her arm.

"Don't," I whispered.

"Connor, this is bullshit!" she yelled.

"Yes, it is bullshit. I need to meet with my personal attorney," I said.

As we got up from our seats, I grabbed Ellery's hand and led her out of the courtroom. When we reached the hallway, I pulled her into me and held her tight.

"Everything's going to be fine, Elle; I don't want you worrying about this."

"I hope you're right," she said.

I kissed her on the head and called Lou, my personal attorney. When I hung up the phone from him, I walked over to the bench where Ellery was sitting and talking on the phone. When she hung up, she looked at me with sadness in her eyes.

"Who where you talking to?" I asked.

"Peyton. I was checking on Julia."

"Is everything okay?"

"Yeah. She wants to keep Julia a little while longer and then when Henry gets home from the hospital, they'll bring her home. I invited them for dinner. I hope you don't mind."

"Not at all, sweetheart," I said as I took her hand and softly kissed it. "I think we could use some good friends tonight," she said.

I helped her up from the bench and put my arm around her as we walked out of the building. As I opened the door to the limo, Ellery climbed in and, instantly, Denny knew something was wrong. I sat down next to her and shut the door.

"What happened in there?" Denny asked.

"Ashlyn changed her plea to not guilty by reason of insanity, and she's blaming it on mental distress caused by me."

"What?!" he exclaimed.

Ellery's eyes started to swell with tears as she looked out her window. I wrapped my arms around her and pulled her closer as I buried my face into her neck.

"I don't want you upset over this. Things are going to work out," I said.

"She's an evil bitch, Connor, and she'll go to whatever lengths necessary to destroy you."

"Ellery, I'm not going to let that happen."

"Yeah, well neither am I," she said.

I pulled back and looked at her. "You are to stay away from Ashlyn. Do you understand me?" I said in a firm voice.

She looked at me with those blue eyes. They had a look in them that I knew all too well; the look of defiance and anger. She tilted her head as her lips formed a small smile.

"Yes, Connor, I understand you."

Chapter 9

Ellery

When we arrived home, I went upstairs to change. A few minutes later, Connor came into the bedroom.

"Are you mad at me?" he asked.

I turned around and looked at him as I slipped off my skirt. "No. Why would you ask that?"

"Because you're not saying anything and you have that look."

The fact of the matter was that I was a little upset with him for using a firm tone with me in the limo.

"Connor, I'm not mad at you. I'm just a little—"

"A little what?" he asked as he walked over to me and started unbuttoning my blouse.

"Okay, you need to stop," I said as I put my hand up and backed away.

He inched closer to me with a smile on his face as he slipped off my blouse.

"Why do I need to stop? I thought you loved it when I undressed you."

"I do. It's just you're distracting me from my thoughts. To be honest with you, I'm pissed that you used that tone with me earlier."

"You use that tone with me all the time, and I find it sexy," he whispered as his hot breath on my neck made me quiver.

I bit down on my bottom lip and closed my eyes. He knew damn well what he was doing.

"Connor."

"Shh, baby. Just enjoy what I'm doing to you," he whispered as his hand pushed my thong to the side and he slipped in his finger.

I gasped as pleasure overtook my body. He stared at me while slowly moving his finger in and out of me as a small smile escaped his lips.

"You were saying?"

"Damn you," I moaned as I unbuttoned his pants and slid them down.

I wrapped my fingers around his cock and stroked him up and down. He threw his head back as a groan came from the back of his throat. He removed his fingers and pushed me against the wall. His mouth crashed into mine as I wrapped my legs around him and he buried himself inside me with force. He moved at a fast pace. Our hearts were racing and our breathing was shallow as he moved in and out of me, bringing me to orgasm.

"Oh God, Connor," I yelled as my body shook.

"You feel so good, baby," he shouted as I felt his warmth shoot inside me.

He stood there, my legs still wrapped around his waist, and his hands firmly cupping my ass.

"Now what was it you were saying?" He smiled.

I tilted my head back as he slid his tongue across my throat. "We better get ready. Peyton and Henry will be here soon." Connor pulled out of me, kissed me on the lips, and walked to the bathroom. I pulled a pair of jeans from the drawer and got dressed. As I sat on the edge of the bed, I started to cry. Connor came out of the bathroom and kneeled down in front of me. He took my hands in his.

"Baby, what's wrong? Did I hurt you?" he asked in a panic.

I shook my head. "I miss Julia, and I want her home," I cried.

"Aw, Ellery. Come here, baby," he said as he wrapped his arms around me. "She'll be home soon."

Suddenly, I heard voices coming from downstairs. I jumped up from the bed and flew down the stairs. When I saw Peyton and Henry by the door, I grabbed the car seat from Henry's hand.

"Julia, Mommy missed you so much," I cried as I took her out of her car seat and held her tight.

"God, Elle. Are you okay?" Peyton asked.

"She's fine," Connor said as he came walking down the stairs. "She just missed Julia."

Connor walked over and kissed Peyton on the cheek. "Thank you for looking after her," he said, and then walked over and shook Henry's hand. Connor kissed Julia on the head and told her how much he missed her.

"What's going on with you?" Peyton asked as she sat down next to me.

"I missed her, Peyton. It was the first time we'd been apart since I found out I was pregnant, and it was hard."

"Aw, sweetie," she said as she put her arm around me. "I'm sorry; I should have just brought her home sooner."

"No, it's fine, and thank you again for taking care of her."

"How did it go at court today?" she asked.

I looked at her with a sullen look, but I didn't have to say a word. The single tear that fell from my eye said enough.

"What the fuck, Elle? What did she do, or didn't, or whatever? What the fuck happened?" she whispered.

"We'll talk about it over dinner. I don't want to talk about it now and then again."

As Julia started to cry, Connor walked over and took her from me so I could get a bottle ready. I got up from the couch and walked into the kitchen. Peyton followed behind.

"We need to get you fitted for your maid of honor dress," she said.

"Ugh, I know. I just have a few more pounds to lose."

"I think you look great, but if you insist, then I suggest you hit the gym and hit it fast. You have one month and then you're going for your fitting," she announced.

I took out the pizza menu from the drawer and looked it over. I grabbed my cell phone and called an order for delivery. I warmed up a bottle and Peyton and I walked back into the living room where Henry and Connor were.

"I'll feed her, babe," Connor said.

"I can feed her, Connor."

"Aw, Henry, look at them. They're fighting over who feeds Julia. That's so sweet!" Peyton squealed.

I smiled at Connor and gave him the bottle. I walked over to the bar and Peyton sat down on the stool.

"Pour me some hard liquor, bartender," she said with an accent.

"Let's do some shots." I smiled.

I took down two shot glasses and grabbed the bottle of Jack Daniels. I poured a shot into each glass.

"Here's to a fucked up day!" I smiled as I held up my glass.

Peyton smiled as we both downed our whiskey and slammed our glasses on the granite top of the bar. The burn made its way down my throat. Peyton looked at me.

"Remind me again why you drink this shit," she said.

I laughed as I poured another shot and Connor came walking over to me with Julia in his arms.

"Keep that up and you'll be drunk before you know it," he said.

"Last shot. I promise." I smiled.

Julia fell asleep, so Connor took her upstairs and put her in her crib. The pizza had arrived and we all went into the kitchen and sat down at the table.

"Are you going to tell us what happened today?" Peyton asked as she grabbed a slice of pizza.

"Ashlyn changed her plea to not guilty by reason of temporary insanity due to the distress *I* apparently caused her," Connor explained.

"What?! That stupid bitch!" Peyton yelled.

"Connor, that's crazy," Henry said as he shook his head.

"She's crazy," I said.

"Well, we all know that bitch is crazy. So now what?" Peyton asked.

"Now, we get to rehash the past and all the shit that went on between her and Connor."

"Ellery, don't," Connor said as he looked at me.

I looked away because I didn't want to go through this again. Not now; not ever.

Chapter 10

Connor

Peyton and Henry left, and Ellery went upstairs to check on Julia. I walked over to the bar and poured myself a scotch. I could see how upset Ellery was and it killed me not to be able to make it better for her. This was just the beginning of a long and painful road, and I'd do whatever it took to shield my family from it. I walked up the steps and stopped in the doorway of the nursery. Ellery was sitting in the rocking chair, rocking Julia. As I stood there and smiled, she looked up at me with her sad eyes. I walked over to her and knelt down, placing my hands on her legs.

"I want you to listen to me, Elle. We're going to get through this. I talked to Lou and he said not to worry about it, and that we'll talk in the morning. He's going to do some investigating. You know he's the best lawyer in the country, and he'll take care of this."

"The only way we'll get through it, Connor, is together. There can't be any secrets."

"I know that, baby, and there won't be. You'll be with me every step of the way," I said.

She smiled at me as she ran the back of her hand down my cheek. "I love you so much."

I took her hand and held it against my lips as I closed my

eyes. "I love you too, and you better never, for even one single moment, forget it."

I stood up and took Julia from her arms. I kissed her tiny head and laid her down in her crib. Ellery took my hand and we walked down the hall to our bedroom. She changed into her satin nightgown and I undressed. We climbed into bed, and I wrapped my arms around her as she snuggled against me and fell sound asleep.

When the buzzing alarm went off, Ellery rolled over and looked at me. We looked at each other and jumped out of bed.

"Oh my God, Julia never woke up last night!" she said in a panic.

We ran to her room to check on her. As we looked in her crib, she looked at us and smiled. Ellery gasped and put her hand over her mouth.

"Connor, she smiled! Did you see it?" she asked excitedly.

"Yes, I saw her." I smiled as I picked her up from her crib and stared at her. Her smile was just like Ellery's, and I knew right then and there, I was in trouble. "She has your smile, Ellery. That means all the boys are going to fall in love with her, and we're going to have quite a problem on our hands."

Ellery laughed and put her arm around my waist. "The only problem we're going to have is if you become one of those overprotective fathers that scare all the boys away."

"She's not allowed to date. I know what boys are like and they're not getting their hands on my daughter."

"Connor," Ellery paused. "Do you realize that our little girl slept through the night?"

I looked at Ellery, who was beaming from head to toe. "You're right. She did sleep through the night." I smiled as I held her up in the air.

I passed Julia to Ellery as I ran to the other room to grab my ringing phone. I picked it up and saw that Lou was calling.

"Hey, Lou," I said as I answered.

"Good morning, Connor. I have a quick meeting this morning and then I'll stop by your office, let's say around eleven."

"I'll be there, Lou, and thank you."

"No problem, buddy. I'll see you then."

I hung up the phone and turned around. Ellery was standing behind me.

"What time is our meeting?" she asked.

"Our meeting?"

"We're in this together, babe, and I'm meeting Lou with you."

I sighed as I kissed her on the lips. "Eleven o'clock at my office. I'll make sure to have Denny drive you there."

"Thank you," she said as she turned and walked downstairs with Julia.

* * * *

I stepped into the shower and stood under the hot water. Thoughts of Ashlyn kept entering my mind and how she could potentially destroy my life, especially with her lies. The thought of my relationship with her and our arrangement coming out made me sick to my stomach. I finished up in the shower, wrapped a towel around my waist, and walked into the bedroom. Ellery was standing in front of the mirror in her bra and panties, staring at herself.

"Are you admiring that beautiful body of yours?" I asked as I walked up behind her and put my hands on her hips.

"No, I'm disgusted by how much weight I still have to

lose."

"Nonsense. Your body is just as amazing now as it was before you got pregnant."

"You're only saying that so you can get laid."

"Oh, yeah! Is that what you really think?" I laughed as I picked her up, threw her on the bed, and started to tickle her until she couldn't take it anymore.

I stopped and stared into her beautiful blue eyes. The smile that I loved so much didn't leave her face as she stared back. I pushed her hair behind her ear.

"I love you, Ellery."

"I love you, Connor," she replied as she traced my lips with her finger.

All I wanted was to make love to her at that moment. I didn't care what time it was. The world could wait when I was with her. I lowered my head and gently nipped her bottom lip. As she softly moaned, Julia's screams, coming from downstairs, snapped us back into our little family world; a world where it was no longer just the two of us, but now the three of us.

We smiled at each other as I sighed and got up from the bed.

"I guess we're going to have to get used to working our sex schedule around Julia," I said as I walked to the closet and pulled out some clothes.

"I guess so." Ellery laughed as she got up, got dressed, and headed downstairs.

* * * *

When I arrived at the office, I sat down at my desk and went through my messages. As I turned my chair around and stared out onto the city of New York, Phil walked in.

"Did you have your meeting with Lou yet?" he asked as he sat down.

"Today at eleven o'clock."

"Damn that bitch. She's crazy and she's trying to avoid going to prison for the next 25 years. You do realize that she'll destroy you and this company in the process, right?"

I got up from my chair. "Don't you think I know that?" I scowled.

"She needs to be stopped, Connor."

"There's nothing I can do. I'll talk to Lou and see what he says."

"I have to finish some things up. I'll be back at eleven for that meeting." Phil sighed as he walked out of the office.

Chapter 11

Ellery

Julia was being fussy. She was continuously crying, and I felt like I was going to pull my hair out. She wouldn't take a bottle, she didn't want her pacifier, and she didn't want to be put down. Even as I held her, she still screamed. I felt so bad because I didn't know what to do. Tears started streaming down my face as I paced the floors with her. I didn't want to call Connor because he had enough to worry about. Just as I was thinking that, my phone rang and it was him.

"Hello," I said as I tried to sound as if I wasn't crying.

"Hi, baby. Why is Julia screaming like that?"

I couldn't hold it together anymore as I broke down. "I don't know. She just won't stop and I don't know what to do for her," I cried.

"Is anyone else there with you?" he asked.

"No, I'm here by myself. Connor, I don't know what's wrong with her. She just won't stop crying."

"I'm on my way, Ellery," he said as he hung up the phone.

I tried to tell him not to come home, but he had already hung up. I held Julia up over my shoulder and patted her back. She screamed. I bounced her as I walked up and down the stairs. She screamed. I sat in the rocking chair and tried to rock her. She screamed. I literally was going to lose it. As I walked back down the stairs with her, Connor stepped out of the elevator. He walked over to me and took Julia. As he looked at me, he wiped the tears from my eyes.

"Maybe I should call the doctor," I said.

"How long as she been like this?" he asked.

"About an hour and a half. All she's been doing is screaming." I started to cry again.

Connor walked around the penthouse with her. He tried the same things as I had done and nothing was working. When I grabbed my phone and started to dial the doctor, the doorbell rang. I put my phone down and opened the door. I was shocked when I saw who was standing in front of me.

"Mason! What—"

"Girl, what the hell is wrong? Why are you crying?" he interrupted as he walked through the door.

Before I could answer, Connor came back into the room with a screaming Julia.

"Oh my God, give me that baby!" Mason said as he walked over and took her from Connor.

The minute Mason held her over his arm, Julia stopped crying.

"What the hell!" Connor said as he looked at me.

"Hi to you too, Connor." Mason smiled.

"Mason, how did you—she has been—"

"She's gassy. You couldn't tell that?" he asked.

Connor and I stood there and just looked at him as he rubbed Julia's back.

"Elle, I love you, but you're a hot mess right now. You need to go clean yourself up." Mason smiled.

"I've missed you so much." I said as I walked over and

hugged him.

"Go on. We'll talk when you come back down," he said as he kissed my cheek.

I went upstairs and into the bathroom. Mason was right; I looked like a hot mess. As I was standing in front of the mirror, wiping the mascara stains from my face, Connor walked in.

"You should see him with her. He's a natural," Connor whispered.

"I saw that the minute he took her and she stopped crying."

"Come here, baby," he said as he turned me around and wrapped his arms around me.

I stood there, wrapped safely in his arms, when suddenly, something dawned on me. "Connor, the meeting with Lou!" I exclaimed.

"It's okay. I rescheduled for later this afternoon."

"I'm sorry. I'm a bad mother and wife." I began to cry.

"Aw, baby. You're not a bad mother or wife. Don't ever say that again. You're overwhelmed. Henry thinks that maybe you're going through post-partum depression."

I pushed back and looked at him in anger. "I'm not depressed, Connor."

"I didn't say you were depressed."

"Yes, you did! You just said you think I have post-partum depression. Do you hear the word depression, Connor? Depressed, depression; same thing, you idiot."

Connor rolled his eyes and walked away. I followed behind him down the stairs. When I reached the living room, Mason was sitting on the couch talking to Julia and she was cooing. Connor and I looked at each other.

"Hey, she's happy." I smiled as I sat down next to them.

"Of course she is. She's with her Uncle Mason." He smiled.

Connor sat down next me and kissed me on the head. "A kiss from an idiot," he whispered.

"I'm sorry. I'll make it up to you later." I smiled as I kissed the tip of his nose.

Mason looked at us and smiled. "It's so good to see both of you again."

"It's good to see you too. What are you doing in New York, and why didn't you tell me you were coming?" I asked.

"Landon got a job with a top modeling agency, and they wanted him to move here. So, here we are!"

"Where is Landon?" Connor asked.

"He had a meeting with his agent, so I decided that I'd take my chances and see if you were home."

"Where are you and Landon living?" I asked as I reached over and took Julia from him.

"I was hoping you'd ask that!" he exclaimed. "We've rented a loft over on the next block."

"That's wonderful. That means we can see you whenever we want." I smiled.

"We can take this little princess shopping, and we can hang out at Starbucks! He smiled as he touched Julia's hand. God, Elle, I'm so excited!"

Connor looked at his watch. "Lou's going to be at my office in thirty minutes. We better get going. I'll grab the diaper bag," Connor said.

I nodded my head and got up from the couch. "Mason, we have a meeting with Connor's lawyer, so we have to get going. Why don't we get together for dinner tonight?"

"That sounds great. I'll ask Landon if we have plans. You're not taking Julia with you, are you?" he asked.

"Yes, we are, why?"

"Leave her here with me. Please, Ellery, let me watch her," he begged.

Connor walked up behind me. "I can't find the diaper bag."

"It's over there," Mason said as he pointed by the door.

"Ellery, hand Julia over to Mason so we can leave," Connor said.

A wide smile spread across Mason's face. "Give me the little princess, Ellery."

I suddenly became nervous. I didn't want to leave her again, but then the thought of her screaming her head off during the meeting frightened me. I kissed her on the head and handed her over to Mason, who was standing there with his arms out.

"Don't worry, Momma; she'll be safe with me," Mason said.

I smiled and followed Connor to the elevator. I stopped, turned around, and looked at Mason.

"How did you get Julia to stop fussing?" I asked.

"The gas drops in the diaper bag, Elle."

"Ah, so that's what that little white bottle was for," I said as I stepped in and the doors closed.

* * * *

Denny was on the other side of town, so Connor drove the Range Rover to the office. Before we reached the building, he called his secretary, Valerie, to send someone down to park it. He pulled up to the curb, walked around, and opened my door.

He grabbed my hand as we walked into the building and took the elevator up to the top floor where Connor's office was. As we stepped off the elevator, I could see the women looking up from behind their cubicles at my husband. I could see the look and hunger in their eyes when he walked by. I proudly held my head up and smiled as I said, "Good afternoon, ladies." Connor looked over at me and smiled.

When we reached his office, Lou and another gentleman were already sitting down and waiting. Phil came in behind us.

"Lou, thanks for meeting me," Connor said as he shook his hand.

"Connor, I want you to meet Ben. He just joined the firm."

As Connor shook Ben's hand, Lou leaned over and kissed me on the cheek.

"It's good to see you, Ellery." He smiled.

I took a seat in between Lou and Ben as Connor walked around and sat behind his desk. Lou folded his hands.

"I'm not going to lie to you, Connor. This could get very ugly. I've decided we're going after her personally for the Chicago fire. I know you didn't want to do it, but if she wants to claim that she was temporarily insane because of the mental stress you put her through, then we'll fight back. I've already alerted the district attorney's office that we're proceeding with this."

"Damn it, Lou. That's not even an option," Connor snapped.

"We have no choice, Connor. Ashlyn is forcing your hand on this. She's going to make sure you go down with her."

Connor stood up, put his hands in his pockets, and turned towards the window. "This is bullshit, Lou. I need you to make this go away," he said.

I sat there in silence as I listened to the conversation between Connor and Lou. I could tell Connor was worried, although he'd never admit it. My phone chimed and, as I pulled it from my purse, I noticed a text message from Mason.

"I'm in love with your little princess."

I smiled, and Connor asked me if everything was okay. I nodded my head and then watched him glare at Ben. I noticed he did that quite a bit since we sat down. Lou got up from his seat and told Connor that he'd get back with him in a couple of days. As Phil walked Lou and Ben out of the office, Connor called Ben back. He turned around and started walking towards Connor. I stood up from my chair because I didn't like the look on Connor's face.

"Do you find my wife attractive?" he asked.

I gasped as my eyes widened. "Connor!" I exclaimed.

"Well, do you? Answer the damn question," he said firmly.

"Um, yes, Mr. Black," Ben answered nervously.

"Then that explains why you've been staring at her."

"Connor, that's enough!" I snapped at him.

Ben looked at me and apologized. "I'm really sorry for staring, but I feel like we've met before." Suddenly, it must have hit him. "I know; you were Kyle's girlfriend back in college."

I looked at him, trying to figure out who he was, and then it came to me. "Ben? As in Ben Winston, Debate Club President and tech geek extraordinaire?"

"Yep, that's me!" He laughed. "I knew you looked familiar, but I couldn't put my finger on it."

Just as I gave him a hug and Connor gave me a dirty look, Cassidy walked in.

"Oh, I'm sorry. I thought you were alone, Connor," she said.

"It's okay, Cassidy. Come on in," he said.

Cassidy walked over to me and gave me a hug. "Where's my niece?"

"She's at home with Mason. I would like you to meet Ben Winston. Ben, this is my sister-in-law, Cassidy."

They lightly shook hands as I turned and looked at Connor. "You owe Ben an apology."

"For what?" he asked.

"You know for what, Connor. That was rude and uncalled for."

Connor took in a sharp breath and shook his head. "Ben, I apologize for being rude."

"It's okay, Mr. Black. If some dude was staring at my beautiful wife or girlfriend, I'd be upset too. Well, it was nice seeing you again, Ellery, and nice to meet you, Cassidy. Mr. Black, we'll be in touch in a couple of days," Ben said as he started to walk out of the office.

"Hold on. I'm leaving too. I'll walk out with you." Cassidy smiled.

"But, Cass—"

I walked over to Connor and put my hand over his mouth. "She thinks he's hot. Let her go."

"Seriously?" he mumbled.

I removed my hand from his mouth and kissed him softly. "Leave your sister alone."

"I didn't say anything," he said.

"Not yet you didn't. But you have that look."

Connor looked at his watch. "Let's get the hell out of here."

He smiled as he put his arm around me.

Chapter 12

Connor

We both climbed into the Range Rover, and I sat there with my hands on the wheel. I looked over at Ellery as she looked at herself in a small mirror. When she stopped looking at herself, she turned her eyes to me.

"What?" she asked.

"I can't believe what Cassidy did in there."

"Why? She saw a hot guy and she took advantage of the situation."

"Oh, so you think he's hot?"

"Yeah, he's cute," Ellery replied as she put on her lipstick.

"I bet you thought he was hot back in college too," I said as I pulled out of the parking space.

"Are you jealous because I said he was hot, Mr. Black?"

"Don't be ridiculous. I'm not jealous."

"Yes, you are. I can tell by that look on your face." She smiled.

"I don't want to talk about this anymore."

"Okay, babe, but there's no need for you to be jealous. You know I think you're the sexiest man alive," she said as she stroked my cheek and gave me a small smile.

I smiled and we drove home. Ellery became impatient with

the traffic because she wanted to get back to Julia. We didn't talk about the meeting, but I could tell Ellery was upset about it. I didn't want her involved in this at all. If I had my way, she wouldn't know anything. I only wanted to protect me and shield her from this bullshit. She didn't deserve to have to go through this because of my past mistakes and poor judgment.

When we arrived at the penthouse and the elevator doors opened, Ellery threw her purse on the table and walked into the living room. Mason was sitting on the floor and had Julia under her play gym. I walked over to the bar and poured myself a scotch. I pulled out my phone and sent a text message to Cassidy.

"Why did you need to see me earlier?"

"I wanted your opinion on a color for the office I'm redoing."

"Then you should have stuck around instead of chasing after that guy."

"Lol, Connor. Tell Ellery I'll call her later. Bye."

I shook my head and set my phone down on the bar. I stared across the room at Ellery as she sat on the floor and played with Julia. She looked up at me with her beautiful eyes and a small smile graced her face. Mason got up from the floor and said that he needed to go. He picked Julia up, kissed her, and then kissed Ellery goodbye. I gave him a simple wave from across the room and told him to take care. When he left, Ellery came walking over to me with Julia. I took the baby from her, kissed her head, and held her in my arms.

"I want to talk to Mason about working for us as Julia's nanny," Ellery said.

"What? I thought you didn't want a nanny for Julia."

"I didn't at first, but did you see how he was with her? He's a natural, and Julia seems to really like him. Plus, it's time for me to start painting again and, with the whole Ashlyn ordeal, I'm going to need help."

I smiled as I pushed back a strand of her blonde hair. "I'm happy you've decided that you needed help, and I think Mason would be perfect."

"Good. I'll set up lunch and discuss it with him." She smiled.

"I thought we were having dinner with him and Landon tonight."

"Landon told Mason they'd have to take a rain check because they have some event with the modeling agency to attend tonight."

"Grab Julia's diaper bag and car seat. We're going out to dinner," I said.

"Good, then we need to stop at the store and pick up some diapers and formula," she said as she walked away.

* * * *

We put Julia in the Range Rover and drove to the restaurant. As we were eating, she decided she was hungry and started to scream. Ellery instantly took her from her seat as people in the restaurant started to stare. I grabbed a bottle from the diaper bag and handed it to Ellery as fast as I could. The second the bottle hit Julia's mouth, she stopped crying. We both let out a sigh of relief. It didn't last long, because when Ellery went to burp her, she screamed the minute the bottle came out of her mouth. This was an upscale restaurant and the patrons weren't happy that their quiet dinner was being interrupted by a screaming baby. I gave Ellery a look indicating that she needed to do something.

"What do you want me to do, Connor?" she growled.

"I don't know; don't burp her."

"She has to be burped."

Suddenly, Ellery looked over at the couple that was sitting at the table next to us and staring. "What? Have you never heard a baby cry before? Turn yourselves around and mind your own business."

"Ellery!" I snapped.

"You know what? I'm over this," she said.

Ellery got up from the table and headed out of the restaurant. I sighed and called over the waitress for the bill. As soon as she gave it to me, I threw the money on the table and walked out after her. I found her walking down the street, carrying Julia over her shoulder. I quickly caught up with her.

"You know, that was inexcusable back there," I said.

"I know it was, and I'm sorry," she said as she kept walking.

I lightly took ahold of her arm. "Elle, stop and look at me. I love you, no matter how much you embarrass me." I smiled. "It's going to take time to adjust to having to go out with a new baby. We'll make mistakes along the way, but we'll get it right eventually."

Ellery laughed when I said that. "Trial and error, right?"

"That's right, baby, trial and error," I said as I kissed her head.

She handed Julia to me and we walked back to the Range Rover. After we stopped at the store to pick up diapers and formula, we went home.

* * * *

After we gave Julia a bath and changed her into her pajamas, I sat on the bed and fed her a bottle while Ellery took a shower. I stared down at her as she was looking up at me. She had the same eyes as Ellery, which made me melt. This little girl was going to be my undoing, and I had a feeling she was going to take advantage of it when she was older.

"I think it's time me and you had a talk, Julia. You're beautiful just like your mommy and some issues are going to come up that we're not going to see eye to eye on. The boys are going to fall all over you and they're going to want to date you. I just want you to know that you're never allowed to date boys. You're Daddy's little girl, and you always will be. I should be the only man in your life. When I pass away, then you can date."

"Connor!" I heard Ellery snap. "Don't talk like that, and you cannot keep her from dating boys." Ellery laughed.

"I can try, can't I?" I smirked.

I put Julia over my shoulder and burped her. She laid her head down on my shoulder and fell asleep. When I got up from the bed, I walked her over to Ellery so she could kiss her goodnight. When I approached the nursery, I carefully laid Julia down in her crib so as not to disturb her. I needed her to sleep so I could spend some alone time with my wife. Ellery was sitting on the edge of the bed with a towel wrapped around her, putting lotion on her legs.

"Let me do that for you." I smiled as I took the bottle of lotion from her hands.

"You're a bad boy, Mr. Black."

"I fully intend to be, Mrs. Black."

I squirted some lotion on my hands and began rubbing her leg. I moved my hands slowly up and down, applying a light pressure with my thumbs. As I began to rub the top of her foot, she threw head back and moaned.

"That feels so good, Connor," she said.

My hands made their way to the sole of her foot. I smiled while I watched the look on her face. Pleasuring her was the only thing I wanted to do. Moving my thumbs up to her heel, I applied more pressure as I moved my thumbs in circles. Her groans grew louder as I reached the ball of her foot and massaged it deeply.

"Oh God, Connor. I could come right now."

"Baby, don't say things like that, and you better not. Not yet."

Before massaging her toes, I took them in my mouth and lightly nipped at each one. I was driving her crazy, and I loved every minute of it. I put more lotion on my hands and started on her other leg and foot. As I reached her thighs, I pushed the edge of the towel back and began rubbing small circles all the way up, focusing on her inner thigh. Ellery's moans grew louder as she lay all the way down on the bed. Since I couldn't take my lips not touching her skin, I leaned forward and began to kiss each area of her thigh that I massaged. Taking her towel in my hands, I undid it, and I let it fall to the sides of her, exposing her fully naked body. My hands made their way up her torso as they clasped on to her beautiful breasts, pinching and kneading her hardened nipples.

"I'm so hard, Ellery. The things you do to me," I whispered as my lips made their way up her thigh.

I pushed her legs further apart as she lay there, open, and begging me to make her come. My mouth explored her moist skin as my tongue lightly circled around her clit. I dipped my finger inside her as she lifted her hips and moved them around as my finger played inside her. I placed my thumb on her swollen clit and began to lightly rub it as her body stiffened and she grabbed each side of the bed. As she let out a scream of pleasure, my tongue licked its way up her breast and my mouth closed itself around her hard nipple. Ellery was panting and staring at me as I stood up and took down my pants and boxers. I smiled at her as she lifted her arms above her head and crossed her wrists. I slowly climbed on top of her and clasped her wrists tightly. She gasped as my hard cock, which sat between her legs, thrust into her. I leaned my face in closer and tugged at her bottom lip with my teeth as I pounded into her over and over again.

"Harder, Connor," she begged.

I tightened the grip around her wrists and moved quickly in and out of her, smashing my mouth against hers in a passionate kiss. She swelled around me as her legs tightened and her body shook with ecstasy.

"Christ, baby," I yelled as I exploded inside her.

As I collapsed on top of her, I let go of her wrists. She wrapped her arms around me and held me tight. I lifted my head and kissed her on the lips.

"Do you realize that we made it through a full round of sex without one whimper from our daughter?"

"I know. Wasn't it wonderful?" She smiled.

"It sure was, baby."

As my lips traced her jawline, we heard Julia whimper. We looked at the monitor and saw her stirring in her crib. I started to get up from the bed when Ellery grabbed my arm.

"Where are you going?"

"To check on Julia," I said.

"Why? She's only whimpering. Maybe she's having a nightmare about you chasing all her boyfriends away."

"Very funny, Ellery."

"It's okay, Connor. She'll be fine. If she starts to scream, then we'll get her, but until then, she's just probably trying to get comfortable."

I pulled on my boxers and lay back in bed. "You're right, babe," I said as I wrapped my arms around her and stared at my daughter through the monitor.

Chapter 13

Ellery

One month later...

Ashlyn's trial had been going on for about three weeks, and Connor was under a lot of stress. Julia had started to sleep through the night, so that made things a little easier for us. Connor and I worked out at the gym every morning before he went to the office, and Mason watched Julia. He was so good with her, and it was easy to see how much he loved her. Landon confided in me that he was happy that we hired Mason as Julia's nanny because all Mason had been talking about in California was adopting a baby, and Landon wasn't ready for that kind of responsibility yet. So, taking care of Julia had kept Mason busy enough to get his baby fill.

It was a typical morning. Mason was downstairs with Julia. I was putting on my workout clothes and Connor was getting his things together for work. He seemed really on edge this morning, and it was bothering me.

"Don't forget we have Camden's birthday party this weekend at your parents' house," I said casually to him.

"I don't know if I can make it. With this trial and everything, I'm behind at the office, so I may have to work all weekend."

I walked over to him and wrapped my arms around his

waist. "Camden will be crushed if you're not there, and you've never missed anything."

He took a hold of my arms and removed them from his waist. "Don't start with me, Ellery. I've got a lot going on right now."

"Excuse me, Connor!" I snapped.

I sighed and walked out of the room. I didn't want to start my day off with an argument, and I needed to get to the gym because I was meeting Peyton for fittings and lunch. I went downstairs and into the kitchen. I grabbed my bag and kissed Julia goodbye.

"Mason, tell Connor that I already left."

"Umm, all right, Elle. Have a good day," he said.

I took the elevator down and when the doors opened, Denny was standing there.

"Are you ready to go, Ellery? Where's Connor?" he asked.

"Who cares, and I'm taking a cab. Bye, Denny," I said as I stepped onto the sidewalk and hailed a cab.

* * * *

I was on the treadmill in the gym, listening to my iPod, when Connor stepped on the treadmill next to me.

"You never cease to amaze me. I hope you know that," he said.

"Sorry, can't hear you. Music's playing," I said loudly.

"Ellery, take out the damn ear phones."

I rolled my eyes and took them out. "There. Happy?"

He shook his head as he ran on the treadmill. "Why the hell would you not wait for me?"

"Because you were being an ass and giving me an attitude."

"All I said was that I didn't think I was going to be able to make it to Camden's party."

"You told me not to start with you in an irritated tone. So, I left because I didn't want to bother you."

"Baby, you weren't bothering me."

"And you're not talking to me. I know you're not telling me things, and it's eating you up inside."

"I don't want to discuss this any further right now, especially here," he said.

I shook my head, and I got off the treadmill. "Fine. I'm going over to the spin bike."

I walked across to the other side of the gym where a row of spin bikes sat. I knew Connor wouldn't come over there because he hated the spin bikes. He was irritating me with his attitude and not wanting to talk about the trial. I could understand him being upset and trying to protect me, but he needed to understand that I didn't need protecting. I was a big girl and I could handle it. What I couldn't handle was him neglecting his family.

I stayed on the bike for about forty-five minutes, and then I looked around for Connor. I went to his usual machines but he wasn't around. I saw Toby, one of the personal trainers, and asked him if he'd seen Connor. He said he that he'd left already. My blood started to boil as anger shot through my body. I couldn't believe that he left without saying goodbye. I stomped off to the locker room, grabbed my phone from my locker, and quickly sent him a text message.

"You're an asshole."

"If you say so," he replied.

I rolled my eyes. I didn't have time for this. I needed to shower quickly and meet Peyton down the street in less than an hour. After I finished getting dressed, I packed up my bag and left the gym. When I walked out the door, I saw Denny leaning up against the limo. I couldn't help but smile at this all-too-familiar sight.

"Denny, what are you doing here?"

"Just seeing if you need a ride home."

"Thank you, but I'm meeting Peyton down the street." I smiled as I started to walk away.

"Ellery!" Denny called out.

I stopped, turned around, and looked at him.

"You know that you and Julia are the things that matters most to Connor."

"I know that, Denny," I said as I looked down.

"He may not always be right, but he loves you more than his own life, and he would do anything to protect you."

Tears began to fill my eyes as I looked up to keep them from falling. I walked over to where Denny was standing, and I gave him a hug.

"I love him more than life too," I whispered in his ear.

Denny kissed me on the cheek and smiled. "Go on and get out of here."

Smiling back, I turned away and walked down the street to the café where I was meeting Peyton. Upon arrival, I stepped inside and saw her sitting down at a table.

"There you are. What took you so long?" she asked.

"Ugh. I've had a bad morning, thanks to my husband," I said as I dug for my phone in my purse.

"What did he do? He's too perfect to cause you to have a bad day."

"Hold on, I need to text him."

"I just wanted you to know that I don't think you're an asshole and I love you."

Within seconds, a reply from him came through. *"I love you too and we'll talk when I get home. See if Mason can watch Julia tonight and we'll go out; just the two of us."*

"Elle, what's wrong? You look like you're stressed," Peyton said as she pushed a cup of coffee towards me.

"Connor's been under a lot of pressure with this trial, and he's been uptight and irritable lately. I need to do something."

"What do you want to do?"

I had the idea in my head that if I went to the jail and paid a visit to Ashlyn that maybe we could talk, woman to woman, and I could convince her to change her plea. I know, wishful thinking, but it was worth a try.

"Are you busy tomorrow?" I asked as I looked at Peyton.

"No, why? What are you planning to do?" she asked with knitted eyebrows.

"I want to go to the jail and pay Ashlyn a little visit."

Peyton's eyes widened. "Are you fucking crazy?!" she voiced rather loudly.

"Peyton! Keep your voice down!"

"Sorry, but you're crazy. Connor will kill you, Elle."

"I'll handle Connor, and he won't know anyway. I just want to pay a friendly visit, woman to woman."

Peyton kept shaking her head. I knew she didn't agree with me, but she was the only person I could trust.

"Whatever, Ellery. I'll go with you, but I don't agree."

"Thank you." I smiled.

We got up from our seats and headed to the bridal shop for our fitting. As I saw Peyton step out of the dressing room in her wedding dress, my eyes began to fill with tears. She looked stunning, and it reminded me of the day Connor and I were married. I hated the way we left things, and I needed to stop by Black Enterprises to see him. As the tailor was pinning my dress, I called Mason to check on Julia. I missed her terribly.

"Hello, doll face. If you're calling about the princess, she's wonderful. We're getting ready to go to the park."

"Hi, Mason. I'm calling to see if you could babysit her tonight while Connor and I go out."

"Of course I can. I'll watch her at my place and then Landon can have some Julia time too!"

"Thanks. I'll be home in a while," I said as I hung up.

* * * *

I told Peyton we needed to stop at Connor's office for a minute because I needed to pick something up. She gave me a look of disbelief. I never could pull anything over on her. We stepped off the elevator and headed down the hallway towards Connor's office. Valerie was sitting at her desk.

"Hi, Ellery." She smiled as she looked up at me.

"Hi, Valerie. Is he in there?"

"Yes, he is. Do you want me to tell him you're here?"

"No, I'll surprise him."

"He's in a mood today," she said.

"I know he is," I said as I put my hand on the handle. "Peyton, I'll only be a few minutes."

I slowly turned the handle and opened the door. Connor was looking down at some papers.

"Valerie, I thought I gave strict instructions that I didn't want to be bothered," he said in an irritated tone without looking up.

"Even for your wife?" I smiled.

Connor looked up and a smile lit up his face. He got up from his desk and walked towards me. I subtly locked the office door and met him halfway across the room. As I approached him, he wrapped his arms tightly around me.

"What are you doing here, baby?"

"I just needed to hug you and tell you that I'm sorry for everything that happened today."

"Baby, there's no need to apologize. I'm the one who's sorry," he said as he rubbed his cheek through my hair. "Where's Peyton? I thought you had plans with her."

"She's waiting outside the office. I told her I'd be quick." I smiled as I started to unbuckle his belt.

Connor's smile grew as he looked at me. "Make up sex, eh?"

"You bet, and I can't wait until tonight," I said as I unbuttoned his pants, took them down, and pushed him on the couch.

He sat there staring at me as I did a little strip dance. "Oh, God, Elle."

As I smiled and climbed on top of him, he grabbed my hips and gently eased me down onto him.

"You're already so wet," he whispered as he took my nipple in his mouth.

"That's what you do to me, babe. You don't even have to touch me. Your looks are more than enough."

As I began to slowly thrust my hips back and forth, Connor threw his head back and a soft moan came from the back of his throat. He was so hard as I moved my hips around in a circular motion, slowly and fluently. He took his hand and reached down for my clit. I grabbed it as I looked at him and winked.

"Put your hands behind your head, Mr. Black."

"You're a bad girl, Ellery."

"I fully intend to be." I smiled as I reached over.

As I held onto his wrists, my breasts brushed up against his face. He moaned as he took turns sucking each nipple. Reaching one hand behind me, I softly caressed his balls as his body tightened.

"That's it, baby, I can't hold it anymore," he whispered.

Suddenly, I felt a warm sensation shoot into my body as I dug my nails into him and released myself all over him.

"Damn it, Ellery, you're making me want to come again." He smiled.

As I buried my face into his neck and tried to catch my breath, he whispered, "You're fucking amazing."

I looked at him and kissed him on the lips as I put my hands on each side of his face. "Now, I can go about my day." I smiled.

He laughed and shook his head as I got off of him. I stood up and quickly pulled on my clothes. As I walked to the door, I put my hand on the handle, stopped, and turned around.

"I'll bill you for services rendered." I winked as I walked out the door.

Chapter 14

When I arrived home after my day with Peyton, I was surprised that Mason and Julia weren't home from the park yet. As I pulled out my phone, a text message from Mason came through.

"Princess and I made a Starbucks run. Be home in five."

"You better have an iced latte in hand when you walk through the door," I replied.

When I walked into the kitchen to grab a bottle of water, I saw Denny on the phone, sitting at the table. He instantly hung up when he saw me.

"Hi, Denny. What's up?" I asked casually.

"Not much, Ellery. How was your day with Peyton?"

"It was fine," I replied as I took a bottle of water from the refrigerator.

He seemed to be nervous. Almost as if he had just gotten caught doing something or he was afraid that I had heard something while he was on the phone. When I heard the elevator doors open, I ran out of the kitchen and straight to Julia. I smiled as I unbuckled her and held her tight.

"One iced latte for you, my dear." Mason smiled as he handed me the cup.

"Thank you, darling. How was Julia today?"

"Glamorous and perfect, like always. You should have seen

the people at the park going crazy over her."

"That's because she's her daddy's girl." I smiled as I held her and kissed her cheek.

I told Mason that Connor and I would be dropping her off at his place around seven o'clock. He smiled, kissed her goodbye, and stepped onto the elevator. As I was walking up the stairs with Julia, Denny emerged from the kitchen.

"Did you work things out with Connor?" he asked.

"I sure did." I winked.

He rolled his eyes and smiled as he left the penthouse.

* * * *

I laid Julia down in the center of our king-sized bed as I got ready for my date with Connor. While I was in my closet looking for something to wear, I heard Connor walk into the bedroom. He walked over to the bed and sat down next to Julia. The moment she saw him, her little legs started moving all around.

"Look at how excited she is to see her daddy." He smiled.

"I don't blame her. I get excited when I see her daddy too."

"Elle, don't say things like that," he warned with a smile.

I walked over to him. Julia had her hand clasped around his finger.

"I'm still thinking about our little office romp," I whispered as I wrapped my arms around him and kissed his cheek.

"God, baby, I am too." He smiled as he turned his head and his lips brushed against mine.

"Where are we going tonight?"

"Anywhere you want to go," he said. "I've been thinking a lot about something lately, and I want to talk to you about it."

As I pulled my jeans from the drawer, a sick feeling

overtook me because I was afraid to hear what he'd been thinking about.

"I want to get a tattoo, and I was thinking we could go to the place where you got yours."

My eyes lit up as I turned around and looked at him. "Are you serious? What kind of tattoo do you want?"

"I can see that you're pleasantly surprised by the idea." He smiled. "I want something with yours and Julia's names on it, but leave enough room in case we have another child."

While pulling up my jeans, I stopped midway and looked at him. "Another child?"

"Yeah, why not? Let's make us a four-person family."

"We can talk about this again in about two years, Connor. I'm not ready to even think about having another baby yet, especially with the problems I had while I was in labor with Julia."

As I finished pulling up my jeans, he got up from the bed, walked over to me, and put his hands on my hips. "Don't worry; I don't want a baby now. I was just thinking in the future," he said as he kissed me on the head.

"How about if we go out to dinner first and then we'll go see Jack about that tattoo you want to get."

"Sounds good, sweetheart. I'm going to take a quick shower and then we'll go."

Julia started fussing, so I picked her up from the bed and took her downstairs. As I was warming up a bottle, I heard my phone chime. I picked it up from the counter and saw that I had a text message from Cassidy.

"I'm going on a date tonight with Ben! I'm so nervous, Elle."

"That's great, Cass. Don't be nervous. You'll have fun."

"It's been a long time since I've been on a date."

"Just relax and be yourself. Call me tomorrow and let me know how it went."

Just as I hit the send button, Connor came walking into the kitchen and took Julia from me.

"Let me finish feeding her. I missed her today."

Connor sat down in the chair and couldn't stop smiling at Julia as he held the bottle in her mouth.

"Cassidy just texted me, and she's going on a date with Ben tonight."

"What? Are you serious?" he growled.

"Yes, I'm serious, and what's your problem? Your sister deserves to be happy."

He sighed. "Don't get me wrong. I want nothing more than for Cassidy to find the man of her dreams that will come in and sweep her off her feet and make her happy, but I'm afraid she'll get hurt because of Camden."

"Because of Camden? Why?" I asked.

"Because of his autism. It's going to take a pretty special guy to get involved with my sister under those circumstances. Not a lot of guys want to jump into a relationship like that."

"Maybe Ben is that special guy." I smiled as I got up from the chair and grabbed the diaper bag.

"Doubt it."

I sighed as I looked over at Connor. "Are you still being pissy because I said he was hot?"

He wouldn't look at me and he had a smirk on his face. "You're lucky you're holding Julia, because if you weren't—"

"If I weren't, then what, Ellery?"

"Oh, nothing." I smiled as I walked out of the kitchen and

into the living room to get Julia's blanket.

Before I knew it, Connor had followed me. He laid Julia down on her blanket, which was on the floor and looked at me.

"If I weren't ... what?" He smiled as he began moving towards me.

I started to back up as I bit down on my bottom lip. Once again, his look, his walk, his whole demeanor—I knew all too well. I ran up the stairs, but before I could make it, Connor grabbed me from behind and carried me back down.

"Now, tell me again what you were going to do to me if I wasn't holding Julia?" he whispered in a sexy voice that sent shivers down my spine.

His grip on me was tight, and he wouldn't let me go. I didn't want him to let me go. When he held me, I felt safe from the world and all my worries disappeared. He put me down, but continued to hold me from behind. I could tell he didn't want to let go as he buried his face into my neck. Finally, I broke the silence.

"Everything's going to be okay, baby," I whispered as I freed my arm and brought my hand to the back of his head.

Chapter 15

Connor

I held onto Ellery, and Julia started to fuss on the floor. I removed her hand from the back of my head and placed her palm against my lips.

"Let's get Julia packed up and ready to go," I said.

As I walked over and picked her up, Ellery got the diaper bag ready. I put Julia in the car seat and we stepped onto the elevator. We dropped Julia off with Mason and Landon and headed out for dinner.

"Where do you want to go for dinner?" I asked.

"The Shake Shack," she replied.

I looked at her as I twisted my face. "The what, what?"

"The Shake Shack, silly! We can get burgers and shakes, plus it's right by Jack's Tattoo Parlor."

"It sounds dirty and greasy."

Ellery laughed as she cocked her head at me. "You're so adorable. Now, let's go. I'm hungry."

I sighed and we headed to the Shake Shack. As I sat there, eating my grilled chicken sandwich, Ellery shoved her burger in my face.

"Here, taste this. It's the best burger in the world."

"No thanks. It looks greasy and disgusting," I said.

"Suit yourself, Mr. Black. I remember a time when you would taste anything I shoved in your face."

I sat there and stared at her as she ate her burger and fries. I was mesmerized by how adorable she was, eating that burger full of grease. I couldn't resist her, so I gave in.

"Bring it here, and let me taste it," I said as I held out my hand.

A smile spread across her face. The one thing that I loved most about her was that the littlest things made her happy. I took a bite as she held it up to me and was pleasantly surprised that it was good.

"Well?" She smiled.

"It's not bad."

"I knew it! I knew you'd like it."

We finished up dinner, if that's what you wanted to call it, and headed out the door. The tattoo parlor was a couple of blocks over, and Ellery wanted to walk. I took her hand in mine and we headed to the parlor. We were walking down the street and looking in the various shop windows as we passed by, when Ellery suddenly stopped.

"Hi, Elle."

"Hi, Kyle," she replied.

"Connor." He nodded his head.

"Kyle." I nodded back.

He introduced us to his girlfriend and asked Ellery how she was doing. She pulled out her phone and showed him pictures of Julia. I was uncomfortable and just wanted to get the hell out of there. I could see by the way he looked at her that he still had feelings for her. We said our goodbyes and continued walking down the street.

"That was awkward," I said.

"Not really. I've run into him before."

"You have? You've never mentioned it."

"It was no big deal. Just a quick 'hi' in passing."

"I can tell he still has feelings for you."

"Oh well. His loss, right?" She smiled.

"That's right, baby, his loss and my gain. If he never would've left you, I never would've met you, and who knows where I'd be right now?"

She squeezed my hand lightly as we stood in front of Jack's Tattoo Parlor.

"Are you sure you want to do this?" she asked.

"Of course I'm sure. I've never been surer about anything in my life, except for you." I winked at her.

As we walked through the door of the parlor, Jack looked up from behind the counter.

"Well, look who decided to drop by; my girl, Ellery." He smiled as he stepped out from behind the counter.

"Hi, Jack," Ellery said as she gave him a hug. "I want you to meet my husband, Connor. He wants to get a tattoo."

"Hey, Connor, nice to meet you, bro," Jack said as we shook hands. "Take a seat right over here and tell me what you're thinking."

"I was thinking about the double infinity symbol in thick black ink, with Ellery's name at the top and Julia's name at the bottom. I want it on my right bicep."

Ellery looked at me, grabbed my hand, and I could see the tears swell in her eyes. I shook my head at her lightly.

"Sounds good, buddy. Are you ready? Jack asked.

"As ready as I'll ever be."

As Jack was halfway into the infinity design, I asked Ellery how she handled getting the tattoos on both wrists.

"I was in a very bad place and nothing could hurt worse than the pain I'd felt from losing you."

I took in a sharp breath because my heart ached when she said that.

"Ellery was a good sport. She didn't even flinch," Jack said.

"She's a strong woman." I smiled.

Two hours later, and my tat was finished. I looked at it through the mirror and it was exactly what I wanted.

"Connor, it looks great! I love it!" Ellery exclaimed.

"Thank you, Jack. You did a great job," I said as I pulled out my wallet and Ellery grabbed it out of my hand.

"Here, Jack. Thank you for everything." She smiled as she handed him the money, plus a hundred-dollar tip.

I looked at her as she looped her arm in mine and we walked out the door. "What is with you giving people such large tips?" I asked.

"He deserved it. Look at the wonderful job he did on your tattoo. I must say that I'm very turned on by it," she said as a wide grin graced her face.

"Well, then, it was worth it."

We walked down the streets of the city and back to the Range Rover. Ellery pulled out her phone and sent a text message to Mason, telling him that we were on our way to get Julia. As we reached the garage where the Range Rover was parked, I opened the door for Ellery and kissed her passionately before letting her get in.

"What was that for?" she asked with a smile.

"Just because I love you, and I want to have sex right here and right now."

"Here? In the parking garage?" she asked as her teeth slid across her bottom lip.

"Yep, right here, in our SUV, in the parking garage."

"You're a kinky man, Connor, but what if someone sees us?"

I leaned closer into her and traced her jaw line with my finger. "No one's going to see us, baby; the windows are tinted."

She reached her hand down and felt my erection through the fabric of my pants as I reached for her breasts from underneath her shirt. She moaned and closed her eyes when my bare fingers touched her nipples.

"Wouldn't you rather do it here, without the risk of Julia disturbing us?" I whispered as my tongue softly licked the tender spot behind her ear.

"Backseat, and I'm on top," she whispered back.

"I'm not going to argue with you," I said as I opened the back passenger's door and we both climbed in.

Chapter 16

Ellery

A couple of days later, as I was getting Julia dressed, my phone rang. I reached over, grabbed it from the bed, and saw it was Sal from the art gallery.

"Hi Sal," I answered.

"Hey, Ellery. My brother is opening up a large art gallery in Chicago, and he wants you to be a part of it. He was going to call you, but I told him to hold off until I talked to you first. His art show is going to be big, and he has a lot of influential people and critics attending. This could be a big break for you as an artist. He said he wants at least five of your new paintings to showcase."

My heart began beating with excitement as I said yes right away. The thought of painting again thrilled me.

"Thank you, Sal. Tell your brother to call me and that I'm very excited."

"I will, Ellery, and congratulations. I know you'll do fantastic," he said as he hung up.

I picked up Julia and did a little happy dance with her. I hadn't painted since before she was born, and I missed it. Connor had already left for the office, and I was dying to tell him about the phone call from Sal, so I decided that we'd stop by his office after we picked up Camden's birthday gift. When

I took Julia downstairs, Claire took her from me.

"Good morning, Ellery." She smiled.

"Good morning, Claire. Can you keep an eye on Julia for me while I finish getting ready? We're going to go shopping today for Camden's birthday and then we're going to pay a surprise visit to Connor."

Claire smiled as she looked down at Julia. "Of course I can keep an eye on this little doll."

"Thank you, Claire. I won't be too long."

* * * *

As Denny was driving Julia and me to FAO Schwarz to meet Cassidy, his phone rang. He looked at it and then at me through the rearview mirror. I found it odd that he didn't answer it. A few seconds later, his phone rang again.

"You better get that. It may be important," I said.

He picked up his phone and answered it. He kept watching me through the mirror. He didn't offer much to the conversation except a few "Okays." This was the second time he had behaved strangely with a phone call while I was around. I was beginning to think that something was going on that he didn't want me to know about. I decided not to ask him about it just yet.

Denny pulled up to the curb and Cassidy was waiting outside the store for us. She walked around, opened the door, and took Julia from her car seat. After I thanked Denny for his help, he said goodbye and drove away.

"I want to hear all about your date with Ben," I said as the man dressed as a toy soldier held the door open for us.

"It was a lot of fun. Not only is he hot, but he's funny too."

"I think I remember him being on the funny side." I smiled.

"Connor was upset that I said he was hot." I laughed.

"Tell Connor he has nothing to worry about."

"I already did, but he wants to be the only hot man in my life."

"Of course he does. He's madly in love with you. But the weird thing is, I didn't think he was the jealous type."

"I quickly put his fears to rest." I winked.

Cassidy and I walked around the store for over two hours. Julia had just woken up and she was starting to get fussy. When I stopped the stroller and took her out of it, Cassidy lightly touched my arm. I looked over at her as she stared ahead. My eyes diverted over to where she was looking, and I saw my husband standing there, next to the big piano, with a wide smile on his face.

"What are you doing here?" I smiled as I walked over to him and he took Julia from my arms.

"I was hoping to take my three favorite girls to lunch."

"Oh, so, now I'm one of your favorite girls?" Cassidy asked him as she kissed his cheek.

"You've always been my favorite sister." He winked.

"Julia and I were going to surprise you and come to the office."

"Well, it looks like I surprised you first," Connor said as he kissed my lips.

Cassidy walked over and stepped onto the big piano with one foot. "Connor, do you remember when we were kids?" she asked with a smile.

"I sure do. Mom and Dad used to bring us here, and the both of us would try to play a song on that."

"Come play with me; just for fun. Like we used to," she said as she held out her hand.

There was nothing I wanted more than to see Connor playing on the big piano, but there was no way he was going to do it. As he handed Julia to me, he took Cassidy's hand and stepped onto the toy with her. I stood there in shock. He took two steps to the left as she took two steps to the right. I put Julia in her stroller and pulled out my phone. This was something that I never wanted to forget, I thought as I hit the video record button. As Cassidy stepped off the piano, Connor stepped a little tune. When he was finished, Cassidy stepped on and played the same tune. Both of them were smiling and laughing. It was so good to see Connor having fun and relax a bit. They were both out of breath when they finished. Cassidy walked past me and I high-fived her. As Connor walked up to me, he wrapped his arms around me tightly and swayed me back and forth.

"You looked really sexy doing that." I smiled.

"We used to come here all the time. Sometimes when Cassidy and I would be playing on it, one of the other keys would light up that we didn't step on, and I'd tell her that Collin was here playing with us. It sort of freaked her out."

I broke our embrace and put my hand on his chest. "I bet he was here. He's always with you in spirit."

Connor smiled and kissed my head. "Come on; let's go eat. I'm starving."

While we stood in line, waiting to make our purchases, Connor took Julia from the stroller and held her up while making funny faces at her.

"Well, look at Daddy Connor," I heard a voice from behind say.

Connor and I turned around and we saw Sarah standing there. Instantly, Connor became nervous.

"Sarah. How are you?" he asked politely.

"I'm good, Connor. It's nice to see you again." She smiled. "Ellery, you look wonderful."

"Thank you, Sarah," I replied as I watched her move closer to Julia.

Seeing her always put a sick feeling in my stomach. Just knowing how she and Connor had used each other for years, and the things they did, made me irritated, but not as bad as when I looked at Ashlyn.

"Ellery, she's adorable, and she looks just like you."

I smiled politely as she backed away. "It was good seeing both of you again. You're a perfect little family, and I would be lying if I didn't say that I was jealous. Have a good day," she said as she walked away.

Cassidy looked at me and then looked at Connor. She didn't say a word and neither did he. Suddenly, I blurted out, "Well, that was awkward."

Connor put Julia in her stroller, stood behind me, and whispered in my ear, "Like it was awkward running into Kyle."

I looked around and saw that Cassidy was making her purchase. I discreetly reached my hand back and placed it on Connor's crotch, giving it a light squeeze. I leaned my head back and whispered, "He was my boyfriend, not my fuck buddy. There's a difference."

Connor placed his hand on mine as I released my light grip. "Baby, that's not nice, and we'll discuss it when we get home."

"You bet we'll discuss it when we get home; just not with words."

"Oh God," he whispered.

I paid for Camden's birthday gifts and the four of us

walked out of the store. As Connor pushed the stroller, I looped my arm around his and smiled.

* * * *

While we were waiting for our food to be served, I asked Connor how he knew we were at FAO Schwarz.

"Babe, you told me last night you were going there, and when I talked to Denny, he said he'd just dropped you and Julia off."

"But we had already been in there for over two hours. How did you know we were still in there?"

"I took my chances, Ellery. What's with the million questions?"

I shook my head and apologized. Something wasn't sitting right with me, and I couldn't put my finger on it.

"Oh my God! I completely forgot to tell you, Connor!" I exclaimed.

"What?"

"The reason Julia and I were coming to see you at the office. Sal called me and his brother is opening an art gallery in Chicago, and he wants me to do a showing with five of my paintings."

"That's great news, Ellery." Cassidy smiled.

"Baby, that's wonderful. I don't think you have five paintings done, do you?" Connor asked.

I looked down as the waitress set my club sandwich down in front of me. "No, I don't. I need to start painting, and quick."

"When's the opening?" Cassidy asked.

As I gave her a perplexed look, I bit down on my bottom lip. "I don't know. I was so excited, I forgot to ask."

"I'm so happy for you." Connor smiled as he leaned over and kissed me.

While eating our lunch, we talked about Camden's party and then Cassidy had to go and say something she shouldn't have.

"Ben's coming to Camden's party."

Julia began to whine, so I reached over and took her from her stroller. I didn't want to look at Connor because I knew he was going to be pissed.

"Don't give me that look, Connor. I'll have you know that he's a very nice guy, and I like him. In fact, we're going out tonight, with Camden."

Connor leaned across the table. "You're letting him into Camden's life?"

"I like him and, from what I can tell, he likes me."

"Does he know about Camden?"

"Of course he does! Do you think I would hide that from him?"

Putting my hand on Connor's arm to try and diffuse the situation didn't help. Cassidy stood up and threw some money on the table.

"I think I'd better leave before you or I say something we'll regret. Ellery, I love you and we'll talk later," she said as she kissed me on the cheek.

She walked out of the restaurant, and I looked at Connor. "Are you happy now?"

Connor shook his head and rolled his eyes. "She had no reason to get upset like that," he said.

By this point, Julia was tired and getting fussy. "I don't want to talk about this now. I need to get Julia home for a nap."

"Come here, baby girl," Connor said as he took her from me. "You'll never get mad at your daddy."

"Just wait until she's a teenager and wants nothing to do with you," I said.

"Ellery, don't say things like that," he said with a shocked looked on his face.

I smiled as we got up from our seats and walked out of the restaurant.

Chapter 17

Connor

Denny was waiting for us outside the restaurant. Once we reached the limo, I handed Julia to Ellery and I folded up the stroller and put it in the trunk. Ellery buckled in Julia as I slid in and shut the door. When I looked over at her, she was staring at me.

"What?" I asked.

"What is your problem?"

"I don't have a problem, Ellery."

"Yes, you do, Connor. Why would you start about Ben?"

"I didn't say anything about Ben. I simply asked if he knew about Camden. That's all."

"You gave Cassidy a look of disgust when she told you he was going to be at the party."

"Listen, I love my sister and Camden very much. She needs to be careful of who she brings into Camden's life."

"Wait a minute," Ellery said as she glared at me. "You're afraid that Camden will push a guy away and break your sister's heart."

As I looked out the window, I couldn't say anything. She was right. I only wanted Cassidy to be happy, but if Camden didn't like someone or felt threatened, he could be a handful. I didn't want my sister getting attached and then having her heart broken when the guy left because of him. Ellery reached over and grabbed my hand.

"Connor, I understand that you're concerned for Cassidy. Trust me, I don't want to see her or Camden get hurt either, but she's a grown woman and is capable of making her own decisions."

"I know she's capable of making her own decisions, Ellery. I just don't want her to get hurt. I've always protected her and Camden, and I'm not about to stop now because some guy wants a piece of ass."

"Connor!" Ellery snapped. "I can't believe you just said that."

As Denny pulled into the parking garage, I opened the door and took out Julia's car seat. Ellery grabbed the diaper bag and followed me into the elevator.

"I'm sorry I said that. Maybe I didn't mean it. Hell, I don't know what I meant. I guess we'll just have to wait and see what happens. But I promise you this: if he hurts her, he'll have me to deal with."

Ellery looked over at me and smiled. "Or me, and I'm not really sure which one of us is worse."

"Oh, that would be you, my love." I smiled as I stepped off the elevator.

Ellery slapped me on the ass for that comment, and I felt a twinge below. "You shouldn't have done that, baby."

"Calm down, Black. I have a baby's diaper to change."

While Ellery took Julia upstairs to change her diaper, I went into my office. A few moments later, Denny came in, shut the door, and sat down.

"Are you going to tell Ellery about Ashlyn?" he asked.

"I don't feel like I have to. I'm keeping her in the loop about the trial and she seems content with that. I don't want to upset her any more than she already is."

"But you promised her no secrets, Connor, and this classifies as a secret."

"She can't focus on Ashlyn and the trial anymore. She's going to be doing a showing at an art gallery in Chicago, and they need five paintings. She needs to focus on that without any distractions. Between painting and Julia, she'll be too busy even to think about Ashlyn and the trial."

Denny sat there and shook his head at me. "Will you ever learn?"

"Trust me. I know what I'm doing."

"You know what you're doing about what?" Ellery asked as she opened the door and stood there.

I had to think fast or she'd start asking a million questions. "Damn it, Ellery. You ruined the surprise," I said.

Denny glared at me. I held out my arms for her and told her to come sit on my lap.

"Denny and I were just talking about your art studio." I smiled.

A beautiful smile graced her face as she looked at me. "What art studio?"

As I glanced over at Denny. He rolled his eyes. "The one I'm building you so you can paint."

Ellery threw her arms around my neck and hugged me. "Connor, I'm so excited! So tell me about this studio of mine!" she said excitedly.

"Yes, Connor, tell Ellery your plans for the studio," Denny said smugly.

"We can discuss it later," I said as I tapped her on the nose and shot Denny at look. "You'll love it, but I have to finish something up. Please let me surprise you, baby."

"Okay, but you know how impatient I am."

"Yes, I know you are," I said as I heard Julia cry.

Thank God for Julia, I thought to myself. Ellery got up from my lap and walked out of the office. Denny got up from his chair and shook his head. "You better get moving on those plans for that art studio you just promised her."

"I'm going to do that right now," I sighed.

I pulled out my phone and dialed Paul. It went to voicemail, so I left a message for him to call me back right away. He could locate a place for Ellery's art studio.

* * * *

As I walked out of my office and passed the living room, I noticed Ellery sound asleep on the couch. I grabbed a blanket from the closet and gently covered her with it. I needed a scotch, so I walked over to the bar and poured myself one. The smoothness going down the back of my throat soothed me, as did the sight of my sleeping wife. My eyes gazed at her as my mind was punishing me for keeping something from her. A few moments later, she opened her eyes and looked at me from across the room.

"How long have I been sleeping?"

"I'm not sure. You were asleep when I came out of my office," I said as I walked over to her, sat down on the edge of the couch, and pushed a few strands of hair from her face.

When she sat up, she took the glass from my hand and took a sip. As always, she made the same face when she drank it.

"Why do you take a sip when you don't like Scotch?"

"I was thirsty." She smiled.

I leaned closer towards her and brushed her lips with mine. Her lips responded seductively as she hardened our kiss. Just as I laid her back and hovered over her, kissing her passionately, my phone rang. Taking in a sharp breath as I broke our kiss, I pulled my phone from my pocket and saw that Paul was calling.

"Baby, we have to continue this later. I have to take this; it's Paul."

"It's all right. Go ahead and take your call. I'll go check on Julia."

"Hey, Paul," I answered as I walked into my office and shut the door. "I need you to find me a space that I can convert into an art studio for Ellery."

"I'll get on that right away, Connor. Do you have a certain area in mind?"

"Somewhere close to the penthouse. I think she'll like it better if she's close to home."

"Got it. I'll call you when I locate something."

I had a good feeling about this art studio. It was something that I should've done a long time ago, but with Ellery's illness, the wedding, and now Julia, she didn't really paint too much, and I didn't give it any thought. Perfection was what I needed the studio to be. It needed to be a distraction from the daily grind of the trial.

Chapter 18

Ellery

As I picked up Julia from the changing table, my phone started to ring. I held her up over my shoulder and walked over to take it from where it was sitting on her dresser.

"Hi, Peyton."

"Hey, Elle. I thought we were going to see that bitch in jail."

"We are. The day we talked about it was visiting day, so now we have to wait until next week."

"Oh okay. I was just wondering because you were really adamant about going and then you never mentioned it again. I thought that maybe you'd changed your mind. Actually, I was hoping you'd changed your mind."

"No, Peyton, I haven't changed my mind."

"Okie dokie, Elle. What are you doing?"

"Staring at my sexy husband as he's standing in the doorway. I'll call you later."

As I hit the end button, Connor walked over, took Julia, and sat in the rocking chair. My greatest love was watching my husband with his daughter. I took the new clothes I bought for Julia and hung them in the closet. My stomach tied itself in knots when Connor asked me a question.

"What haven't you changed your mind about?"

I stood facing the inside of the closet as I hung up the clothes one by one. My skin started to feel fiery and nerves set in. I needed to think of something fast.

"What?" I innocently asked.

"I heard you say to Peyton that you haven't changed your mind."

"Oh, that. It was about going with her next week to look at flowers for the wedding."

"Why would she think that you'd change your mind?"

"She didn't. She was just making sure that I didn't change my mind," I said as I looked at him in confusion.

"Shouldn't Henry be going with her?" he asked.

"Did you go with me, Mr. Black?"

"Good point." He smiled.

Emerging from the rocking chair, he took Julia downstairs and put her in her swing. I followed behind as I let out a sigh of relief. If he ever found out that I was going to see Ashlyn, I didn't know what he'd do.

I picked up toys around the living room and put them in a basket, then walked to the kitchen to make a cup of coffee. Connor came from behind and wrapped his strong arms around me, taking in my scent as his hot breath traveled down my neck. As I put my hands on his arms and tilted my head to the side, his lips began their journey across my skin.

"I wish Mason was here right now to take Julia for a while so I could fuck you on this kitchen counter."

"We don't need Mason. You can still do it. Julia's being good in her swing. We may not have a lot of time, but we can certainly try."

A low growl developed in the back of his throat as he reached his hand between my thighs and started cupping me below. I quickly turned around to face him. He picked me up and set me on the counter while his hands made their way up my shirt and to my breasts. I brought my hands to his head and ran my fingers through his hair. Our mouths devoured each other. Suddenly, we heard someone clear their throat. I jumped, and Connor looked across the kitchen.

"Am I interrupting something?" Denny asked as he walked to the refrigerator.

"Damn it, Denny."

"Relax, Connor. Julia would have made sure you two didn't get any further."

I couldn't help but laugh at his comment as I got off the counter and straightened my shirt. Just as I was about to say something, my phone rang. I looked over to where it was sitting.

"It's a call from Chicago. I bet it's Sal's brother. I'll be right back," I said as I walked out of the kitchen.

"Hello."

"Ellery?" a male voice spoke.

"Yes, this is Ellery."

"Hi, this is Vinnie, Sal's brother. He said he was going to call you about my art gallery showing here in Chicago."

"Yes, Vinnie, Sal did call me, and I'm very interested in doing a showing."

"That's great, Ellery. I've seen your work and I think you're an amazing painter. Is there any way you can fly out to Chicago and we can meet for dinner to discuss the opening?"

"Sure. When would you like to meet?"

"The sooner, the better. That way, you can get a feel for what I'm expecting."

"I can probably fly out tomorrow," I said.

"That'll be great. Call me or send me a text to confirm, and I'll make reservations for dinner. I look forward to meeting you, Ellery."

"Thank you, Vinnie. I'll be in touch."

Excitedly, I walked back to the kitchen, where Denny was holding Julia and Connor was sitting across from him.

"Well?" Connor asked.

"I'm flying to Chicago tomorrow to have dinner with Vinnie. So make sure the plane's ready."

"Yes, ma'am!" Connor smiled. "I'll clear my schedule for tomorrow and fly with you."

"You don't have to go, Connor. I know how busy you are."

"You're not going alone, end of discussion, Ellery," he said in a serious tone.

I looked over at Denny as he raised his eyebrows at me. When I slowly walked over to where Connor sat, he looked up from his phone at me.

"What?"

"I love you, but if you ever take that tone with me again, I will hurt you. Do you understand?"

The corners of his mouth curved up into a sinister smile. "Then I'll make sure to use that tone more often, especially in the bedroom."

"Or in the kitchen, if that's what you prefer," Denny chimed in.

I couldn't help but laugh as I walked over and kissed Denny on the cheek.

* * * *

After having the best sex with Connor, first in bed and then again in the shower, we packed a light bag, grabbed the diaper bag, put Julia in her car seat, and headed to Mason's loft to pick him up. Opening the door, he slid into the seat across from us and sat down next to Julia.

"Hello, princess! We're going to have so much fun in Chicago. Uncle Mason is going to take you to the American Girl store."

"Don't you think she's a little young for that?" Connor asked.

"Bite your tongue! You're never too young for those beautiful and fun dolls."

Once we arrived at the airport, we boarded Connor's plane and headed to Chicago. Upon arriving in the Windy City, we checked ourselves into the Trump Towers and headed to our rooms. Connor handed Mason a key to his own room. Mason looked at him in confusion.

"I have my own room? Aren't nannies supposed to stay with the couple and their child?"

"You have your own room where you can hang out with Julia when we need you to. Your bar is fully stocked with the best liquor, so please enjoy. But not while Julia's with you."

"Have I told you how much I love you?" Mason winked at him.

Stepping into the suite, I threw myself on the luxurious king-sized bed. Connor asked Mason to take Julia to his room while we got ready for dinner.

"Dinner isn't for a few hours," I said.

Connor walked towards the bed, unbuttoning his shirt. He slid it off and laid it across the chair. I stared at his sexy, ripped abs and shivers ran across my skin. He climbed on the bed and hovered over me while he gazed into my eyes.

"I want to make love to you, Ellery Black; right here and right now. I want to touch and feel every inch of your bare skin, and I want to feel your excitement all over me. Then I want to take you into the bathtub and soap up your naked body while making love to you again."

I gasped. His effect on me was riveting, and I was already wet just from his words. He always made me feel like I was the only woman on Earth, and his constant hunger for me made my body tremble. I stared into his mesmerizing eyes as he slid his hand down my yoga pants, not stopping until he felt how aroused I was.

"God, you're so wet, baby," he moaned as dipped his finger inside me.

I arched my back and threw back my head, begging for more as he ripped off my pants and tossed them on the floor.

* * * *

While I freshened up my makeup and fixed my hair, Connor went and brought Julia and Mason back to the room. Mason walked into the bathroom and looked at me.

"Look at your glowing face, Miss Ellery. You must've had amazing sex."

I didn't turn around. I looked at him through the mirror and smiled.

"I knew it!" he exclaimed.

"Oh, stop it. You knew we were going to when he had you take Julia to your room."

Mason took a few steps forward and leaned in closer to me. "Just tell me one thing: is he as amazing in bed as he looks like he'd be?"

I knitted my eyebrows at him and then smiled. "Yes, and amazing doesn't even describe how skillful he is."

"Damn, I knew it." He sighed.

"Stop dreaming about my husband and help me pick out a dress to wear."

As I walked over to the closet and looked at the four dresses I brought, Connor walked into the bedroom with Julia. He laid her down on the bed and dangled her animal keys in front of her. I looked over and smiled, then pulled the red dress and the blue dress from the closet.

"Which one?" I asked as I held both dresses up.

"The blue one. The red one," both Connor and Mason said at the same time.

I looked at both of them with a twisted face. "Okay, the black one it is," I said as I put the red and blue dresses back, and I pulled out the black one.

"Thank you, gentlemen. Now if you'll excuse me, I have a dress to put on."

"Okay, black works," I heard Mason say as I walked into the bathroom and shut the door.

When I finished putting on my dress and black heels, I kissed Julia goodbye while Connor had his hand on the small of my back, pushing me out the door. We met Vinnie at a restaurant called Spiaggia. He had already arrived and stood up when the hostess showed us to the table.

"Ellery Black. It's nice to finally meet you," he said as he kissed me lightly on the cheek.

"It's nice to meet you as well, Vinnie. This is my husband, Connor Black."

The two of them shook hands, then we took our seats and opened our menus.

"I took the liberty of ordering us a bottle of their finest Pinot grigio. I hope you don't mind."

"No, not at all." Connor smiled.

After deciding what I wanted for dinner, I closed the menu and folded my hands on the table. "So, tell me about your art gallery."

"The gallery is about ten thousand square feet. I would like to show you it tomorrow morning, if possible."

"We need to fly back to New York in the morning. How about tonight, after dinner?" Connor said.

"Okay, tonight will be fine." Vinnie smiled.

"The opening of the gallery will take place in forty-five days," Vinnie said. "Is that something you can work with?"

I took a sip of my wine and swallowed hard. I didn't know if I could do it. But I wasn't going to let him know that.

"Of course I can work with that," I said as I took another sip of wine.

"Great. When we go and tour the unfinished gallery, I'll show you the space I have picked out for your paintings."

As we ate our fine cuisine and drank our wine, Connor and Vinnie mostly talked about the business aspect of the art gallery. I pulled out my phone and sent a text message to Mason.

"How's my baby?"

"I'm fine, thank you. Oh wait, you mean the princess. She's adorable and she's sleeping."

"Great. We'll be back to the hotel later. We're going to take a tour of the art gallery."

"No hurry and have fun."

* * * *

After we toured the art gallery, Connor and I said goodbye to Vinnie and slid into the back seat of the limo that was waiting for us. Connor reached over and took my hand.

"Did you like the gallery?"

"I loved it. It's going to be amazing once it's finished."

"It'll be amazing when your paintings are hanging on the wall." He smiled.

After I kissed him on the cheek, I laid my head on his shoulder while I was worried about whether or not I'd be able to finish all five paintings in time. When I was single, the worry would never have crossed my mind. But now that I was a wife and a mother, it was going to be difficult, even with Connor's and Mason's help. I took in a deep breath as Connor kissed me on my head.

Chapter 19

Connor

After we had a nice breakfast, we flew back to New York. I had Denny drop me off at Black Enterprises so I could catch up on business before he drove Ellery, Julia, and Mason home.

"I'll see you later, baby," I said as I kissed Ellery and then Julia goodbye.

"Bye, sweetheart. Don't work too hard."

I shut the door and walked into the building. As I stepped onto the elevator, my phone rang. It was Paul.

"I'm on my way up to see you. I'm in the elevator."

When the elevator doors opened, I walked down the hallway to Paul's office. I opened the door and sat down across from him.

"I found a place for Ellery's art studio."

"Great; where's it at?" I asked.

"In your building."

I looked at him in confusion. "What do you mean, in my building? What building?"

"Where you live, Connor," he sighed.

I knitted my eyebrows while I got up and walked over to his coffee pot. "I don't know if that's such a good idea. I wanted it outside of the building."

"Listen, Connor. It's perfect, and I think she'd love it. It's on the tenth floor, and it's the end apartment. It has more windows for natural light, kitchen, bathroom, and a bedroom, which can be converted into a storage room. She'll have everything she needs there and, most importantly, it's safe. I know how you are with her about safety."

I stood there, sipped my coffee, and nodded my head. "Perhaps you're right. I'll go have a look at it before I head home. Thanks, Paul," I said as I walked out and headed to my office.

Later in the day, I decided to call Cassidy. I dialed her number and waited patiently for her to answer. I wasn't sure if she would or not, considering how we left things the other day.

"If you're calling to harass me about my love life, save it," she answered.

"Now that's a clever way to answer the phone. I take it you're still pissed at me."

"Pissed isn't a strong enough word, Connor."

"I'm sorry about the other day. I really am. Now, if you'll forgive me, then I can tell you the reason I'm calling."

"You didn't call to apologize?" she asked.

"Well, yes, that too, but I also wanted to ask you for a favor."

I heard a long sigh on the other end. "What do you want?"

"I'm looking at an apartment in my building to convert to an art studio for Ellery, and I would love for you to look at it with me. But please don't tell her; it's a surprise."

"When do you want to do this?"

"What time is good for you?" I asked her.

"How about an hour?"

I looked across my office and I saw the door open. Cassidy was standing in the doorway. I smiled and hung up the phone, getting up from my chair as she stepped into the office. I gave her a tight hug.

"I'm sorry, sis. You know how much I love you and Camden, and I only want the best for you."

"I know you do, Connor, and I love you too, but you can't think that you can rule my life. Let me fall. I'll get back up and try again. I'm not as weak as you think I am."

"I don't think you're weak at all." I smiled as I broke our embrace.

"I have a couple of things to finish up in the other office and then we can go."

"Great, I'll call Denny to come pick us up."

"No need. I have my car. You can just drive us there." She smiled as she left the office.

There was nothing I hated more than New York City traffic and she knew it. Perhaps it was her way of getting back at me.

* * * *

Cassidy and I stepped into the apartment and, instantly, I knew it was perfect for Ellery.

"I love it, Connor," Cassidy said. "She'll love it!"

"It's nice. Tell me your vision for the place. Remember, it's to be an art studio."

As Cassidy walked around the apartment and showed me what she envisioned, I knew that Ellery was going to adore it. The more I thought about it, I knew that Paul was right. It was a lot safer here for Ellery to have an art studio, and I wouldn't have to worry so much about her. Pulling out my phone, I called the owner and bought the apartment. Cassidy and I walked out the door and, as I pushed the button to the elevator, I hugged Cassidy goodbye. The doors opened and I jumped when I saw Ellery standing inside the elevator.

"Connor, Cassidy. What are you doing?" she asked with a weird look on her face.

Fuck, I thought to myself. "Baby, what are you doing?"

"I believe I asked you first, Connor," she said as she stepped off the elevator. "Why are you on this floor?"

"Oh, hell," I said as I shook my head. I grabbed her hand. "Come on; I'll show you the reason."

I opened the apartment door and motioned for her to step inside. "I'm confused," she said.

"Welcome to your art studio."

A shocked expression overtook her face. "What?"

I wrapped my arms around her waist. "This is your art studio, baby. I bought it for you as a surprise and Cassidy is going to decorate it. This is where you'll come and do all your painting with no interruptions."

"Oh, Connor, I love it! Thank you," she said as she kissed me.

She thanked Cassidy with a hug and then Cassidy announced she had to leave.

"I need to get home. I still have a lot to do for Camden's party tomorrow."

Ellery asked her if there was anything she could help her do. Cassidy politely said no and that she had everything under control. After she walked out of the apartment, Ellery shut the door and stood up against it with a smile on her face. I could tell she was up to something.

"We should get going," I said.

"We will, after we christen my new art studio." She smiled.

I felt a twinge below when she said that. She walked over to where I was standing, grabbed the bottom of my shirt, and lifted it over my head.

"I'm going to give you a proper thank you, Mr. Black," she said as she unbuckled my belt.

I was grinning from ear to ear with that thought.

* * * *

We pulled up to the long, winding driveway of my parents' house. The porch was decorated with balloons and a big sign that said *Happy Birthday, Camden*. Ellery and I both smiled when we saw the sign, knowing that, in the not-too-distant future, we'd be doing the same for Julia. We stopped at our beach house first to drop off our bags and to check on things. It'd been a while since we'd been there because of everything that was going on. Mason and Landon were driving up for the party as well as Peyton and Henry, and Denny and his wife, Dana. I parked the Range Rover and unbuckled Julia's car seat. Ellery grabbed the diaper bag and Camden's gifts. As we walked into the house, Camden came running from the family room. I quickly put down the car seat as he ran into my arms.

"Happy birthday, buddy," I said as I kissed his head. He smiled at me and then looked at Ellery and held his arms out to her. She set the gifts on the table and took him from me, hugging him and wishing him a happy birthday.

As Ellery took Julia from the car seat, Camden led me by the hand out to the backyard. All of our family and friends were there, laughing, talking, and having a good time. The minute my mother saw us, she ran over and took Julia from Ellery. As we made our rounds, Aunt Sadie came up to us and gave us both a hug. She took Ellery's hand and turned it over.

I really hated when she was at family functions. As she looked at Ellery and smiled, she squeezed her hand.

"You're very healthy, my dear."

"Thank you, Aunt Sadie; that's good to know." She smiled.

Aunt Sadie asked Ellery to bend down and she whispered something in her ear. I watched as Ellery smiled and thanked her.

"What was that about?" I asked when Aunt Sadie walked away.

"Oh, she just told me that she sees a little boy in our future." She smiled as she hooked her arm around mine.

I raised my eyebrows at her. "We're going to have a son?"

"According to Aunt Sadie, we are." She laughed.

The thought of having a son thrilled me. A boy that I could groom to take over Black Enterprises like my dad did with me. I leaned over and kissed Ellery on the head.

"What was that for?" she asked.

"Just because I love you."

She smiled as she gave my arm a squeeze. We walked over to where Denny and Dana were sitting and took a seat next to them. It wasn't too long after I sat down that my father asked to see me. I followed him into the house and into his office, where he shut the door.

"How are things going with the trial, son?" he asked.

I ran my hand through my hair as I walked over to the bar and poured a glass of scotch. "It's going like all trials go, Dad. I just wish this bullshit was over."

"You got yourself into this mess, Connor. What the hell were you thinking, getting into a relationship with that whore?"

I took in a sharp breath as I looked at him. "I had my reasons."

"You never said what those reasons were, and I want to know. I don't want my company dragged through the mud because you couldn't keep your dick in your pants."

His comment burned throughout my body. "Black Enterprises is my company now. I turned that company around when you weren't paying attention to it because you were off with your whore in the Caribbean and your accountant was robbing you blind," I spat through gritted teeth.

My father didn't know that I knew about the woman that he took to the Caribbean two years before I took over the company. He was supposed to be on a business trip for a month in Germany, at least that's what he told my mother. His accountant had embezzled money and his V.P. made some very bad business deals. My father turned around and wouldn't look at me as he spoke.

"You never told your mother about that. Why?"

"Because, it would've killed her and I didn't want to see her hurt. My relationship with Ashlyn was out of control. I was in a dark and bad place at that time. Thank God Ellery came into my life when she did. Listen, Dad, Lou has this under control. I don't want you to worry about it. Hopefully, it'll all be over soon."

As he turned around, he looked at me and smiled. "You're right, son, and I'm sorry for what I said."

I gave him a small smile as he walked from behind his desk and patted me on the back. I opened the door and Ellery was standing there.

"There you are. I wondered where you had disappeared to," she said.

"Sorry, Ellery. I had to steal my boy and go over a few things with him. Now where's that granddaughter of mine?" My father smiled at her.

As we walked out to the backyard, we heard screaming. I looked over to my right and saw Camden on the ground, kicking and screaming at the top of his lungs. I started to go to him and Ellery grabbed my arm. "Connor, don't."

Just then, I saw Ben go over to him. He laid down on the ground next to him and made Camden look at him. He started making gestures with his hands and pointing up at the sky and told Camden to do the same. Ellery looked over at me and smiled as Camden instantly calmed down and did what Ben had asked. Everyone went about their business and continued to eat and talk amongst each other. Cassidy stared at me from across the yard. When I walked over to her, Ben and Camden got up from the ground and walked over to us.

"That was impressive, Ben," I said.

"My brother is autistic and I practically raised him before I went off to college. My mom worked double shifts at the hospital and my dad took off when I was nine. Camden is a great kid." He smiled as he looked at Cassidy.

At that moment, I saw something between them. Ellery walked over to and handed me Julia.

"Admit you were wrong about Ben," she said.

"I was wrong about Ben. He's a great guy." I smiled.

Chapter 20

Ellery

Connor seemed to be more on edge lately and more irritable. He would go to the courthouse every day and then to the office. He was coming home later than normal because he was behind on work. I did as much as I could to try and take the stress off of him. Even though my studio wasn't ready yet, I started painting and panic set in, as I was scared that I wouldn't be able to finish.

It was ten o'clock in the evening, and I had just put Julia to bed. As I sat down at my easel, I heard the elevator doors open.

"Hey, baby. I'm sorry I'm so late. I had a lot of work to do," he slurred as he kissed me on the cheek and the stench of alcohol overtook my senses.

"Have you been drinking?" I asked.

"I had a couple drinks," he said as he sat on the couch.

"At the office?"

"No, I stopped at the bar before I came home."

He stretched out on the couch and put his arm over his eyes. I got up from my seat and walked over to him. "How did you get home?"

"I took a cab."

I was furious with him for not telling me that he was stopping at the bar before coming home. I was also mad at the fact that he didn't even come home to see Julia before she went to bed. This wasn't like him, and something else was going on.

"You couldn't come home to spend some time with Julia before she went to bed?" I asked with a raised voice.

He lifted his arm and looked at me. "Are you pissed off or something?"

"Yes, I'm pissed off, Connor. You didn't tell me you were going to the bar after the office. I just assumed you were there working. Who did you go to the bar with?"

"I went with Paul. What's the big deal? Fuck, Ellery, you're pissing me off."

"*I'm* pissing *you* off? You come home at ten o'clock at night, reeking of alcohol, and you expect me not to be upset? It would've been different if you would've called and told me."

Connor got up from the couch and headed towards the stairs. "I don't need to explain my whereabouts to you, Ellery."

I stood there in shock as he walked up the stairs; this wasn't my husband. I decided it was best to leave him alone and let him sleep it off, but I couldn't shake the feeling that something else was going on. Taking my phone from the table, I dialed Peyton.

"Hello, sexy mama. Henry and I are about to have sex, so I need to make it quick," she answered.

"Why did you answer the phone, then?"

"Because it's you, and what if it was important?"

"Connor came home drunk."

"Really? That's not like him."

"I know. It's this fucking trial and that bitch Ashlyn. I need to go and pay her a visit tomorrow and you're coming with me. Remember; don't say a word to Henry or anyone else."

"Okay, I'll see you tomorrow for the fitting."

"Thanks, Peyton," I said as I hung up.

Turning off all the lights, I walked upstairs and checked on Julia before heading to the bedroom. Stepping into the shower, I couldn't stop thinking about what Connor said to me, and it made me angry. The hot water streaming down my body felt good as I shampooed my hair. I didn't want to wake up Connor, so I didn't stay in the shower very long. As I stepped out, I was startled by him going to the bathroom.

"Jesus, Connor, you scared me."

"Sorry. I just had to take a piss."

I wrapped the towel around me and as I went to step into the bedroom, Connor grabbed my arm and pulled me into him.

"I'm sorry, baby. I'm sorry about tonight, and I'm sorry for what I said."

"I know you are, Connor. You're under a lot of pressure."

"It's no excuse, Ellery," he said as he kissed me. "Please let me make love to you."

I smiled at his drunken words, and I nodded my head as he removed the towel from me, picked me up, and carried me to our bed.

* * * *

"So what are you going to say to her when you see her?"

"I don't know. I tried a million conversations in my head," I replied as we drove to the jail where Ashlyn was.

"What did you tell Connor you were doing today?" Peyton

asked.

"I told him that you and I were going for another fitting and then going to do some cake tasting."

I hated lying to him and it was killing me inside. But I didn't have a choice. I needed to try and save my family and, most importantly, my husband. I parked the Range Rover and walked the distance from the parking lot to the building. The clerk sitting behind the glass window asked me the name of the prisoner I was visiting. Once I gave him Ashlyn's name, he typed in the computer and then gave me a strange look.

"I'm sorry, ma'am, but she was released from this facility a couple of weeks ago. She's currently under house confinement."

My skin started to get prickly, and suddenly, I didn't feel well. The thought of that bitch out of jail made me sick to my stomach. As I looked at Peyton, her eyes widened.

"How the fuck did that bitch manage to get out of here?!" Peyton snapped.

"She must have one hell of a lawyer, because according to my records, she was granted bail."

"Thank you," I said to the clerk as I grabbed Peyton's arms and hurried out of the building.

We walked back to the Range Rover, and all I thought about was if Connor knew this. But I knew there was no way he did because he would've told me. My husband would've told me something as crucial as that.

"Do you think Connor knew about this?" Peyton asked, as if she read my mind.

"No. There's no way Connor knew."

We climbed into the vehicle, and I put my forehead on the steering wheel.

"Now what, Elle?"

"Now, we go to Ashlyn's apartment."

I heard Peyton gasp when I said that. I didn't care if it was wrong or not. I was going to see her one way or the other.

"Do you even know where she lives?"

"Of course I do. Remember, Connor was the one who bought her the damn apartment."

We drove an hour back to the city and headed straight to Ashlyn's apartment. I was furious that she was out on bail, and I couldn't wrap my head around it.

"FUCK!" I screamed. "How the hell did she get out on bail? I yelled as we pulled into a parking space."

"Calm down, Ellery."

As Peyton and I took the elevator up to the floor that her apartment was on, my body was shaking with anger. The fact that she could burn down a building, admit it, then change her plea, and get out on bail was too much for me to handle. We stood in front of her door, and I gently knocked. A few seconds later, the door opened and Ashlyn stood there. Her eyes grew wide as she stared at me.

"What the fuck are you doing here?"

"I want to talk to you," I replied.

"Get the hell out of here!" she exclaimed as she tried to shut the door.

"Oh, no, you don't," Peyton said as she threw her body against the door to stop it from shutting.

The two of them struggled while Ashlyn tried to shut the door and Peyton tried to keep it open.

"Please, Ashlyn. I just want to talk to you," I pleaded.

Peyton managed to push the door all the way open and

knock Ashlyn back a few steps. We walked inside and Peyton shut the door.

"You better make it quick or I'm calling the police," she said.

My pulse was racing, and my skin was on fire as I stood in front of the woman who was ruining my family.

"Why, Ashlyn? Just tell me why you want to ruin my family."

As she looked at me, her eyes grew even darker. "You ruined my life."

"How did *I* ruin your life?" I asked.

"You took the only person I ever loved away from me. You walked into his life, and he completely ignored me. He was the only person that ever paid attention to me."

Standing there, I could see how unstable this woman really was.

"You burned down Connor's building. You hired someone to destroy it. Now you have to suffer the consequences for your actions. Did you think you wouldn't get caught?"

"I wouldn't have gotten caught if that weasel wouldn't have said anything."

"Ashlyn, do you have any regrets about what you did?"

"No, I don't. Connor hurt me deep down to the very core, just like he did my sister, and now I'm going to make him pay for what he's done. I'm going to make sure he never hurts me again, even if I have to destroy you and his precious little baby."

A fire burned through my body like never before and an anger I never knew I had emerged from deep within my soul. She threatened my daughter. To threaten me was one thing, but to threaten my child was another. She had just crossed a dangerous line. I felt like my body was out of control as I lunged at her and knocked her ass to the ground. I sat on top of her as I clutched her face with both my hands.

"Don't you ever threaten my daughter. Do you understand me, you psychotic bitch?"

Ashlyn struggled and managed to break from my grip as she pushed me off of her.

"I'm going to fucking kill you, bitch! It's something I should have done instead of burning down that building!" she screamed.

She came at me and grabbed my hair, knocking me down as I hit my forehead on the table. I heard Peyton scream as she tried to grab her. Suddenly, the door flew open and two men came running in. Connor grabbed me from behind and Denny grabbed Ashlyn and restrained her.

"Ellery, you're bleeding," Connor said as he wiped the blood from my head.

"She threatened Julia," I said.

"What?!" Connor yelled as he looked at her.

Peyton went and got a cloth from the bathroom and handed it to Connor as he held it over my cut.

"You're in big trouble," Connor said as he applied pressure to the wound.

"How did you know I was here?" I asked.

"We aren't talking about that now."

"Believe me, we're talking about it, Connor."

Two police officers walked into Ashlyn's apartment and took her from Denny.

One of the officers walked over and asked me what had happened.

"She just went crazy and came after me. She knocked me down, and I hit my head on the table," I said innocently.

"Would you like to press charges for assault and battery, ma'am?"

"No, I don't think that'll be necessary," Connor said.

I glared at him in disbelief at what he just said. "Yes, I do want to press charges," I said.

Suddenly, Ashlyn yelled. "She came after me first. It was self-defense!"

The officer looked at Peyton. "Were you a witness, miss?"

"Yes, I was, and that woman made a clear threat to kill her and then she came at her and pushed her into that table. I was so scared, I couldn't move."

As Ashlyn was screaming in her defense, the officer handcuffed her and escorted her out of the apartment. Denny looked at me and smiled as he walked over to me.

"Are you okay?" he asked as he took my hand.

"Yes, I'm fine."

Connor removed the cloth from my wound, and it was still bleeding. "You're going to need stitches, Ellery," he said as he shook his head. "I'm so angry with you right now."

"Save it, Connor. I'm in no mood for a lecture."

"Henry's at the hospital. I just talked to him, and he's waiting for us. I'll drive the Range Rover and meet you there," Peyton said.

I looked at her and nodded my head as I asked, "Did you get it all?"

"I sure did." She smiled as she held up the little device she had in her hand.

As Peyton walked out of the apartment, Connor and Denny

helped me up.

"It seems to me I've done this with you before." Denny smiled.

"What did Peyton get?" Connor asked as we walked out of the apartment.

"Evidence." I smiled.

Chapter 21

Connor helped me into the limo and then shut the door. He walked around and slid in next to me. The pain in my head was starting to get worse, and I didn't need him yelling at me.

"What the hell did you think you were doing?" he asked through gritted teeth.

"Trying to save our family."

"I told you to stay away from her and you disobeyed me. You know how unstable she is. She could have killed you, Ellery."

"Connor, please stop yelling. My head really hurts," I said as a tear sprang from my eye.

"Lay off, Connor. The two of you can talk about it later. The most important thing is that we get her head looked at," Denny said.

Connor turned away and looked out the window. I reached for his hand, but he pulled away. The last time he was this mad at me was back in Michigan when he found out about the cancer. Denny pulled up to the emergency entrance, and Peyton was waiting for me with a wheelchair. I opened the door myself and started to get out. Connor came around and grabbed my arm. I jerked away from him.

"Don't touch me," I snapped as I sat down in the chair.

Peyton looked at him and then at me. She wheeled me to

the registration desk and the nurse took me back into a room right away. She took the cloth from my head and looked at me.

"Dr. Henry can fix that up for you." She smiled as she patted my hand.

After she walked out of the room, Connor stood at the side of the table. I couldn't stop thinking about how he and Denny knew that I was at Ashlyn's apartment. It was bothering me on a whole new level. As I was about to ask the dreaded question that I wasn't sure I wanted to know the answer to, Henry strolled into the room. He stood in the entrance with a smirk on his face.

"Is this déjà vu?" he asked.

"Sort of feels like it, doesn't it?" I replied.

While Henry stitched me up, he started to ask questions. "So, why were the two of you over at Ashlyn's place, but most importantly, what was she doing there? I thought she was in jail."

"Apparently, she posted bail and they let her out on house arrest," Peyton said.

He put the final stitch in and kissed me on the head. "All fixed up, again." He smiled.

Connor didn't say a word. He just kept staring at me with a look of disappointment and anger. "Peyton, I'll drive you home and Connor can take Ellery home in the Range Rover," Denny said.

Great, I thought to myself. I didn't want to be alone with him. I knew the biggest of arguments was coming, and I didn't feel good or strong enough to fight with him. He extended his hand to me and helped me off the table. I turned and looked at Peyton.

"I want you and Henry to come over tonight for dinner."

"NO, Ellery. You need to rest," Connor said.

"Don't worry about me. We have some things to discuss."

"We'll bring dinner. So don't worry about anything," Peyton said as she walked over and hugged me.

Connor pulled the Range Rover up to the entrance and sat there. I thought he would've gotten out and opened the door, but he didn't. He was being a complete asshole, and I didn't appreciate it. My heart started beating faster when I climbed in and shut the door as he took off out of the hospital parking lot and drove us home.

* * * *

The ride home was silent. He didn't say a word and neither did I. I walked up the stairs and into our bedroom. Mason had texted me earlier, saying that he was at the park with Julia and they'd be back later. I sat on the edge of the bed and waited for Connor to come and start yelling at me. He walked into the room and handed me a white pill and a glass of water.

"What the hell were you thinking?" he snapped.

"Before I say a word, you are to answer two questions."

His angry eyes glared at me. "You are in no position to tell me what to do, Ellery."

"Did you know that Ashlyn was out of jail?" I asked.

Connor ran his hands through his hair and took in a sharp breath as he turned away and walked across the room. "Yes, I fucking knew!"

As my body shook, I set the glass on the nightstand. "You knew and you didn't tell me? You lied to me, Connor."

"And you lied to me, Ellery!" he said with a raised voice. "I told you a hundred times that you were to stay away from her and you didn't listen. That's your problem: you never listen. You're always going off and doing whatever the fuck you want to without any consideration for me or my feelings."

"She's going to destroy you, destroy us, and our family. I couldn't sit back and let her do it."

Connor became enraged as he stepped closer to me and pointed his finger in my face. "I told you that I wouldn't let her do that, yet you didn't believe me and had to take matters into your own hands. You could've been killed. She's crazy like that!"

"How did you know I was there?" I asked as I got up from the bed.

Once again, he wouldn't look at me and he turned around. "It doesn't matter how I knew."

"Were you having me followed?"

"No."

Then suddenly, my mind kept going back to the times when he would randomly show up at the places where I was. I remembered when he showed up at FAO Schwarz and he knew exactly what floor I was on and what section Cassidy and I were in. I looked over at my phone, which was lying on the bed.

"You motherfucker! You were keeping tabs on me through my phone?! You were tracking me?!" I yelled.

The air was thick and he didn't need to say anything, because his silence said it all. I closed my eyes as I felt dizzy, and I needed to lay down on the bed.

"You had no right," I whispered as a tear streamed down my face.

"You gave me no choice, Ellery. I knew you would do something like this," he said calmly as he took a few steps closer to the bed.

"I want you to get out of this bedroom and leave me alone. My head hurts and I need some space."

"I think we both need some space," he said as he walked out and shut the bedroom door.

Chapter 22

Connor

After grabbing the bottle of Motrin from the bathroom cabinet, I walked into the living room and straight to the bar. Shaking two pills into my hand, I popped them in my mouth and chased them down with a glass of scotch.

"Don't you think it's a little early to start drinking?" Denny said as he walked in the room and sat down in the leather chair.

"It's never too early to start drinking. Would you like one?" I asked as I held up my glass.

With a wave of his hand, he politely declined. "Did you and Ellery have it out already?"

"Sort of." I sighed.

"I told you she was going to find out that you knew Ashlyn was out of jail. Did she find out how you've been tracking her?"

"Yes," I said as I sat down on the couch.

"I warned you, Connor. I told you that it wasn't a good idea to keep secrets from her."

"Like I had a choice. Look at what she did."

"Exactly! She would've done it anyway. So wouldn't it have been better to tell her from the start? Because if you ask me, the pain she's feeling now is far worse."

"Yeah, well, what about me and how I'm feeling, Denny? She lied to me. She lied about what she was doing and where she was going today."

"You lied, she lied. You two are perfect for each other. Listen, Connor, I know why you did what you did, and I know why Ellery did what she did. The truth of the matter is that at the end of the day, regardless of all the bullshit that went on earlier, you two love each other more than you did yesterday. I'll tell you something, though; you were one cold-hearted bastard to her in the limo and at the hospital."

I got up from the couch, walked over to the bar, and poured another scotch. "Don't start with that, Denny." I sighed.

"Damn right I'll start it. Your wife, the mother of your baby, is upstairs with stitches in her head because of that psycho girl you used to date, and instead of apologizing to her and comforting her, you're down here, throwing back scotch."

"And talking to you, may I add," I said with irritation. "You know Ellery, and you know how she can be. She's pissed off, and she told me to leave the bedroom because she needed space."

Denny got up from the chair and started walking towards the elevator. He stopped, turned around, and shot me a look. "You'll feel like an ass soon enough." He smiled.

"What the hell is that supposed to mean?" I yelled as the elevator doors shut.

As I sighed and walked over to the bar to set down my glass, I heard the elevator door open. At first, I thought it was Denny, but I was pleasantly surprised when I looked over and saw Mason and Julia.

"There's my baby girl." I smiled when I took her from

Mason's arms. "Did you have fun at the park?"

"We had a fabulous time. She has made the most amazing friends and all the mannies love her."

I looked at Mason in confusion. "What?"

"Once a week, I meet the other mannies with their babies in the park. You wouldn't believe the stories they tell me about the families they work for, and I just sit there and brag about you and Ellery. Speaking of Diva Girl, where is she?"

"She had a little accident earlier, and she's upstairs lying down."

"What?!" Mason exclaimed. "What happened?"

"She fell and hit her head and needed a few stitches. She's okay."

Mason put his hand over his mouth. "Did she fall here?"

"No. It's a long story. She'll tell you all about it tomorrow. She needs to rest."

"Do you need me to take care of the princess for a while longer?" he asked.

"No. Consider yourself done for the day. Go home and relax." I smiled.

"If you need me, just call."

"Thanks, Mason. I will," I said as the elevator door shut.

I looked at Julia and kissed the tip of her nose. "I love you, baby girl."

I took Julia upstairs, changed her diaper, and then walked to my room. Ellery was still asleep across the bed. The bandage on her forehead started to bring back the memories of when I almost lost her. But it also reminded me of how close we became during that time. I smiled as I looked at her and then at Julia, who was also looking at her. My emotions were running deep from the events of the day. I was still so angry with her for lying to me and going to see Ashlyn. Julia started babbling, and Ellery opened her eyes. As she looked at Julia, she held out her hand. I walked over to the bed and sat down so Ellery could touch her.

"Hi, baby girl," she said as she took ahold of Julia's hand.

"How's your head?" I asked her.

"It hurts," she said as she looked down. "I'm still really angry with you."

"And I'm still angry with you."

Ellery sat up and held her arms out. I handed Julia over to her and she took her and hugged her tight. Then Ellery began to cry. It broke my heart to see her sitting there, holding Julia and crying.

"Baby, don't," I whispered.

"You weren't there. You didn't hear how that bitch threatened our daughter."

I sighed as my phone rang. I pulled it from my pocket and saw it was Lou calling.

"Hello, Lou," I answered as I got up from the bed. "Yeah, tonight will be fine; see you then."

"What was that about?" Ellery asked.

"Lou's coming over tonight to discuss the events of today."

Ellery didn't say anything. She laid Julia on the bed and got up and walked to the bathroom. After a few moments, I went in to check on her. She was standing in front of the sink, looking at herself in the mirror.

"I have no regrets for what I did today," she said.

"I don't want to discuss it any more right now," I said as I stood in the doorway.

"That's fine. I just wanted you to know that because, like you, I will not let anyone hurt or destroy my family," she said as she pushed me out of the way and walked out of the bathroom.

She picked up Julia from the bed and took her downstairs. As I stood there, contemplating what to do next, a text message came through from Cassidy.

"Ellery's studio is finished if you want to come take a look at it."

"Thanks, Cassidy, we'll be right down," I replied.

Ellery was in the kitchen, heating up a bottle for Julia when I walked down to let her know about her art studio.

"Cassidy just texted me that your art studio is ready. I told her that we'd be right down."

"Okay," she said as she held Julia and grabbed her bottle.

We stepped onto the elevator and rode it down to the tenth floor. As we stepped off, Cassidy was standing there with the door open. She took one look at Ellery's head and instantly became concerned.

"Ellery, what happened?" she asked sympathetically as Ellery handed Julia to her.

"I fell and hit my head. I'm okay."

We walked inside the apartment, and it was finished to perfection. As Ellery smiled, I could tell she was pleased with the way it turned out.

"Thank you, Cassidy. I love it!" she exclaimed. "I can't wait to start painting."

I walked over to Cassidy and gave her a kiss on the cheek. "Thank you, sis. It's beautiful. You've really outdone yourself."

"You're welcome. Now, I have to get going. Ben and I are taking Camden out to dinner."

"Have fun." Ellery smiled as she gave her a hug.

I took Julia from her and continued to feed her as Cassidy left the apartment. Ellery stood in front of the easel that held a big blank canvas on it.

"I'll start this painting tomorrow," she said.

"Are you happy?"

She looked at me with an angry look and left the apartment without saying a word. I looked down at Julia and sighed.

Chapter 23

Ellery

I walked over to the bar and poured myself a shot of Jack. As I slammed it back, Connor stood there with Julia, staring at me.

"What?"

"I don't think it's a good idea to be drinking when you took a pain pill," he replied as he put Julia in her swing.

"It's fine, Connor. One shot isn't going to kill me."

"No, but Ashlyn could've and you seem to think that's okay."

"I'm not listening to you anymore," I said as I tore up the stairs.

"You never do anyway!" I heard him yell.

As I glanced at the time on my phone, I noticed that Peyton and Henry were going to be over soon. After I changed into more comfortable clothing, I went into the kitchen and took out a bottle of wine. I heard the elevator doors open and Connor greeting Peyton and Henry. When they walked into the kitchen, Henry walked over to me and gave me a light kiss.

"How's your head?"

"It's sore, but I'm okay." I smiled.

I stood there thinking that at least someone cared. Peyton walked over to me and put her arm around me.

"Are you and sexy man still fighting?"

"Yes. God, I'm so mad at him for keeping that from me."

"I understand, but don't forget you kept something from him too."

I rolled my eyes and then flinched at the pain from the stitches. I reached up in the cabinet, grabbed four dinner plates, and then Peyton finished setting up the rest of the table. As the four of us sat down and ate our dinner, Peyton took out the recorder she had earlier. First, she looked at me and then over at Connor.

"Do you want to hear this or not?" she asked him.

"No, actually I don't," he replied. "It doesn't matter what's on there. You shouldn't have been there in the first place."

"Fuck you, Connor," I said as I got up and threw my plate in the sink and it broke.

"Way to go, Elle!" he exclaimed.

As I was on the verge of tears, the doorman rang and said that Lou was on his way up. I opened the door just as he stepped off the elevator in the hallway.

"Hi, Lou," I said as he leaned over and kissed me on the cheek.

"Are you all right?" he asked.

We gathered into the living room and Connor poured everyone their drinks. Lou looked at me as he asked, "Can you tell me what happened today?"

"This is what happened today," Peyton said as she pressed play on the recorder.

Connor handed Lou a drink and then sat down in the chair

across from where I was sitting. He stared at me and he listened intently. He slowly closed his eyes when he heard Ashlyn say how she was going to destroy not only him, but me and Julia as well.

"Talk about fatal attraction. Right, Lou?" Peyton said.

When Lou finished listening to our horrific altercation, he looked at me and smiled. "That is one damn good confession and threat Ashlyn made. I'm taking that to her lawyer and then submitting it as evidence. If she isn't advised to change her plea, then we'll continue to press the charges of assault and battery and she'll get added time for that. Ellery, I have a question for you and I need you to be completely honest with me. Did you physically attack her?"

"Hell, yeah, she did!" Peyton spoke up. "You should've seen her. She knocked her ass to the ground and then grabbed a hold of her face and wouldn't let her go and told her she better never threaten her daughter again. Well, you heard it."

Connor looked at me with an expression of shock. "Oh, please. I already punched her out once; did you honestly think I wouldn't go after her when she threatened our daughter?" I said to him.

Lou sat there, nodding his head. "We're just going to keep that information to ourselves. She doesn't have a mark on her and you have stitches. So, once the judge and jury hear what she had to say, they won't believe her anyway."

He got up from the chair, and we walked him to the door.

"Thanks, Lou," Connor said as they shook hands.

"No problem." He smiled. "Take care of that head, Ellery. I'm asking for a postponement and this could all be over within a week."

A feeling of relief flowed through me when I heard Lou say

that. Peyton took Julia from her swing and walked over to me. "It's almost over, sweetie. Henry and I are going to leave. He has to be at the hospital in a few hours. Go take a pain pill, down a couple shots of that shit you like, and you'll sleep great."

I smiled at her and took the baby as we said our goodbyes. Connor picked up the dirty glasses from the table and took them into the kitchen. He still didn't say anything to me, even after hearing what Ashlyn had said. Taking Julia upstairs to change her, I couldn't stop thinking about how hurt I was finding out that Connor knew Ashlyn was out of jail and how he was tracking my every move. A sick feeling emerged in my stomach as I laid Julia down in her crib. The only thing I wanted and needed was a hot bath.

As I started the bath, I poured a capful of bubbles under the stream of the hot water. Closing the bathroom door, I undressed, twisted up my hair, and lay back in the tub. If there was one person I needed the most right now, it was my mom. Tears started to fall down my face as the bullshit of the day settled inside me. I brought my knees up to my chest and wrapped my arms around my legs as I sobbed into them.

"Ellery," I heard Connor whisper as he opened the door and walked in.

He climbed into the bathtub, behind me, fully dressed, and wrapped his arms around me.

"I'm so sorry, baby," he began to cry. "I'm sorry for everything you've been through today. I just wanted to shield you from the scariness of the world. I wanted to protect you, Ellery. I need you to try and understand why I did what I did and why I behaved the way that I did. I love you so damn much."

Bringing my arms to his, he loosened his grip around me

and I turned around to face him. He tilted his head as he stared at me and tried to wipe away the mascara stains from under my eyes. Bringing my hand up to his face, I gently wiped away each tear that fell from his eyes.

"Look at you; your clothes are soaking wet." I smiled softly.

"It doesn't matter as long as I'm holding you." He smiled as his hand softly swept across my cheek.

"Do you forgive me?" I asked.

"Of course I forgive you. Do you forgive me?"

"Yes, I love you way too much not to."

* * *

I sat down at my easel to start my third painting. A peaceful feeling was restored throughout my body now that Ashlyn had been found guilty and sentenced to twenty-five years in prison with no possibility of parole. Connor was more relaxed, and so was I without the trial hanging over our heads. Julia was growing so fast, we could barely keep up with her. As the sunlight beamed through the windows, I decided to take advantage of the beautiful day and take Julia to Central Park. I grabbed my sketchpad and headed up to the penthouse. As I stepped off the elevator, I saw Mason and Julia in the living room.

"I'm giving you the afternoon off because I'm taking Julia to Central Park."

"Oh goody, can I come?" Mason asked as he handed me the baby.

I felt bad telling him no, but I wanted to spend some time alone with my daughter.

"Aw, Mason. I'm sorry, but I really just want to spend some time alone with Julia. Considering all the shit that went on, I feel like a horrible mom that I haven't spent as much time with her as I should."

"I understand, Mama." He smiled as he kissed me on the cheek.

"I do need you to do me a favor, though. I need you to go to the spa for me," I said as I grabbed my purse and pulled out my wallet.

"What do you need from the spa?" he asked.

"I need you to get the works done: massage, manicure, and facial."

"Are you serious?"

"Yes," I said as I handed him some money. "Consider this a perk because you have done so much for Connor and me, and we appreciate it. I know it isn't much, but it's a start."

"Are you kidding? It's awesome. Thank you, doll face!" he said excitedly as he kissed me and headed towards the elevator.

As I smiled and kissed Julia on the nose, I desperately wished that Connor could join us in the park, but he had back-to-back meetings all day, plus a conference call. I put Julia in her stroller, packed her diaper bag, grabbed a blanket, my drawing pad, pencils, and bottled water. After I made sure I had everything I needed, I pushed the stroller onto the elevator and walked to Central Park.

The flowers in the Conservatory Garden were as beautiful as always. As I was pushing Julia, I looked ahead and noticed there was no one in my favorite spot. When I reached it, I spread out the blanket on the grass, kicked off my shoes, and took Julia from her stroller.

"This is my favorite place, Julia. I hope that it'll be yours too someday."

I laid her down on the blanket and took off her socks. She started kicking and moving her arms around while making the cutest cooing sounds. I opened up my drawing pad and began drawing the picture I had envisioned for my painting. Looking over at Julia, I started to sketch a field of flowers. A few moments later, I heard my phone ring. As I pulled it from my bag, I smiled when I saw it was Connor calling.

"Look; it's your daddy," I said as I showed Julia the phone. "Hello," I answered.

"Hey, baby, I was thinking we could have lunch together."

"That sounds nice. What time?"

"How about now? Turn around," he said.

I turned around and watched as Connor walked towards me with a bag in his hand. Grinning from ear to ear, I hung up and set my phone down.

"How did you know I was here?"

Before sitting down on the blanket, he kicked off his shoes and took off his socks. "I talked to Mason. I tried to call you earlier and it went straight to voicemail, so I called him and asked him to put you on the phone, and he told that me you and Julia were here," he said as he sat down and kissed me.

"I thought you had back-to-back meetings and a conference call today?"

Connor picked up Julia and started playing with her. "I did. I had a couple of meetings already, but when I found out that my wife and daughter were in Central Park, I wanted to spend the day with them, so I cancelled the rest of my meetings."

"I'm so happy you're here with us." I smiled as I stroked his cheek. "What's in the bag?"

"Open it and find out."

I picked up the bag and looked inside. "Aw, you brought us

hot dogs."

"I know how much you love them here." He smiled.

As I took the hot dogs from the bag, Connor put Julia in her stroller.

"There's something I need to discuss with you," he said.

"Okay. What's up?"

"I don't want you to be mad that I didn't discuss this with you first because it just sort of happened suddenly."

As I gave him a worried look, he smiled and cupped my chin in his hand. "Don't worry, it's nothing bad."

I let out a sigh of relief as he began to tell me what he did. "I've invested in Vinnie's art gallery in Chicago. I'm now his partner."

"What?" I asked in confusion.

"His partner pulled out at the last minute and left him with a half-finished gallery and not enough funds to complete it and get it ready for the opening. He called me and asked if I would be interested in investing in the gallery and being his partner. I had my business attorney draw up the legal papers and he's coming to the office tomorrow to sign them."

As I sat there and stared at him, I needed to tell him something that I'd been thinking about for a while.

"Can I be totally honest with you about something?"

"Of course, baby. What is it?"

"I thought you already owned the art gallery and that you didn't want to tell me."

The look on his face was dumbfounded. "Why would you think that?"

"I don't know. It's just a feeling I had."

"Well, you were wrong. I had nothing to do with that

gallery until this morning. I can't believe you would think that I wouldn't tell you something like that."

"Really?" I said as I cocked my head and pursed my lips.

"Right. Point taken," he said while nodding his head.

After we ate our hot dogs and Julia had fallen asleep, Connor and I lay down on the blanket. I snuggled up against him as he put his arm around me, and we looked up at the sky.

"This is a perfect day," he said as he kissed my head.

"Every day is perfect when we're together." I smiled.

"I'll never forget the day I found you lying here, in the rain. You were so sick, and I was so scared. You broke my heart that day, baby."

"How?" I whispered.

"By telling me you were lying here so that no one would know you were crying. You have no idea how that killed me inside to hear you say that."

I lifted up my head and looked at him. "I'm sorry. My life was so different then. You saved me from myself."

He looked down at me and his lips brushed against mine. "We saved each other."

Even though I wanted to stay in this spot forever, our heartfelt moment was soon interrupted by Julia's cry. We both smiled as we got up and Connor took her from the stroller.

"I think it's time we head home," I said as I started packing up.

"I think you're right."

After kissing Julia on both cheeks, Connor put her in the stroller and pulled out his phone.

"Who are you calling?" I asked.

"Denny. I'm telling him to come pick us up."

"Tell Denny I said hi!" I smiled as I took the stroller and started walking.

"Ellery Rose Black! Come back here with that baby!" he said rather loudly.

I turned my head and looked at him with a big smile on my face. "Have fun in the limo by yourself, Mr. Black! My baby and I are walking home."

Before long, Connor was right behind me. "You are so stubborn."

"I know, and that's one of the reasons why you love me."

"Just one of a million, baby. Just one of a million," he said as he put his arm around me.

Chapter 24

Connor

Ellery had been working hard on her paintings. The opening was next month and she still had two more pictures to paint. Mason had gone to California for a week with Landon, so I helped out as much as I could with Julia so Ellery wouldn't worry about taking care of her. I had given Claire the day off to take her husband to the doctor, and Peyton was out of town with Henry. I had planned to stay home and work, but my attention was needed at the office. I tried to call my family for help, forgetting they were all out of town as well. Ellery had just left for the studio and Phil called, stating that I needed to be at the office for a meeting regarding the new Chicago building, and today was the only day it could be done. I looked at Julia as she sat in her bouncy seat.

"Listen, Julia. Daddy is going to take you to the office and I need you to be extra good. Okay?"

As she smiled at me, she screeched. She thought it was funny that I asked her to be extra good. I put her in her car seat, grabbed the diaper bag, and stepped into the elevator. Today was Denny's day off, so I would have to drive the Range Rover to work. I stopped by Ellery's studio to let her know that I was taking Julia with me. As I walked through the door, she turned around and looked at me.

"Hey, honey, what's up?" she asked as she walked over and

kissed me.

"I'm taking Julia to the office. I have a few things that I need to do."

"By yourself?"

"Yes, by myself. Do you think I'm not capable of spending the day with my daughter alone?"

"No, I think you're capable. Good luck, sweetie." She smiled as she bent down and kissed Julia's head.

I put my hand on the knob, turned it, and opened the door. Turning around and looking at her, I said, "Was that good luck for me or for Julia?" I asked in confusion.

"It was for both of you." She laughed.

As I put Julia in the back and buckled the car seat, she started to cry. Shit, I thought to myself, and I was already running late for the meeting. She had just eaten so I knew she wasn't hungry, and I had just changed her diaper before we left. I reached in the diaper bag and pulled out her pacifier. Ellery wasn't too keen on her having it, but this was an emergency. When I put it in her mouth, she stopped crying. I let out a sigh of relief as I climbed in the driver's side and headed to the office. Traffic was horrible, and Julia started crying again. I looked in the rearview mirror and her pacifier had fallen out of her mouth. Her screams grew louder as I tried to reach back and grab it. After I finally found it, I put it back in her mouth, but she didn't want it. She spit it out and started screaming. I didn't want to call Ellery because I didn't want her to worry, so I dialed the next best person: Mason.

"Hel—Connor, why is the princess crying like that?"

"Mason, I need your help. I'm taking Julia to the office."

"By yourself?" he interrupted.

"Yes. I'm stuck in traffic, and she won't stop screaming.

She won't take the pacifier either."

"You gave her the pacifier? Does Ellery know this?"

"No, and you're not going to tell her either. Help me; I don't know what to do."

"Do you have any classical music with you?"

"I don't think so."

"Look in the diaper bag. There may be a CD in there."

Reaching in the back, I grabbed a hold of the diaper bag and, as I was bringing it up to the front, items started falling out onto the floor. Julia was still screaming, and I was about to have a nervous breakdown.

"There's no fucking CD in here!" I screamed into the phone.

"Connor, I'm sorry, but there's nothing you can do until you get to the office."

After hanging up, I looked at my phone and had an idea. Still stuck in traffic, I downloaded some classical music onto my phone. Beethoven's "Ode to Joy" was the first song on the list. I hit play and turned the volume up as loud as it would go. I held the phone towards the back and closer to Julia. She didn't stop crying right away, but the noise was becoming softer. As traffic started moving, Julia fell asleep, and I felt like I could breathe again. Finally, we arrived at Black Enterprises. I pulled into the parking garage and parked in my spot. As I looked behind me, I saw that Julia was still asleep, and I needed her to stay that way. I carefully opened the door and started picking up all the things from the diaper bag that fell on the floor. As I gently unbuckled the car seat, Julia's eyes opened, and I froze. Grabbing the pacifier that was sitting next to her, I put in her mouth and her eyes slowly closed. I started to sweat at the thought of her screaming bloody murder again.

Stepping off the back elevator that led to my office, I was instantly surrounded by a flock of women who wanted to see Julia. When I walked down the hallway to my office, I realized that Valerie wasn't sitting at her desk. Shit, her vacation started today, I remembered as I was counting on her to keep an eye on Julia. Opening the door to my office, I set the car seat on my desk, while I gathered some files for the meeting.

"Whoa, Connor! Why is Julia here?" Phil asked in shock.

"Because I didn't have anyone to watch her, Phil," I replied with irritation.

"Don't you have a manny or nanny or whatever?"

"He's on vacation, and Ellery is working on her paintings."

"You can't bring a baby to a meeting," he said.

Glaring at his stupidity, I calmly said, "Have you forgotten that Black Enterprises is *my* company and I can do whatever the hell I want? If I want to bring my daughter to the meeting, then I'll damn well do it!"

Phil sighed and walked out of the office. "The meeting starts in five minutes," he said.

Julia opened her eyes. I grabbed my files and the car seat and headed to the boardroom.

Upon entering the room with fifteen men and women, all eyes glared at me when I walked in. "Sorry I'm late, but as you can see, I have my daughter with me today and if any one of you has a problem with it, the door is right over there. Are we clear?"

While I stood and looked at the people in the room, there was silence. "Very good. Now let's proceed."

* * * *

As I changed Julia's diaper, I looked up and saw Ellery standing in the doorway of the nursery with a smile on her face.

"Hey, baby, how long have you been standing there?" I asked.

"Long enough to hear that little conversation the two of you were having."

"That was a private conversation between me and my daughter." I smiled.

She walked into the nursery, gave me a kiss, and picked up Julia from the changing table.

"How did it go today with your daddy?" Ellery asked her as she held her in the air.

"Things went fine. I don't know why you have a hard time believing that I can't handle my daughter by myself," I said as I threw the diaper away.

"What's that, Julia? You screamed all the way to the office, and daddy was having a meltdown?"

Damn it. She must have talked to Mason. "That's not how it went down, Ellery."

"That's not what I heard, Connor." She grinned at me.

"Why would Mason tell you that I called him?"

"What's that, Julia? Daddy gave you the pacifier?" She glared at me.

"Can't I do anything without someone telling you everything?"

"Mason didn't tell me, well, not technically. I was on the phone with him when you called, and I made him put it on three-way so I could listen."

"Ellery Rose! That's an invasion of privacy."

"Oh, please. I found it amusing and as much as I wanted to come rescue you, I knew you'd figure out what to do."

"Thank you for the confidence," I said as I put my hands on her hips and softly kissed her on the lips.

"After all, you are the CEO of a billion-dollar company. You've dealt with worse. I wasn't worried that one little baby would be the thing to break you. I'll admit that I was a little worried about something else."

"What were you worried about?"

"There's nothing sexier than a man with a baby, and I could see those vultures at your office taking advantage of that."

Smiling at her, I took Julia from her arms and laid her down in her crib.

"What are you doing?" Ellery laughed as I picked her up.

"There's only one vulture I want taking advantage of me, and I want it right now."

"Connor, what about Julia?"

"She'll be fine. She's safe in her crib, and if she starts to cry, then we'll stop. But, I want to make love to you now. I don't want to wait another second."

Before laying her down on the bed, my fingers tugged at the bottom of her shirt, lifting it over her head. As my mouth smashed into hers, she reached her arms back and unhooked her bra, letting it fall to the floor. After my hand cupped her breast and tugged at the hardness of her nipple, I picked her up and she wrapped her legs around me as I laid her gently on the bed. I wanted to devour her as I took her breast in my mouth. Her fingers were quickly unbuttoning my pants as I was unbuttoning hers. I stood up and took them down as fast as I could. I ripped my shirt from me and threw it on the floor as she sat up and took her pants off, throwing them across the room. She looked at me with a seductive smile and laid down on her stomach.

"Christ, Ellery, you have me so hard."

"Then put that erection to good use, Mr. Black."

A growl came from the back of my throat, and I swore I almost came right then and there when she said that. I dipped my finger inside her to make sure she was ready for me, and sure enough, she was more than ready. Hovering over her, I slowly pushed myself inside and began thrusting in and out of her when, suddenly, Julia began to cry.

"Don't you dare stop, Connor!" she exclaimed.

"I won't, but—"

"There are no 'buts'! You cannot and will not stop! I'm so close. Oh God. Oh God!" Ellery screamed as her body tightened and released itself, causing me to explode inside her.

We lay there as our hearts raced and we tried to catch our breath. All of a sudden, it was quiet. Ellery turned her head and looked at me.

"Of course she stops crying now." She laughed.

That's my daughter. My love, my life, and my little angel.

Chapter 25

Ellery

As I stood in front of my easel, putting the final touches on my fourth painting, I looked out the large window that overlooked the city. So many thoughts ran through my head about the showing at the gallery, Connor's new Chicago building, and Peyton's bachelorette party, which was starting tomorrow at ten a.m. Connor and I had a slight argument about it because he wanted Denny to drive us around the city all day and night. I told him no, and he wasn't happy. Needless to say, I won. I didn't understand what he was so worried about, because he was having Henry's bachelor party tomorrow night as well. I heard the door open and, as I turned around, Connor walked in, set his briefcase on the chair, and then wrapped his arms around me.

"Hi, good looking." I smiled.

"It feels so good to hold you. I missed you, baby," he said as he buried his face into my neck.

"I missed you too. What's wrong?"

"It's just one of those days where if everything could go wrong, it did. Where's Julia?" he asked.

"She's at home with Mason."

He broke our embrace and looked at me. "Now tell me exactly what you're doing tomorrow for Peyton's bachelorette party."

I looked at him with knitted eyebrows. "Why do you want to know?"

"I'm your husband, and I should know what you're doing."

I was hoping to get away without having to go over the party detail by detail because he wasn't going to be happy when he heard what I had planned. This could be the start of a huge fight.

"Please have a seat, Mr. Black, while I explain to you the details of Peyton's bachelorette party. You will in no way say a word or comment on the upcoming events. There will be no arguments, no harsh words, and I forbid you to become jealous. If you decide you want to start an argument, then you'll be cut off from sex for a very long time. This is my best friend's party and I'm putting everything sexy into it before she gets married. It's what we women do, and if you can't trust me, your wife, who loves you more than life, then you need to go and see your therapist."

He sat there, with his legs crossed and his hands folded in his lap, and stared at me as I finished my last sentence. "Okay, and the same goes for you."

After he said that, I started to get a little worried and a sick feeling crept inside my stomach. But I wasn't going to let him know that. He didn't know what I had planned, and I didn't know what he had planned. We were both going to do our own thing and trust each other. I knew how much he loved me and he knew how much I loved him.

"Okay, fine," I said as I faked a smile.

He got up from the couch, kissed me, and said he had some plans to confirm. I knew he did it on purpose because it was killing him that he didn't know what I had planned, so he was trying to get back at me. I told him that I'd be upstairs in a bit after I finished my painting. Connor's mom and dad were taking care of Julia for the weekend because Mason and Landon were joining the bachelorette party.

* * * *

The next morning, I awoke before Connor. We had dropped off Julia at his parents' house last night and then we had sex all over the penthouse, taking advantage of the fact that Julia wasn't here to interrupt us. While I stood in front of the mirror, I put my blonde hair up in a high ponytail. As I brushed my teeth, Connor stood in the doorway of the bathroom in nothing but his pajama bottoms, with his muscular arms against the doorframe.

"What?" I smiled.

"Nothing. I'm just admiring your beauty before we part ways in a couple of hours."

I spit in the sink and rinsed my mouth before walking over to him and placing my hands on his bare and sculpted chest.

"I hate the fact that we aren't going to see each other until tomorrow."

"I know. Me too," he said as he held my face and kissed my lips.

"So, what are your plans?" I asked casually.

"I'm not telling you a thing. You're so secretive about your party, so I'm being secretive too."

"You do realize you sound like a baby, right?"

"Yes, but only your baby," he whispered as he licked behind my ear and then slapped me on the ass.

I giggled as I packed the last of the things I needed for the party. When Connor was done showering and getting dressed, he grabbed my bag and we took the elevator down to the parking garage, where two limos were waiting for us.

"Your limo, my love," Connor said as he opened the door.

"Thank you, darling." I smiled.

He wrapped his arms around me and pulled me into him. "Be careful, behave, and be safe."

"Don't worry, Connor, I'll be fine. You do the same."

"I love you, Ellery."

"I love you, Connor," I said as I got in the limo and we pulled away.

* * * *

We picked up Mason and Landon, since they lived around the corner, and then we picked up Peyton and the other girls in the wedding party. Peyton was wound up and ready to get the party started. She didn't have any idea of what I had planned. In fact, nobody did, not even Mason.

"Okay, bestie, tell me what's on the agenda for today and tonight and why we had to pack an overnight bag!"

"You'll see when we get there." I smiled.

The limo pulled up to the curb of the Waldorf Hotel and all eyes grew wide.

"Elle, what did you do?" Mason asked.

I smiled as the driver opened the door and we all stepped out of the limo. "Our day starts here," I said.

As we walked through the doors of the hotel, we were instantly greeted by the concierge. "Mrs. Black, welcome to the Waldorf."

"Thank you," I said as the bellhop took our bags and led us to the elevator. When we reached the Presidential Suite, I put the card key in the slot and opened the door.

"Look at this fucking place!" Peyton squealed.

"I think I've died and gone to Heaven," Mason said as he

looked around the suite.

"I have hairstylists and makeup artists for each of us coming in to do our hair and make up for tonight." I smiled.

"Shut the fuck up!" Peyton screamed as she threw her arms around me.

I grabbed my phone from my purse and looked at the time. "Okay, everyone, we have spa appointments in five minutes. We're all getting the works. Massage, facial, manicures, and pedicures."

As we walked out of the suite, Mason looped his arm around me. "You sure know how to do it up, girl!" He smiled.

We all changed into our luxurious robes and slippers from the spa. I realized that I had left my phone in the suite, and I needed to keep it on me in case there was an emergency with Julia.

"I'll be right back. I left my phone in the room," I said as I got up and walked out of the spa.

While I stood and waited for the elevator, I couldn't stop thinking about Connor and how I already was starting to miss him. I was beginning to regret not telling him my plans, but I knew he wouldn't approve of the nightlife with his safety issues and all. When the elevator doors opened, I gasped and I stood there, unable to move. The man inside of the elevator looked at me. I looked at him. As I swallowed hard, my heart began beating rapidly from the way he was staring at me. His mysterious eyes studied me as they looked me up and down.

"Which floor, miss?" he asked.

"Thirty-fifth, please."

"Spa?" he asked as he stared at the robe I was wearing.

"Yes, I'm throwing a bachelorette party for my best friend," I answered as I bit down on my bottom lip.

The elevator stopped at the thirty-fifth floor and we both stepped out. "Have a good time at the bachelorette party. Hopefully, I'll run into you again." He smiled as I turned right and he turned left. I smiled and nodded my head as I thanked him and walked to my room. I took the key from the pocket of my robe and, as I slid it in, I turned my head and looked in the direction he went, only to find him six rooms down, staring at me. As I opened the door, I quickly stepped inside the room and shut it. Backing up against the door, I let out deep breaths as my heart pounded rapidly in my chest. *What the hell is wrong with me?* I walked over to where my phone sat on the table and checked it. There weren't any messages from my in-laws or Connor.

As I lay on the massage table, I couldn't stop thinking about the elevator, the man in it, and the way he looked at me. My heart began to rapidly pick up pace just from the thought. My mind needed to snap back into reality if I was going to pull this party off. After all of us were finished with our spa appointments, we went back to the room and Peyton screamed when she walked in and saw two hot, buff men wearing nothing but little aprons, cuffs and bow ties.

"Oh my God, Ellery! I fucking love you!"

As I laughed at her reaction, Landon walked over to me. "Nice touch, Ellery." He smiled.

The buff butlers opened a bottle of champagne and handed each of us a glass. It wasn't too long after that the stylists arrived. I pulled out a rhinestone studded, silver tiara that said "Bride to be" and handed it to Peyton's hairstylist. While we were getting ready for our big night out, room service was delivered. The butler answered the door as the trays of sushi, and cheese, and crackers were delivered to the room. Taking the card from the tray, the buff butler handed it to me. It read:

Forever Us

"A little gift for you and your girls.

I hope you enjoy it.

Regards, the man from the elevator."

"Who's it from?" Peyton asked.

"It's just from the hotel staff," I lied.

"Butlers in the buff, bring those trays over here!" she said.

I smiled as I read the note and, once again, my heart started racing at the thought of him. The mystery of him got under my skin. I couldn't believe he sent the trays and that he was thinking about me.

"Hello, Elle! What world are you lost in?" Peyton said as she snapped her fingers.

I looked at her in confusion. "What?"

"You looked like you were stuck in space or something. What's going on with you?"

"Nothing. I was just thinking about Julia," I replied as I sipped my champagne.

Once my hair and makeup were done, I stepped into my bedroom and took out the dress I had bought. As I slipped it on, I looked in the mirror. The low cut, short silvery beaded dress was perfect for tonight.

"Look at you, hot and sexy mama!" Mason said as he walked into the room. "That dress is hot and your up-do hairstyle really complements it. I don't think Connor would approve of you looking like that without him by your side."

"Connor's not here, is he?" I smiled.

"No, he's not, but you better be careful because you're going to have all the guys drooling on the floor."

I laughed as I put on my silver, high-heeled, Jimmy Choos. Everyone looked amazing. Before leaving the suite, I took out

165

the white sash that was embellished with the words "Bride to be" on it and put it on Peyton.

"There! Now your outfit's complete." I smiled.

Peyton hugged me and there was a knock at the door. As I opened it, the bellhop handed me a piece of white paper. I opened it and it read:

> *"I'm sitting at the bar in the hotel.*
> *If you can join me, even for a few minutes,*
> *I'd appreciate it.*
> *Regards, the man from the elevator."*

My rapidly beating pulse was about to give away my nervousness as I turned to the group and told them I'd be right back, that the concierge needed to see me downstairs. As I grabbed my small clutch, I told them I'd meet them in the limo in about twenty minutes. I took the elevator down to the lobby and walked to the bar. As I saw him sitting on the bar stool, the nervous butterflies in my stomach were fluttering their wings like crazy. *Why was I doing this? How could I do this?* He turned his head and his eyes burned through me. I nervously walked over and sat down on the stool next to him.

"I wasn't sure if you'd show," he said as he picked up his glass.

"I wanted to thank you for the sushi and cheese trays you sent to my room. That was very nice of you, but you didn't have to do that."

"I know I didn't, but I thought you and your female companions would enjoy it. Did you enjoy it?" he asked as he stared into my eyes.

"Yes, very much. Thank you," I replied as my heart felt like it was going to jump out of my chest."

"Would you like a drink?"

"No, thank you. I have to meet my friends in the limo in about ten minutes."

"Would you object if I told you how stunning you look?"

"Thank you," I said as I looked down.

"I see you're married," he said as he looked at my ring.

"Yes, I am, and I have a baby at home."

I glanced over at his hand to see if he was wearing a ring and he was. "I see you're married as well."

He looked at me as the corners of his mouth curved slightly upwards. "Yes, I am. But that doesn't stop me from looking at beautiful women. Apparently, it doesn't stop you either because you're sitting here with me."

I gulped as I got up from the stool. He reached over and placed his hand on mine as an electrical shock shot through my body. "Thank you for coming down and meeting me."

"I have to go. Thank you again for the trays," I said as I walked out of there as fast as I could.

Everyone was waiting for me in the limo. As the driver opened the door for me, I slid in next to Mason.

"Are you all right? You look flushed," he said.

"I'm fine. Now let's go and have a good time."

Chapter 26

We arrived at the first club and had dinner up on the rooftop. I couldn't stop thinking about the man from the elevator and how it had felt when he touched me. Needing to see if I had any missed calls or text messages, I pulled my phone from my clutch and saw nothing. I wondered what Connor was doing and I felt like I needed to text him.

"Hi, babe. I just want to make sure you're having a good time."

A few minutes later, a reply from him came through.

"Hey, baby. We're having a great time. How about you?"

"Yeah, I am. I just wanted to tell you that I love you," I typed with guilt.

"I love you too. Remember to stay safe."

"I will."

As I put my phone back in my clutch, I grabbed my glass of wine and drank it as fast as I could. I put all thoughts of the man from the elevator out of my mind so I could enjoy the evening that I had spent months planning. We ate, drank, and had a good time. But the fun didn't really start until we walked into the club called X. It was a high-class strip club that was divided in half. One side of the club was male strippers and the other half was female strippers.

We sat at the table, waiting for the show to start. Peyton

was already drunk and so were a few of the girls. I needed a drink and didn't want to wait for the waitress, so I excused myself and walked up to the large bar that was shared by both sides of the club. As the bartender approached me, I ordered a shot of Jack. He put the shot glass down in front of me and I threw it back, allowing the burning sensation to coat my throat. Suddenly, I was startled by a voice in my ear.

"Well, isn't this a coincidence seeing you here. It must be fate," the deep voice whispered as his scent captured me and his hot breath warmed my neck.

Once again, my heart started beating rapidly as the lower half of me started to ache. "Are you following me?" I asked without turning around.

"I was just about to ask you the same question. Do you always come to strip clubs?"

"No. I told you before that it's my best friend's bachelorette party."

"Ah, that's right," he said as he traced little circles on my shoulder with his finger.

My skin started to heat up at his touch. There wasn't anywhere I could go. He had me trapped between the bar and the stool. "Am I making you uncomfortable?" he asked.

"Just a bit," I answered nervously.

"I apologize. You better get back to your friends," he whispered as he leaned in closer to me and I felt his lips slightly touch my neck.

I flinched and he moved his arm so I could get by. As I walked away, I turned around, even though every part of me said not to. But I did, because I could feel his burning eyes all over me. I sat back at the table just in time for the show to start.

"Where were you?" Landon asked. "We were going to start a search party."

"The bar was packed. It took forever to get the bartender's attention."

The show started and one male stripper walked onto the stage. Peyton started going crazy and yelling. I looked over at her and laughed because she was standing on the chair. I needed to use the bathroom, so I got up from my seat and told the group that I'd be right back. I was feeling a little tipsy from the Jack and coke I was drinking and then the champagne I had earlier. I couldn't find the bathrooms, so I had to ask one of the waitresses. She pointed down the long hallway and said they were on the left. After peeing, what seemed like forever, I washed my hands and, when I opened the door, I was startled to see the line of people down the narrow hallway. When I stepped out of the bathroom and tried to make my way through the crowd of people, I felt two hands grab my waist. I turned around and it was him.

"It's okay; let me guide you out of here," he said.

As we were reaching the end of the hallway, two drunken girls stumbled and pushed us up against the wall.

"Hold on. Let them pass," he whispered in my ear.

I gulped as the ache down below came back and my senses were heightened by his tantalizing scent; an unfamiliar scent to me. Once the girls passed by, he grabbed my waist and led me out of the hallway.

"Don't turn around, but hold out your hand," he instructed.

I did what he asked and I held my hand out in front of me. He put a piece of white paper in it and then he closed my hand.

"Don't let anybody see that. It's only for you," he

whispered and then walked away in the opposite direction.

I opened my hand and unfolded the piece of paper. It read:

My room, tonight, after your party.

Room 4709

I'll be there, waiting for you.

As I stood there staring at the note, I heard someone call my name. I looked up and closed my hand tightly as Mason walked towards me.

"What's taking you so long?" he asked.

"Look at the line," I said as I took his hand and we walked back to our table.

Our time at the strip club was finished and we needed to move on to the last club. As I helped Peyton into the limo, she wouldn't stop talking about the lap dance she received from the stripper. Everyone was cracking jokes and having a good time. I was starting to get a bit worried that Peyton was too drunk to go to the next club, but she insisted she was fine. When I opened my clutch to pull out my phone, the white piece of paper fell onto the floor.

"Oops, you dropped something," Landon said as he reached down and picked it up.

"No! I can get it," I said in a sharp tone.

Mason picked up the paper and handed it to me. "Wow, calm down, Elle, it's only a piece of paper. "

"I'm sorry," I said.

* * * *

The club was packed. The music was blaring, and the floor was thumping. I tried to get my mind off of him, but I couldn't. His tall stature and assurance were startling, but in a way that was to be desired. To distract myself from the thoughts of him that seemed to consume me, I lost myself in the music, dancing, drinking, and having a good time. When it was time to leave, Landon had to carry Peyton to the limo as the girls and I stumbled behind, laughing and practically falling on our asses. I pulled my phone from my clutch and there were no messages or missed calls from anyone. Not too long after we left the club, we were back at the Waldorf. Landon carried Peyton to the room and collapsed on the couch. I pulled the white piece of paper from my clutch and stared at the room number. It wasn't the same room he had gone into earlier in the day. This room was on the top floor of the hotel.

I took in a deep breath and stepped off the elevator. I knocked quietly on the door of Room 4709. Immediately, the door opened, and he stood there with a smile on his face.

"Please come in," he said. "I wasn't sure if you'd show."

"I wasn't sure if I would either," I said as I stepped inside his room.

"Would you like a drink?"

"No, thank you. I've had way too much already."

The corners of his mouth curved up when I said that. "Is that so?" he said as he walked closer to me, took my clutch from my hands, and threw it on the chair. He stood in front of me, and as I looked down, he cupped my chin in his hand and lifted it up until I was forced to look at him.

"Someone as beautiful as you should never be looking down."

As I took in a sharp breath, he took his finger and ran it across my jaw line. "You're so stunning. From the moment I laid eyes on you, I wanted you. I know you felt it too. I could tell by the look in your beautiful blue eyes. Did you feel something?"

I nodded my head lightly as his gaze held mine.

"Say it. I want to hear you say that you felt something when you saw me."

"I felt something," I whispered.

He leaned closer to me, gently nipped my bottom lip, and then looked at me. "Do you want me to fuck you? Because I've wanted to since the moment I saw you," he said as he traced my lips with his finger.

The words wouldn't escape my lips, so I nodded my head.

His mouth crashed into mine as my lips parted slightly, allowing his tongue to explore my mouth. Once he had me against the wall, he cupped me below, feeling my soaked panties as his fingers pushed them to the side and he inserted his finger inside me.

"I knew I turned you on," he said as his lips pursued my neck.

While I ran my fingers through his hair, he took down both straps of my dress and let it fall to the floor. "I want you to leave your shoes on," he commanded.

His right hand kneaded my breast as his left ripped the panties right from me. I gasped as he dipped two fingers inside. He moved them in and out of me while he unbuttoned his pants with his other hand and took them down. My breathing was rapid and my moans became louder as he inserted himself into me. He was rock hard and so strong that each time he pushed deeper into me, he sent my body into convulsions. I wrapped my legs tightly around him as he held me up against the wall and continued to thrust in and out of me.

"Oh my God, oh my God," I yelled as my body shook and

he brought me to an amazing orgasm.

"That's right. I want to feel your pleasure all over me," he said as he forcefully pushed himself into me one last time and I felt him explode inside of me.

With my legs still wrapped around him, he looked at me and kissed my lips. "Well played, Mrs. Black." He smiled.

"Touché, Mr. Black." I laughed.

I unwrapped my legs and he gently put me down. "Please say you'll stay with me tonight instead of going back to your room. I don't want to sleep alone."

"Of course I'll stay here. I love you so much, Connor," I said as I wiped the sweat from his forehead.

"And I love you, Ellery."

We climbed into the luxury bed and Connor wrapped his arms around me.

"Did you know I was here? I asked.

"No. I had no idea you'd be here. I had a Vegas room set up in the suite for Henry's party and one of the other guys arranged the strip club. When the elevator doors opened and I saw you standing there, you took my breath away, and I felt like it was my first time ever seeing you. That's why I wanted to pretend that I didn't know you, and when you played along, that's when I decided to play it out."

"We should do this more often." I smiled as I rolled over and his arms tightened around me.

As he softly kissed my back, he whispered, "We're going to have a little talk in the morning about that dress you were wearing."

I smiled as I closed my eyes and fell fast asleep.

Chapter 27

Connor

One month later...

"I don't give a shit if his wife left him. You tell him that the Chicago building better be ready next month for the inspection. I've paid him good money to see that it gets done, and it better be ready! Because if it's not, you tell that son-of-a-bitch that I'll see him in court," I yelled as I threw my phone across the desk.

"What's going on?" Ellery said as she walked into my home office, carrying Julia.

"Just people not doing what they're supposed to be." I sighed as I got up from my desk and walked over to her.

"Is it the Chicago building again?"

"Yeah, baby, it is, but I don't want you worrying about it," I said as I kissed her head and took Julia from her. "Have you finished the last painting?"

"Yes, I have. I just finished it a few minutes ago." She smiled.

"Great. I'll have them wrapped and shipped to the gallery. They'll be there just in time for the opening next week."

I looked at Julia and she stared at me with her big blue eyes as I talked to Ellery. She was growing so fast. Ellery had started her on baby food and she'd learned to sit up by herself.

"Peyton and Henry come home today from their month-long honeymoon," Ellery said.

"They had a great wedding. I can't believe how fast it came and went."

"I know. Time is going by so fast. Look at how big Julia is getting already," she said.

We heard the elevator doors open and Mason announcing that he had arrived.

"Are you ready to hit the gym?" I asked Ellery.

"You bet I am. Let me go and grab my bag."

We walked out of the office and I handed Julia over to Mason. "There's the little princess." He smiled.

While Ellery grabbed her bag, I took mine from the hall closet and grabbed my keys. "I forgot to tell you that I'm driving us today. Denny called me this morning, and he's not feeling well."

Ellery turned and looked at me. "What? What's wrong with him?" she asked with concern.

"I'm not sure. He just said he wasn't feeling well and that he's sorry, but he couldn't work today."

"Denny is never sick," she said.

"I know. I'm a little worried about him, but I'm sure he's just picked up a bug. People at the office are sick."

"I hope he feels better soon."

"Me too, baby," I said as I put my arm around her and we headed to the gym.

* * * *

After our workout, Ellery dropped me off at the office and took the Range Rover with her. I told her that I'd catch a cab home this evening. Valerie followed me into my office, rattling off all the meetings that were scheduled for today. As I sighed, I set my briefcase down on my desk and looked out the large window that overlooked the city. My mind wouldn't stop thinking about Denny. In all the years I'd known him, he had never once been sick, and I was concerned.

"Mr. Black, are you all right?" Valerie asked.

"I'm fine, Valerie. Now, if you'll excuse me, I have a couple of things to do before my first meeting."

She nodded her head and walked out of the office, closing the door behind her. As I turned my computer on, the screen displayed a picture of Ellery and Julia. After a few minutes had passed, Phil and Paul walked into the office, summoning me to the meeting. I left my phone on my desk and grabbed my files.

While I sat in the board room on a conference call with Sakura Nakamora, CEO of Takashi Enterprises, a Japanese company we were trying to negotiate a contract with, Ellery came through the door. As I saw her, I jumped out of my seat.

"Ellery, what's wrong?" I asked, as I could tell she looked panicked.

"Connor, I'm sorry, but it's Denny."

"Finish this meeting without me," I said as I looked at Paul and Phil.

I placed my hand on the small of her back and led her out to the hallway. "What happened?" I asked as we walked to my office.

"Dana called me and said that Denny had a seizure, so she called an ambulance and they immediately rushed him to the emergency room. We both tried calling you, but you weren't answering your phone."

"Shit. I left it on my desk while I was in my meeting. I'm sorry, baby," I said as we walked into my office, and I grabbed my phone.

"I tried to call Valerie, but she wasn't at her desk. I knew you had a meeting, so when you weren't in your office, I figured you were in the board room."

We raced down to where Ellery had parked the Range Rover. We got in and I drove as quickly as I could to the ER. Once we arrived, the nurse took us back to where Denny was. When we walked into the room, Dana got up from her seat and I gave her a hug.

"Connor, Ellery, thank you for coming," she cried.

"What happened, Dana?" I asked her as I looked over at Denny. He was sleeping.

"He woke up this morning, said he wasn't feeling well, but he couldn't describe what was wrong. He said he felt dizzy. So I made him lie down for a while and when he went to get out of bed, he fell to the floor and started seizing."

"Are you sure it was a seizure?" I asked.

"Yes, my sister used to have them all the time," she said as she cried.

As I held her tightly and told her that he was going to be okay, Denny opened his eyes.

"Why the hell are you hugging my wife," he said with a slight grin.

"Why the hell are you lying in that bed in the emergency room? You were supposed to work today." I smiled as I put my hand on his shoulder.

"Yeah, well, I'm sure you'd survive without me," he said.

"I wouldn't be so sure of that," I said with a serious tone.

He looked at Dana and held out his hand to her. She took it as more tears started to fall. Ellery walked over to her and clasped her shoulders.

"Dana, stop the tears," he said. "I'm going to be fine."

The doctor walked in with the nurse and told Denny that they were going to run a CT scan to see what was going on. As they took him out of the room, I took Ellery's hand and we waited in the waiting room of the ER.

"I could use a glass of scotch right now," I said.

"How about some coffee instead?" Ellery asked as she smiled at me.

I put my arm around her and we headed to the Starbucks that was inside the hospital. Ellery handed me my coffee and, on our way back to the waiting room, we ran into Dr. Taub.

"Ellery, Connor; it's nice to see you. Ellery, are you here for your annual blood work?"

"No, Dr. Taub. A friend of ours was brought into the ER and we're here visiting," she replied.

"Oh, well, I hope your friend is okay. Don't forget about that blood work. You know how important that is," he said as he walked away.

We waited an hour before Denny was brought back to his room. As we were sitting there with him, the doctor walked in and asked to speak with Denny and Dana alone.

"Whatever you have to say, you can say it in front of them; they're my family," Denny said.

The doctor cleared his throat before he began to speak. "The CT scan showed a tumor in the brain."

Immediately, Dana broke down and started crying. As I grabbed her, to keep her from falling, Ellery took a hold of Denny's other hand.

"I'm not a specialist, but I've called one in to come see you."

"What's his name and how good is he?" I asked.

"He's one of the best neurosurgeons we have on staff. He's very reputable. His name is Dr. William Armstrong and he'll be in tonight to see you. Until then, we're going to keep you here overnight, and after Dr. Armstrong consults with you, then we'll have a better understanding on how to proceed."

Denny's expression never changed as he listened intently to every word the doctor spoke to him.

"Is the food here any good?" he asked.

Ellery laughed as she squeezed his hand. "It's not that bad," she said.

"Okay then, I'll stay."

The doctor smiled as he walked out of the room. Denny looked over at Dana and squeezed her hand. "Stop crying, woman. Everything's going to be fine. I'll be all right."

"Of course you will be." Ellery smiled at him.

Hearing the news that Denny had a brain tumor sickened my stomach. I didn't know much about them, but what I did know was that they weren't good. As I stepped out of the room to make a phone call, Ellery followed me. I took my phone out of my pocket and dialed Bernie.

"Bernie, it's Connor. I need you to dig up everything you can on a Dr. William Armstrong. He's a neurosurgeon at Mount Sinai Hospital here in the city. I want everything; do you understand me? This is important."

"Yes, Mr. Black, I'll get on it right away and get back with you."

"Thank you," I said as I ended the call.

Ellery grabbed my hand. "What's that all about?"

"I need to make sure he's the best, because if he isn't, then I'm flying in the best."

* * * *

Ellery and I left the hospital to go home and be with Julia for a while, before coming back later when Dr. Armstrong was going to be there. As I set Julia in her highchair to eat and, while Ellery was getting her food ready, my phone rang. It was Bernie.

"What did you find out?" I said as I answered.

"Dr. Armstrong is rated one of the best in his field. His credentials are excellent, Connor. I don't think you have anything to worry about."

"Thank you, Bernie. I appreciate it," I said as I ended the call.

"What did he say?" Ellery asked as she set the jars of baby food on the table.

"He said that he's one of the best. So, we'll have to wait and see."

As I took the baby spoon and dipped it into the jar, Julia started to squeal. I smiled as I brought the spoon to her mouth and she gracefully took it.

"Mason said that he would watch Julia for us tonight while we're at the hospital. Have you called your mom and dad yet?"

"No, I still have to do that. I will as soon as I'm done feeding Julia."

Ellery walked over to me and put her arms around my neck. "I can feed her, babe," she said as she kissed my cheek.

"I want to finish feeding her. I'll call them after."

When Julia was finished eating, Ellery cleaned her up and took her out of her highchair while I went and called my mom and dad. They were upset when I told them the news and said to let them know what was going on and when they could visit. About an hour later, Mason stepped off the elevator with Landon.

"Hey, you two," I said.

"If it's okay with you, we're going to take Julia with us furniture shopping," Mason said.

"Oh, that sounds like fun!" Ellery exclaimed.

"That's fine," I said as I walked upstairs.

I went into the bathroom and splashed some water on my face. Things weren't sitting right with me, and I had a bad feeling. I stood with my hands on the counter when Ellery walked in and looked at me.

"Connor, are you okay?" she asked.

"I don't know, Elle. To be honest, I don't know what I'm feeling right now."

She walked over to me and wrapped her arms tightly around my waist. I needed her now more than ever before. I closed my eyes as she rested her head on my back.

"Let's try to think positive about this, Connor. I know it's hard, believe me, but positivity is the key to staying strong, and we need to be strong for him and Dana. Your strength is what pulled me through my illness, even when we thought there was no hope."

I turned around and held her face in my hands. "I never gave up hope. Hope was all I had. I wouldn't have made it through without it. The thought of losing you to that illness flooded my mind every day, but I never once gave up hope, and I never once gave up on you."

Tears formed in her eyes and her bottom lip started to quiver. "I had given up. I lost all hope for me. Then I met you. You made me fall in love with you, and you showed me there was a reason to fight. You had enough hope for both of us and, if it wasn't for you, I wouldn't be here today."

A single tear fell from my eye as I listened to her words. I pulled her into me and held her as tightly as I could. She was my safety, my saint, and my savior, and I thanked God every day for not taking her away from me. She jumped up and wrapped her legs around me and I carried her to our bed. I gently laid her down and stared into her eyes as I softly kissed her lips. Believe it or not, that was all I wanted. I just wanted to kiss her and nothing else.

* * * *

When Ellery and I went up to Denny's room, Dr. Armstrong had just left and Dana was crying. Ellery walked over to Dana to comfort her, and Denny gave me a sullen look.

"What's wrong? What did Dr. Armstrong say?" I asked as I went and stood at his bedside.

"I have a Grade III brain tumor and it's aggressive. Which means it's growing rapidly."

When I heard Denny speak those words, my stomach twisted itself in knots. "What does that mean?"

"It means I have brain cancer and there's a possibility it spread somewhere else. But he won't know that until they do an MRI."

"When are you having that done?" I asked.

"In the morning," he said as he looked away from me.

I had no words at that moment. I didn't know what to say. The worry that I once thought was gone from my life had returned, just with someone else that I loved, and was very important to me. Ellery looked at me with tears in her eyes as she tried to comfort Dana.

"What about surgery?" I asked.

"He said it's operable and that he'll discuss that with me after the results of the MRI come back."

"I'm sorry, Denny," I said as I looked down.

"Don't be, Connor. I'll be okay."

Ellery sat on the edge of the bed and placed her hand on Denny's. "I'm always here if you need me. If you want to cry, talk, laugh, or even scream, I'm here."

If anyone knew how Denny felt, it was Ellery. She had endured, battled, and fought her cancer, not only once, but twice. As Denny started to grow tired, we decided it was best to leave. Dana walked us out of room as we said goodbye.

"He's going to be fine, Dana. I'm not going to stand here and tell you not to worry because I know you can't help it. Go home and get some rest. You'll be no good to him if you're tired," I said as I kissed her head.

She smiled and nodded her head as she turned and walked back into Denny's room. I sighed and looked at Ellery as she looked like she was lost in a thought.

"What's going on in that pretty little head of yours?" I asked as I pushed her hair behind her ear.

"I know what he's going through, and I know what he's feeling. It breaks my heart that he has to go through this."

"Well, then, it's a damn good thing he has you to talk to," I said as I pulled her into me and hugged her tightly.

I could tell she was as scared as I was. She had too much on her plate already with the gallery showing and with Julia. She had just moved on and put to rest the trial and the incident with Ashlyn. As I glanced over at her while we were driving home, that look of pain and sadness was spread across her face. I grabbed her hand and brought it up to my lips.

"Tell me what you're feeling, Elle."

She sighed and then took in a sharp breath. "I feel like I'm going through this all over again. Even though it isn't me, it's someone that I love and is like a father to me. FUCK," she screamed.

I pulled over to the side of the road, threw the Range Rover in park and got out. I walked around to the passenger's side and opened the door. I grabbed Ellery from her seat and held her as tight as I could.

"It's okay, baby, let it out," I said as tears swelled in my eyes.

Ellery sobbed into my chest and we both slowly fell to the ground.

"Why? Why the fuck did this have to happen to him? It's not fair, Connor. He has brain cancer, and I'm so scared he's going to die. He's the father I never had. He's always there for me. He can't die. He can't die, Connor," she screamed.

She was shaking uncontrollably. I'd never seen her this way before, and it was killing me. The only thing I could do was hold her and try to give her some comfort. The tears pooled from my eyes as I buried my face into her neck. We needed to be strong, but we also needed to let our feelings out.

"He's going to beat this, Ellery."

She didn't say another word. She just cried in my arms until there were no more tears. I told her we needed to get home to Julia, and she nodded her head as I helped her back into the truck. I helped her with her seatbelt, then kissed her on the head before shutting the door.

Chapter 28

Ellery

A few days had passed and Denny's MRI showed that the cancer hadn't spread to any other organs in his body. Connor and I were relieved with the news. Dr. Armstrong had scheduled the surgery for Friday, which was the day of the gallery's opening and my showing. Connor had all my paintings flown to Chicago already, so I had nothing to worry about. I just needed to show up. At this point, I no longer wanted to go. Denny was more important and so was being there for him, Dana, and Connor. I just wasn't sure how Connor was going to take the news.

I gave Mason the day off, and Julia and I drove over to Denny's house for a visit. He seemed to be in high spirits. As he sat in the chair across from me, I reached forward and grabbed his hand.

"I know you're scared, but Dr. Armstrong is one of the best in the country. You know that Connor had him checked out thoroughly."

"Yeah, I know he did, and I don't doubt that he's the best, but the thought of my brain being cut into isn't very pleasant."

"I know it's not, but it has to be done. After, you'll start chemo for a while, and then you'll be cancer free and you can put all of this behind you." I smiled.

"Easier said than done, Elle."

"Not really. I've put it all behind me."

"Do you ever think of the 'what if's'?" he asked.

"Sometimes I do, especially when I'm with Connor. If I can't sleep at night, I'll roll over, wrap my arms around him, and start to think about what if the treatments didn't work. It's who we are as human beings, Denny. Those thoughts will always creep up in your mind, and you're the only one who can put them to rest."

He smiled as I got up from the chair and took Julia from Dana. As I walked over to Denny, I handed Julia to him.

"Give Uncle Denny a kiss goodbye," I told her.

She made her cute noises and proceeded to hit him in the face. "Your daddy taught you that, didn't he?" He laughed.

Denny gave her a kiss on the cheek and a hug. I leaned over, kissed him goodbye, and Julia and I headed home.

* * * *

The penthouse was quiet. No one was home but me and Julia. I set her down on her blanket in the living room and surrounded her with toys. As fall was settling in, and it was getting chilly, I walked over to the fireplace and turned it on. I sat down on the blanket across from her and began playing with her and her toys. I gave some more thought about my showing on Friday and decided that I could fly to Chicago right before the opening and fly back the same night. After an hour had passed, Connor came home. He kicked off his shoes, set his briefcase down on the chair, and joined us on the floor.

"How are my two special girls?" He smiled.

"We're good, sweetheart," I said as I kissed him.

Julia started yelling when Connor sat down. She was becoming very vocal lately. Her high-pitched voice was hard on the ears. Connor leaned towards her, held her arms, and stood her up. Her little legs wobbled as she smiled and shrieked.

"Wow, she's really happy today!" he said.

"She's been very good all day. We went and saw Denny earlier."

"How is he? I stopped by this morning before going to the office."

"He's okay. I can tell he's scared about the surgery."

"That's natural. I would be too," Connor said as he carefully lowered Julia down.

"I need to talk to you about Friday," I said.

"What about it? That's the day of Denny's surgery."

That was all he said. He didn't mention anything about the opening or my showing. It must've slipped his mind with everything going on. I wasn't going to discuss it further. I was going to get in and get out of that gallery as fast as I could. I'd be home before Connor even noticed I was missing.

"I just wanted to tell you that Mason is keeping Julia all day and all night at his place."

"That's fine," he said as he leaned over and kissed me, forcing me on my back as he wouldn't stop.

Our make-out session was interrupted by Julia's screeches. Connor broke our kiss and we looked at her. She was on her knees, rocking back and forth.

"Oh my God, Connor, she's going to crawl!" I exclaimed.

Instantly, he sat up and held his arms out to her. "Come to Daddy, Julia," he said.

She stayed in that position and smiled. When she wouldn't move, I took all her toys and moved them away from her and set one block in front of her, but far enough away so that she would have to crawl to reach it. She started to get frustrated as she kept falling over. Soon, she'd had enough and let out a full-blown cry. Connor picked her up and held her. I would never get tired of seeing him with her. Then I started to think about what Denny said and the what if's.

"I'll go get her a bottle. She's probably hungry," I said as I got up.

As I walked to the kitchen, I remembered that I had to call Vinnie and tell him not to mention the opening to Connor. That was the last thing I wanted him to worry about. I got Julia's bottle ready and walked back to the living room, where I found Connor asleep in the oversized leather recliner and Julia curled up on his chest. Smiling, I snapped a picture with my phone and sent it to Peyton.

* * * *

Since Denny's surgery was scheduled for six o'clock in the morning, Mason had come and picked up Julia the night before. When the alarm went off, Connor rolled over and put his arm around me as I reached over and turned it off. I snuggled closer to him for a few minutes before we had to get up and get ready to go to the hospital.

"Me and you need to have a talk," he said in a serious tone.

"About?" I replied.

"The art gallery and showing tonight."

Shit, I thought to myself. I should have never underestimated him and thought that he'd forget something.

"What about it?"

"I'm a little pissed off that you failed to mention it to me and the fact that you're going without me."

I rolled over and looked at him. "How did you remember

with everything going on, and how did you know I was going without you?"

"My pilot called me last night to confirm."

"Damn him. Why didn't you say anything last night?" I asked.

"Because Mason had just picked up Julia and I wanted to devour your body. I figured if I mentioned it, we'd fight and then no body devouring for me."

I cocked my head in disbelief that he had just said what he did. "Are you serious?" I asked.

"Yes, I am, and I wasn't giving that up. It's not that often that Julia isn't here to interrupt us."

"I'm not talking about this now. We need to get ready and go to the hospital," I said as I got out of bed.

Connor climbed out of bed and followed me into the bathroom. "See, that's where you're wrong, Ellery. We *are* going to discuss it now."

Who the hell did he think he was, starting an argument with me before I even had my first cup of coffee? I slipped on my silk robe and headed towards the kitchen and Connor followed behind.

"I'm coming with you; end of discussion. See, now that wasn't so bad, was it?"

"Connor."

He walked over to me, picked me up, and set me on the counter. "Listen to me. You're my wife and this is something that's very important to you, and it's important to me too. "

"But—"

He cut me off and brought his finger to my lips. "No buts. I love Denny and we'll be here for his surgery. But I'm getting on that plane with you and we're going to that art gallery together. I would never miss your first showing, or any showing, and to think that you were going to go by yourself really hurt me, Ellery."

As I stared into his eyes, I could see the hurt in them. *What the hell did I do?* My eyes started to swell with tears as I wrapped my arms around his neck.

"I'm so sorry. I just feel so guilty having to go to this showing while someone that I love very much will be having brain surgery. I feel so selfish, Connor, and I didn't want you to have to make a decision."

"There was never a decision to be made, honey. I was going with you all along."

"I'm sorry." I began to cry.

"Let's go upstairs and finish getting dressed so we can get to the hospital," he said as he kissed me on my head and picked me up off the counter.

* * * *

Thanks to the morning New York City traffic, we arrived at the hospital just as the nurse was getting ready to wheel Denny out of the room and into the operating room.

"I didn't think I'd see you two before I went under the big knife and got my brain cut open," he said.

"Damn traffic," Connor said. "We'll be here waiting for you when you get out, so make it quick." He smiled.

"Yeah, I'll try." Denny smiled back.

After I gave him a kiss on the cheek, I whispered, "You're strong and you can do this. Remember, I'm out here waiting for you, so you better come back."

"I will," he said as they wheeled him down the hallway.

Connor put his arm around Dana and led her to the waiting room. Dana's family arrived and tried to keep her as occupied as possible. Connor and I left the waiting room and went up to the cafeteria to grab some lunch.

"Are you nervous about tonight?" he asked.

"Yes!" I smiled.

"Don't be. You're a very talented artist, and everyone is going to love your paintings."

"You're just saying that because you're my husband." I smiled and stuck out my tongue at him.

Connor laughed and threw a straw wrapper at me and then he glanced at his watch. "It's been six hours already since Denny went into surgery. We should get back to the waiting room."

He grabbed our trays and then my hand as we walked back to the waiting room. We weren't back very long when the doctor came to speak to us.

"We were able to remove the tumor, but it did cause some cerebral hemorrhaging and there was significant swelling in the brain. During the surgery, he slipped into a coma."

Connor grabbed Dana as she almost fell to the ground. Instantly, a sick feeling washed over me, and I needed to sit down. *This can't be happening.* Doctor Armstrong continued as Connor kept a tight grip on Dana.

"This isn't uncommon, and we're keeping an eye on him very carefully."

"How long will he be in a coma?" Connor asked.

Dr. Armstrong sighed as he looked at us. "There's no telling. It could be up to twelve hours or twelve days. I wish I had an exact answer for you, but I don't. The good news is that the tumor is gone, and the cancer didn't spread to any other organs. So now, we just have to wait. He's back in his room and you may go see him."

"Thank you, Dr. Armstrong," Connor said as he walked away.

He looked over at me and shook his head as Dana sobbed in his arms. "Come on, Dana, let's go see him," he said, leading her to Denny's room.

I got up from my chair and followed behind. When we reached the room and I saw Denny lying there, tears started to fill my eyes. The soft beeps of the machines to which he was hooked up, and the white bandage that was wrapped around his head were horrifying. Dana almost collapsed before Connor sat her down in the chair. He looked over at me as the tears streamed down my face. As Dana reached over and ran her hand across Denny's cheek, Connor came over and pulled me into him.

"He's going to be okay," he said as he kissed my head.

I needed to be strong, and I couldn't let Dana see me fall apart. I pulled back from Connor, kissed him, and told him I'd be right back. When I found the nearest bathroom, I stood and stared at my tear-soaked eyes. The thought of going to Chicago terrified me. I found myself no longer wanting to go for the fear that something bad would happen to Denny while we were gone. But, Denny had made me promise him that I would go; not just for myself, but for him. When I walked back to the room, Connor walked over to me.

"I think she's settled down now. It's time for us to leave."

"Connor, I wouldn't blame you if you wanted to stay with her," I spoke softly.

"We've already settled this, and I'm going with you. Now I don't want to hear another word about it. Do you understand me?" he said in a commanding tone.

I nodded my head and we said goodbye to Dana and her family. Connor told her to keep us posted and that we'd be back tomorrow. As we walked out of the hospital, hand in hand, I could tell Connor wasn't doing well, but he refused to show it. I was worried that if he didn't let his feelings out, he was going to have a break down.

Chapter 29

Connor

Ellery's paintings looked stunning up on the brand new walls of the art gallery. Vinnie did a fine job displaying each piece of artwork. Ellery had never looked more beautiful than she did in her short, lace, cream-colored dress. I felt it was too short and too low cut. We had a slight discussion about it when she put it on, but like always, she shut me down and told me to deal with it. She was breathtaking, and I didn't want other men looking at her. But, that's the price you pay when you're married to the most beautiful and sexy woman on Earth. As I carefully watched her mix and mingle with the other artists and guests, Vinnie walked up to me and handed me a glass of champagne.

"Thank you, Vinnie. You did a fine job with this opening. The gallery looks fantastic."

"Thank you, Connor, but none of this would have been possible without your help." He smiled. "Doesn't Ellery's artwork look fabulous up on the wall?"

"It does. Look at all the people over there, admiring them," I said.

"If you'll excuse me, I see my brother," Vinnie said as he walked away.

The art gallery was filled with influential people. The

Governor of Chicago and some outstanding photographers were only a few. As I walked around, admiring some of the other artwork, I came across a display of paintings of beautiful naked women. Ellery walked over to me as I was staring at them.

"I see you found something to admire," she said as she looked at the paintings.

"They're beautiful and so exquisite, aren't they?" I asked.

Ellery looked at me and then looked back at the portraits. "If you're in love with them so much, the model is right over there. Maybe you could ask her if she would like you to fuck her!" she snapped as she walked away.

What the hell just happened? I couldn't believe Ellery had just said that. I turned around to look for her, but she was gone. I tried to search the gallery for her, but I kept getting stopped by people. When I finally was able to break free, I found her over by her paintings, talking to a group of people.

"Good evening. Please excuse us; I need to talk to my wife for a moment." I smiled as I lightly touched Ellery's arm and let her to a quiet corner.

"What the hell do you think you're doing?" she snapped.

"Me? What the fuck was all that about back there?" I snapped back.

"People are staring, Connor."

"Then I suggest you put on a fake smile, Ellery."

She did just that and she proceeded to yell at me. "You were gushing all over those naked paintings. I simply pointed out that the model is here if you wanted to fuck her, since she was so beautiful and exquisite, and you couldn't stop staring at her."

"Are you serious? Are you fucking serious right now? I

can't believe you would be jealous over something like that. My God, Ellery, I was staring at it and saying those things about the artist's skill, not the actual model. I was picturing you in that painting because I want one of you, naked."

She looked away from me as she bit down on her bottom lip. I had to do everything in my power to keep from putting my hands all over her. "I'm sorry if I gave you the wrong impression. You know I would never want anyone else. I love you, Ellery. I don't know how to make that any clearer to you than I already have since we've been together."

"I know you do, and I'm sorry. It's just my nerves with this opening, missing Julia, and the fact that Denny is lying in a hospital bed in a coma."

"I know, baby," I said as I wrapped my arms around her and hugged her tight. "It's almost over and then we'll be on our way home."

All of a sudden, we heard a voice behind us. "Really? You can't wait until after the showing?" Peyton said.

Ellery's eyes lit up when she saw Peyton and Henry standing there and a huge smile graced her face as looked across the gallery and saw my family smiling at her. I hadn't told her they were coming; I wanted it be a surprise. She took them over to her section and Henry stayed back with me.

"I heard about Denny. I'm sorry, man," he said as he patted me on the back.

"Thanks, Henry, but I don't really want to talk about it right now."

"I understand. If you need anything let me know."

Peyton stood in front of the portraits of the naked woman that Ellery and I had just fought about. Henry and I walked over and stood next to her. Not too long after, Ellery joined us.

"Will you paint me naked, Elle?" Peyton asked.

I looked over at Henry, and he smiled at me.

"Maybe," Ellery answered.

"Can I watch?" I smiled.

The night went smoothly and Ellery sold all five of her paintings. She was very happy, but she just wanted to get back home. We both did. We missed our baby girl, and we wanted to get back to Denny.

It had been a long and exhausting day. Ellery and I were lying on the couch together on the plane. As I held her in my arms, she tilted her head back and looked at me.

"I gave some thought about what you said earlier."

"About what, baby?" I asked.

"About you wanting a nude portrait of me."

"Really? And what did you decide?" I smiled.

"I decided that when we get back to New York, I'm going to call that artist and ask him to do it. After all, I know you wouldn't have a problem with a strange man staring at me for six or seven hours a day while I'm fully naked in front of him, posing."

I took in a sharp breath. "You know what? Let's just forget about that painting. I have the real thing right here and that's all I need." I smiled as I leaned down and kissed her lips. There was no way I was going to let that happen.

Chapter 30

Ellery

I paced back and forth, trying to comfort Julia as she screamed her head off at three o'clock in the morning. I bounced her, walked her around the penthouse, sat down, rocked her in the rocking chair, and nothing soothed her. I even gave her gas drops, thinking she was gassy, but that didn't help either. Connor came up behind me in the living room and took her from me.

"What's wrong, Julia? Daddy's here."

I rolled my eyes because sometimes he thought he was the cure-all where she was concerned. When she didn't stop screaming, he looked at me.

"Don't you have a book or something you can refer to?" he asked as he bounced her up and down and she continued to scream even louder.

I ran upstairs to our bedroom and grabbed the baby book from the bookshelf. As I ran down the stairs, I turned to the section that was outlined for her age group.

"It says she may be teething. Run your finger along her gums and see if you feel anything," I said.

He took his finger and put it in Julia's mouth. "Yep, I feel a lump right here," he said.

When I walked over to him, he took my finger and placed it

on Julia's gums. "Aw, my poor baby," I pouted as I kissed her head.

"I'll go and get the baby Tylenol. That should help her feel better."

Connor followed me into the kitchen, and I took the Tylenol from the cupboard. I gave Julia her dosage and we sat with her on the couch.

"I can take her, sweetheart. You have to get up for work in a couple of hours."

"It's okay. We can do this together." He smiled as he leaned over and kissed me.

The Tylenol took effect and Julia finally fell asleep. Connor slowly got up from the couch, took her upstairs, and laid her down in her crib. I climbed under my warm sheets and closed my eyes. As I began to drift asleep, I felt little kisses all over my back. I opened my eyes and rolled over.

"What are you doing?" I asked.

Connor climbed on top of me and whispered, "I'm going to make love to you and then you can go to sleep."

"Is that so? What if I don't want you to make love to me?"

"Ellery Rose Black! I better never hear those words come from your mouth."

I couldn't help but laugh when he said that. I held his face in my hands as he hovered over me. "Make love to me."

"I changed my mind," he said as he got off of me and rolled over.

"What?!" I exclaimed as I took my pillow and hit him with it.

"So, you want a pillow fight, do you?" He retaliated by taking his pillow and hitting me back.

I stood up on the bed with my pillow in hand and hit him with it again. He jumped out of bed and swung his pillow at me, but missed when I jumped to the other side. As I jumped off the bed, we stood and stared at each other from opposite sides, waiting for the other to make a move.

"You aren't getting off that easy, baby," Connor said.

"Bring it on, Black." I smiled.

He stood there and shook his head. "You wait until I get a hold of you."

It was now four o'clock in the morning, and I couldn't believe we were having a pillow fight. Connor finally made his move and ran to the other side of the bed where I stood. I laughed as I tried to dash across the bed to the other side, but he grabbed my leg and I screamed. As I fell onto the bed, he positioned himself on top of me and covered my mouth with his hand.

"Shh...you're going to wake the baby, and we can't have her waking up quite yet." He smiled.

Lying there, I stared into his eyes as he stared into mine and, with his hand still covering my mouth, he asked, "Do you want me to make love to you?"

I nodded my head, and he smiled as he took his other hand and placed it between my legs.

When the alarm went off, I heard Julia whining. We'd only slept about two hours. He turned and looked at me as I rolled over, and he kissed me on the head.

"Go back to sleep, sweetheart. I'll take care of Julia before I head to the office. You need your rest after your workout last night." He smiled.

I sighed, rolled over, and went back to sleep. I wasn't going to argue with him because I was dead tired.

A couple of hours later, I woke up and headed to the kitchen for some coffee. Mason was already over and feeding Julia in her highchair.

"Good morning, Elle. Oh my, look at those bags under your eyes. Did Connor keep you up all night?"

I poured some coffee in my cup, kissed Julia on the head, and sat down across from Mason. "He did for about an hour, but it was Julia who was up all night screaming. She's teething."

"Yeah, I know. I hope you used the teething gel in the diaper bag," he said.

"I didn't know there was teething gel in the diaper bag! Why didn't you tell me?"

"I forgot, sorry. I figured you go in the diaper bag every day, so you would've seen it."

Just as I was about to answer him, a text message came through on my phone from a restricted number.

"You are one of the most beautiful women I've ever seen and I can't stop thinking about you. You haunt my dreams."

Smiling, I showed the message to Mason. "I have the most romantic husband in the world."

"That's weird; why would he send it from a restricted number?" Mason asked.

"He likes to play games." I smiled.

A shower was required before I headed over to the hospital to see Denny. I got up from the table and went upstairs. After I got dressed, I kissed Julia goodbye and took a cab to the hospital. Dana was the only one in the room and she smiled when she saw me.

"How's he doing?" I asked as I walked over to the bed and touched his hand.

"Still the same, but Dr. Armstrong said that the swelling in his brain went down and that's a good sign."

No matter how many times I visited him, it didn't get any easier. Dana said she was going to take a little break and meet her sister in the cafeteria for coffee. When she left the room, I sat in the chair, took a hold of his hand, and squeezed it tight.

"Denny, it's me, Ellery. We all miss you so much and we need you to wake up. It's so hard seeing you like this. I know you're strong and you're going to pull through this."

Just as I was talking to him, my phone beeped with a text message. It was from the restricted number again.

"I hope you didn't find my last text out of line. I just needed you to know that I find you exquisite and I couldn't let another day go by without telling you."

When I tried to send a reply, the message wouldn't go through. I thought it was strange, but it was Connor, so I would play his game with him until tonight when he got home from work. After leaving the hospital, I had a few errands to run and then I met Peyton for lunch at our favorite restaurant. I walked over to the booth where she was sitting.

"You're late," she said.

"Just by five minutes and you're always late. You were late for your own wedding." I laughed.

She sighed. "I know. Don't remind me."

"So, tell me all about the fabulous honeymoon," I said as I took a sip of water.

"It was amazing! I didn't want to come home." She pouted.

I reached in my purse for my phone when I heard it beeping. As I pulled it out, there was another text message from that same restricted number. Connor must be bored today or something, I thought.

"I hope you're enjoying my text messages. A woman as stunning as you should be told every day, multiple times. To me, you're a queen and you should be treated as such."

I smiled and laughed at the same time as I shook my head.

"What's so funny?" Peyton asked.

"It's Connor and his game playing. Look at the text messages he's been sending me since this morning," I said as I handed Peyton my phone.

"He's so romantic. Why the restricted number, though?"

"I don't know. To keep it interesting, I guess."

She smiled at me and then continued to tell me about her and Henry's honeymoon. Once we finished lunch, we walked out of the restaurant and parted ways. When I arrived home, I was greeted at the elevator by Mason and Julia.

"Girl, wait until you see what's in the kitchen for you." He smiled.

Curiosity got the best of me, so I put my purse down and walked to the kitchen. I gasped when I saw three dozen pink roses sitting in separate vases on the counter.

"Looks like Connor has really outdone himself today," Mason said.

I walked over and pulled the card from one of the vases. It read:

To the most beautiful woman in the world.

No one will ever come close to your beauty.

My heart melted when I read that, and I couldn't wait until Connor came home. As I set the card down, I heard my phone beep. There was another text message from that same number.

"Beautiful flowers for a beautiful woman. I want you to think of me every time you look at them."

A few hours had passed and Connor finally arrived home. As he stepped off the elevator, I wrapped my arms around him and hugged him tight before he even had the chance to put his briefcase down.

"Wow, now I like that greeting." He smiled as he kissed me. "I thought I was going to get yelled at for not calling you all day. You wouldn't believe the shit going on at the office right now. I was in back-to-back meetings all day."

I smiled at him and walked back to the kitchen to take the chicken out of the oven. Connor followed behind me.

"Where did those flowers come from?" he asked.

"From someone who thinks I'm the most beautiful and exquisite woman in the world." I smiled as I set the chicken on the stove.

"Of course you are, baby, but who sent them?"

I turned around and looked at him. "A hot and sexy man sent them to me, along with those romantic texts all day."

Suddenly, Connor got angry. "Ellery, I will ask you one last time: Who the fuck sent you those flowers and what texts are you talking about?!" he yelled.

I couldn't believe how upset he was. This was his game and he had the nerve to yell at me.

"Jesus, Connor, calm down. You're the one who sent them. Why are you yelling at me?"

As he looked at me, his eyes turned dark. "I didn't send you those flowers or any text messages today. I told you I was in back-to-back meetings all day!" he yelled again. "Give me your phone!" he commanded.

He was scaring me and I didn't like it. With shaking hands, I opened the text messages on my phone and handed it to him. As he read them, the look on his face was daunting. He looked at me and then back at the flowers. He picked up the card from the counter and read it.

"When did these flowers come?" he asked.

"I don't know. They were delivered when I was out with Peyton."

Connor pulled his phone from his pocket and dialed it. "Mason, it's Connor. Were you here when the flowers for Ellery were delivered? I see. Thank you," he said as he hung up.

"He said that when he and Julia got home from the park, they were outside the door."

"Connor, I thought they were from you along with the text messages. Now you're scaring me," I said as my bottom lip started to quiver.

"Why the hell would I send you text messages from a restricted number?"

"I thought you were playing with me."

He sighed as he paced around the kitchen, running his hands through his hair. "These aren't from me!" he yelled.

I couldn't stand there and be yelled at anymore. I didn't know what was going on, so I took off up the stairs and went into my bedroom. After I locked the door, I threw myself on the bed, scared and shaking that someone, other than my husband, was saying those things to me and sending me my favorite flowers. While I was lying there, Connor knocked on the door.

"Ellery, open the door."

"No! Stay the hell away from me."

"Baby, please. I'm so sorry. I didn't mean to yell at you like that. We need to talk about this, so please open the door."

He sounded like he had calmed down, so I got up from the bed and unlocked the door. With a turn of the knob, he opened it as I sat on the edge of the bed. Connor walked in and sat on the bed next to me. He put his arm around me and pulled me into him as he held my head against his chest. I started to cry.

"I'm sorry. Please forgive me, Ellery. You just have no idea the terrible thoughts that are going through my head right now."

"You fucking scared me, Connor."

"I know I did. I'm sorry. It's just the thought of someone saying that shit to you is unnerving, and I took it out on you, and I shouldn't have. Please, baby, look at me."

I lifted my head up and Connor wiped the tears from my eyes. He took my face in his hands and softly kissed my lips.

"We need to find out who's doing this. I put a call into Detective James, the private investigator who worked with me on the Chicago fire. He's coming over in a while and so is Paul."

As I nodded my head, I got up from the bed and went into the bathroom. I looked at myself in the mirror and tried to remove the mascara stains from under my eyes. The day that was going so well and made me so happy had all just gone to hell. Connor stood in the doorway of the bathroom and looked at me.

"Are you okay, Elle?"

"Do I look okay, Connor? Some stranger is stalking me, sending me text messages and my favorite flowers, and my husband just got done screaming at me. So to answer your question, no, I'm not okay. I accept your apology, but I really just want you to leave me alone for a while so I can take in everything that just happened."

Suddenly, we heard Julia cry from her crib. "I'll tend to Julia and leave you alone," Connor said with an attitude.

I sighed as I closed my eyes and tried to figure out what the hell was going on. I needed to talk to Peyton, but my phone was downstairs. The last time I saw Connor that angry was back in the hotel room in Michigan. The way he yelled and the look he had in his eye brought back all the memories I never wanted to remember again. Once I finished wiping the mascara from underneath my eyes, I put my hair up in a ponytail and changed into my yoga pants and a sweatshirt. I walked past the living room. Connor was giving Julia her bottle. As I walked into the kitchen, I grabbed my phone from the counter and noticed the roses were gone.

"Did you throw the roses away?" I asked Connor as I walked over to the bar.

"You bet I did," he replied.

The bottle of Jack was already sitting out and so was a shot glass. As I poured myself a shot, I looked over at my husband. "Did you get this out?"

"Yes. I figured you'd be coming down for some," he replied as he looked down at Julia.

"Thank you," I said as I threw the shot back and set the glass down. "I'm scared," I blurted out as I poured another shot.

Chapter 31

Connor

I looked over at Ellery and saw the fear in her eyes. I wanted to go to her, but I was feeding Julia. I never should've yelled at her the way I did. But when I read those messages and saw the flowers and the card, a fear crept up inside of me that someone was after my wife. Ellery continued to slam a couple of shots as I burped Julia. She had just finished her bottle, so I set her on the floor amongst her toys. Ellery stood behind the bar, and I walked over to her.

"Come here," I said as I embraced her. "I know this whole thing is scary, but I promise you that I'll never let anything happen to you or Julia. We're going to find out who's behind this and they're going to pay. I'll see to that."

"Who would do something like this?" she asked.

"I don't know, baby; some sick, twisted individual," I said as I tightened my grip around her.

The doorman rang up and said that Detective James and Paul were downstairs. I told him to send them up right away.

"Mr. Black, it's nice to see you again," Detective James said as he shook my hand.

"I wish it was under better circumstances," I sighed.

Paul walked over to Ellery and gave her a hug. "Are you okay, Elle?" he asked.

I escorted the detective to the living room and offered him a drink. Paul got up, walked over to the bar, and poured himself a glass of bourbon.

"Detective James, you remember my wife, Ellery."

"Yes, I do. It's nice to see you again."

Ellery gave a small smile as she nodded her head. I sat down beside her and held her hand.

"Your husband has filled me in on what's going on. Can I see the messages you received today?"

Ellery reached over, took her phone from the table, and handed it to him. As Detective James scrolled through the messages, I got up, walked into the kitchen, and grabbed the card that came with the flowers.

"He sent her three dozen roses with this card attached," I said as I handed it to him.

"Have you met anyone new recently?" he asked.

"I meet people every day, detective."

"What about the showing at the art gallery?" Paul said as he looked at Ellery.

"I met and talked to a lot of people there."

"Did you notice anyone as being odd or felt like something was off with someone?" Detective James asked.

"No. Not that I can remember," Ellery replied.

"I'm going to take a screenshot of these messages. You didn't change your number already, did you?"

"No, I was going to do that first thing tomorrow morning," I said.

"Well, don't. We need to see how far this person will go. It could just be a couple of messages and then he's done with it. Unfortunately, we can't do anything unless he threatens her in some way."

Julia started getting fussy, so Ellery picked her up. She said she was taking her upstairs to change her diaper. As soon as she was out of earshot, I looked at Detective James and said sternly, "I will use every resource I have to find out who's doing this. I will not stand by and wait until he harms Ellery or Julia. I don't give a shit about the law and I'll warn you now, if I catch him first, I'll kill him."

"Connor, I'll pretend I didn't hear that," Detective James said. "My men and I will be on this. After all, you're paying us very well," he said as he got up from the chair. "I'll start first thing in the morning, and I'll try to find out where those flowers came from."

"Thank you, Detective James," I said as I shook his hand.

"No problem, Connor. We'll find this son of a bitch. Try not to worry."

As I shut the door, Ellery walked into the room with Julia. "Did Detective James leave?" she asked.

"Yes, baby, he did," I replied as I walked over to her and gave her a kiss and took Julia.

"What do you want me to do, Connor?" Paul asked.

"Find me a bodyguard for Ellery and Julia. I'll need two of them. One to go out with Ellery and one for Mason. I want you to get our tech guys on these messages and find out what number they're coming from, and I want to know where the flowers came from. I'm not going into the office tomorrow, so report back here."

"I'll get on it right away," Paul said. He walked over to Ellery and gave her a hug. "Don't worry about this; we'll keep you safe."

"Thanks, Paul. I appreciate it." She smiled.

Paul walked out the door, and Ellery wrapped her arms around my waist. "Do you really think it's necessary to hire a bodyguard?" she asked.

"Yes, I do. I'm not taking any chances, and I can't be with you twenty-four-seven."

"I wish you could be," she said as she kissed my lips.

"I do too, baby. I do too."

* * * *

Ellery tossed and turned all night. I tried to keep her still by holding her, but she was so restless that she would wiggle her way out of my grip. When I got out of the shower, Ellery was sitting up in bed with her phone in her hand.

"What's wrong? Did you get another text?" I asked.

She held out her phone to me, and I walked over and took it from her. Sure enough, there was another message.

"I couldn't stop thinking about you all night. I hope you were thinking about me."

I threw the phone on the bed and ran my hands through my hair. Reading those words that were being said to my wife fueled my anger even more. I took in a deep breath as I walked over to the dresser and pulled out a pair of jeans.

"I'm not letting that bastard run my life, Connor."

I turned around and looked at her. "What do you mean by that?"

"I can't live in fear and I won't. I'm stronger than that, and I won't let some obsessive sick fuck control my life."

I walked over to the bed, sat down, and put my arm her. "Ellery, I'm sorry this is happening, but you'll be protected at all times. You're not allowed to leave this penthouse or building without security."

"So you were really serious about having someone follow me around?"

"Not following you around, sweetheart; protecting you," I said as I kissed the side of her head. "Now go and get dressed. We have to go visit Denny."

When we heard Mason downstairs, Ellery threw on some clothes, and we walked into the kitchen, where he was dancing with Julia.

"Good morning, Momma. Good morning, Daddy." He smiled.

"Good morning, Mason. We need to talk to you," I said as I grabbed a cup of coffee and sat down at the table.

"That doesn't sound good. Did I do something wrong?"

Ellery took Julia from him and asked him to sit down. "It's nothing you did. Do you remember those text messages I received from the restricted number?"

"Yeah, I remember," he said with a confused look.

"They weren't from me," I chimed in.

Mason shifted in his seat as he stared at me. "Who were they from?"

"We don't know," Ellery said as she kissed Julia on the head.

"Oh my God, the roses. They weren't from you either?"

As I sipped my coffee, I shook my head. "No, they weren't. It seems that someone has taken a great interest in my wife."

Mason looked at Ellery, got up from his seat, and gave her a hug. "I'm so sorry, Elle. What can I do?"

"I have a detective working on it, but I'm hiring a bodyguard for you and Julia. Ellery will have her own, just until we find out who's behind this."

My phone rang and, as I pulled it from my pocket, I saw Paul was calling. "Hello, Paul."

"Good morning, Connor. I have two guys lined up as security if you want to interview them. We can be at your place in about fifteen minutes."

"Sounds good; we'll be here," I said as I hung up. "Paul is on his way over with two men he wants me to interview. When we're done, we'll head over to the hospital."

Ellery nodded her head while she poured herself a cup of coffee. Mason took Julia upstairs to change her diaper, and I walked to my office. I was going over some paperwork when Ellery walked in with Paul and two large men. I stood up from my chair and walked over to them. Their grip was strong as I shook both of their hands.

"Mr. Black, it's an honor to meet you, sir," they both said.

"Thank you for coming. Please have a seat. I'm sure Paul has filled you in on what's happened."

"Yes, sir, he has. We want you to know that we have specialized backgrounds in dealing with someone like this and we'd be more than happy to protect your wife and child. Justin and I are both ex-navy seals whom served with the U.S. Special Operations Forces for over twenty years."

As I sat there and listened to their background, I felt they'd be the right choice for Ellery and Julia. "Ellery, what you do you think?" I asked.

"I think they'd be a good choice," she replied as she looked at both of them and smiled.

"Okay, you're hired," I said as I stood up and shook their hands. "You'll both start tomorrow."

"Thank you, Mr. Black. Don't worry, Mrs. Black; we aren't going to let anything happen. You'll be very safe with us."

Ellery gave a small smile and walked out of the office. I could tell uneasiness washed over her. I asked Paul to shut the door while I talked to Justin and Adam.

"There's something you must be aware of. My wife is a very stubborn woman who does whatever she wants. She doesn't like to listen to anybody when it comes to her safety. She's independent and strong-willed, so good luck. Don't let her fool you."

While both of the men laughed, I walked them out of the office and to the elevator. "We'll see you tomorrow." I smiled.

* * * *

We visited Denny and nothing had changed. He was still in a coma and the doctors couldn't give us any answers. Dana asked us if we would join her in the cafeteria for some coffee. I told Ellery to go ahead, but to stay with Dana at all times. I sat in the chair and stared at Denny and put my hand on top of his.

"I wish you'd wake up. There's so much going on that I need to talk to you about. Ellery is being stalked. He keeps sending her text messages, and yesterday, he had three dozen roses delivered to the penthouse. If there was ever a time I needed your smart mouth and advice, it's now. I'm so scared, Denny. If anything ever happened to her, I don't know what I'd do."

"You better find that bastard," he whispered.

I jumped up from the chair as Denny slowly opened his eyes and looked at me. A smile filled my face as I squeezed his hand. I pushed the button for the nurse, and Ellery and Dana walked in.

"Look who's awake." I smiled.

Dana burst into tears as she ran over to the bed. Ellery

walked over and touched his other hand lightly.

"Welcome back." She smiled.

The nurse and doctor walked into the room and examined Denny. He seemed to be okay, except he was complaining of a horrific headache. The doctor told him it was normal and they'd give him something for the pain. He and Dana stared at each other while she cried and told him how much she loved him. I wanted to give them some alone time, so I told Denny and Dana that we'd be back later. As soon as Ellery and I stepped into the hallway, I grabbed her and pulled her into a warm embrace.

"Thank God he woke up," I whispered.

Chapter 32

Ellery

As we drove home, I heard my phone beeping. The restricted number appeared on the screen. Connor looked over at me and could tell by the look on my face that something was wrong.

"What does it say?" he asked.

As I read the message, I instantly felt sick to my stomach.

"I masturbate to your picture, and you make me come so fast. I hope that turns you on. I dream about seeing your naked body and pressing it up against mine. I dream about being inside of you."

When I didn't say anything, Connor grabbed the phone from my hand just as we pulled into the garage of the penthouse. The anger that washed over his face was horrifying. I watched him take in a sharp breath and clench his fist.

"Connor, calm down, right now," I demanded.

"How do you expect me to calm down when some guy says he masturbates to my wife's picture and dreams about being inside you," he yelled as he slammed his fists on the steering wheel. "I can't just sit back and watch this. I need to do something."

I couldn't stand seeing him so angry. When we got out of

the Ranger Rover, I stopped him before we reached the elevator, and I wrapped my arms around him.

"Please, Connor. Detective James is going to find this son of a bitch. Please stop being so angry. I know you're scared and so am I, but I don't need you going all crazy on me."

He held me tightly; so tightly, I could barely breathe. "I'm sorry, Ellery."

We broke our embrace and went up to the penthouse.

"I hope you two didn't eat lunch. I made the most scrumptious salad for you," Mason said as he emerged from the kitchen.

I smiled as we sat down at the table and he served us.

"Is Julia taking a nap?" Connor asked.

"Yes. The princess is down for her nap," he replied as he sat down next to me.

My phone beeped, alerting me I had a text message. Connor's eyes glared at me as I read it. "Relax, it's from Peyton. She wants to drop by."

Connor let out a sigh of relief as I secretly did as well. I wanted nothing more than to get my number changed. Suddenly, Connor's phone started ringing from his pocket. He pulled it out and said it was Detective James. After a brief conversation, he hung up and looked at me.

"They were able to trace the text messages to a cell phone out of Chicago."

"He must've been there that night at the gallery," I said.

As we talked, Peyton came walking into the kitchen. We all stopped and looked at her.

"Hi. What's going on?" she asked.

Connor and Mason both said hello to her, and I told her to

have a seat. Mason got up, took a plate from the cupboard, and served Peyton some salad.

"Those text messages weren't from Connor. Someone is stalking me," I said.

"Stop it. That's not even funny."

"She's not joking, Peyton. This is serious," Connor said.

Peyton looked at me and then reached over and hugged me. "I can't believe this. Do you know who it is?"

"Not yet. But we just found out that the texts were coming from a cell phone in Chicago."

"Could it be someone from the gallery opening? Wait!" Peyton exclaimed as she took out her phone. "I remember this really weird guy there. I was on my way back from the bathroom and I saw this guy, standing in the corner," she said as she showed Connor and me her phone. "He was taking pictures with his phone. It caught my attention because he had one hand on his crotch, like he was playing with himself. I thought it was funny, so I took his picture. I was going to show you, but Henry distracted me and I forgot."

"Who or what was he taking pictures of?" Connor asked.

"I'm not sure, but I do remember looking over to where he was pointing his phone and Ellery was over there."

Connor got up from his seat, walked over to Peyton, and wrapped his arms tightly around her as he kissed her on the cheek. "Do you know how much I love you?"

"Umm...sure," she said as she looked at me.

"Send that picture to my phone, please."

"I will, as soon as you stop smothering me," Peyton said.

"Sorry, Peyton." Connor smiled as he looked at me. "I'm going to call Detective James and then I'm flying to Chicago.

I want to see those tapes from that night. I'm calling my pilot now to get the plane ready."

"I'm coming with you!" I exclaimed.

"That's fine. Mason, can you stay here tonight and watch Julia?"

"Of course I can. You two go and don't worry about a thing." He smiled.

* * * *

Connor and I packed a light bag and stopped by the hospital to see Denny before heading to the airport. We told him what was going on and where we were going. He smiled at us and told us to be careful. Seeing him awake and looking well took one weight off of our shoulders.

We boarded the plane, and I took my seat while Connor poured me a glass of wine and himself a scotch. When we finally took off, we unbuckled our seat belts and sat on the couch. I drank some wine, handed the glass to Connor, and laid my head down on his lap. As I stared up at him, he started playing with my hair.

"You tossed and turned all night," he said.

"I know, and I'm sorry if I kept you up."

He leaned down and brought his mouth to mine, kissing me tenderly on the lips. "I won't give up until this asshole is found. No one is allowed to dream of you but me."

I brought my hand up to his face and softly stroked his cheek. "I love you."

"I love you more, Mrs. Black." Connor smiled down at me. He looked at his watch and then back at me. "We have an hour until we land in Chicago. I'm thinking about taking you into the bedroom and making love to you."

"Is that so?"

"Mhmm," Connor said as he ran his finger over my lips.

"Then what are you waiting for? Take me. I'm all yours."

"You're mine. Mine forever, and nobody will ever take you from me."

"Never," I whispered as I kissed him on the lips.

* * * *

As I walked around the art gallery, Connor talked to Vinnie. He told Connor that the guy in the picture was the lighting man, and he was taking pictures of the way the lighting was set up so he could show a prospective client.

"I can call him in if you want to speak to him," Vinnie said.

"That doesn't explain why the man was holding his crotch like that. Who does that in a public place?" Connor asked.

"He has testicular cancer, and I know he's frequently in pain. So that's probably why he was doing that. Why are you asking about him anyway?"

"Someone's been sending text messages and flowers to my wife. The texts are sex related and when I saw this picture, I automatically assumed it was him."

"Couldn't be him," Vinnie said. "Did I mention that he's gay?"

Connor looked at me with a disappointed expression. I thought for sure it was the lighting man, and this would finally be over. A beep came from my purse, which alerted me that I had a text message. As I fumbled for it, I took out my phone and there was a text from him.

"I stare at your picture and imagine what it would be like to fuck you and hear you moan. I think about you all day, and I can't stop. Your smile drives me insane and your mouth around my cock is what I crave and desire."

My panicked face gave it away that the message was from him. Connor grabbed my phone and I stood there as rage took over his face and settled into his eyes. He put his arm around me and pulled me into him. "When I find out who's doing this, I'm going to kill him."

We thanked Vinnie and left the gallery. When we stepped outside, Connor called Detective James and told him about the latest text message and how the man from the art gallery wasn't the guy. The text messages were starting to get more graphic, and now I was getting more frightened than before. As soon as Connor hung up the phone with Detective James, he pulled me into him.

"Let's go get some dinner and then we'll head back to New York."

I nodded my head and we walked down the street to a Mexican restaurant. I really wasn't hungry, so I only ordered the tacos. As we were eating, I kept noticing two girls sitting at the table next to us, eyeing Connor. I had sort of gotten used to the fact that my husband was the sexiest man alive and that women appreciated his looks, but I drew the line when they wouldn't stop staring at him, even though I was sitting directly across from him.

"Those two women keep staring at you," I whispered.

"I know. I've noticed." He smiled.

"It's irritating, and I'm going to say something if they don't stop."

"No, you won't. There will be no embarrassing me tonight. Now eat your tacos!"

I glared at him from across the table as I took a bite of my taco. He glared at me as he drank his beer. The waiter came over and asked if we wanted dessert. I took the liberty of ordering two desserts.

"It's okay, Ellery, I don't want dessert; I'm full," Connor said.

"You can never be too full for dessert." I smiled.

After a few moments, the waiter set our desserts down on the table. Connor looked at me and sighed. "I'm sorry, baby, but I really don't want this," he said.

"Good," I said as I grabbed his and my desserts and took them over to the women at the next table.

"I would like you to have these desserts on me and my husband. I couldn't help but notice your incessant staring at him as we were trying to enjoy our dinner. Kudos for making asses of yourselves!"

The women looked away as I winked at them, grabbed my purse, and told Connor we were leaving. I heard him apologize as he walked past their table. I stepped outside the doors of the restaurant and Connor caught up with me. I put my hand up as I walked down the street.

"Don't, say a word, Black. They deserved it. I don't appreciate gawkers, especially when it's directed at my husband."

"Where are you walking to?" he asked.

I stopped and looked at him. "I don't know," I said as I threw my hands up in the air and laughed.

Connor wrapped his arms around me and hugged me tightly. "What am I going to do with you?"

"The same thing you've always done. Love me forever, no matter how much I embarrass you." I smiled.

"My dear, sweet wife. I will love you, no matter how much you embarrass me, until the day I die."

Chapter 33

The next few days were pretty much the same. The text messages were becoming more frequent and more graphic. Denny was doing better and was expected to be released in a few days. Connor was working hard at the office, not only on trying to keep up with Black Enterprises, but he was also under a lot of stress trying to find out who was sending me the messages. My security guy, Justin, followed me everywhere I went, and Detective James wasn't any closer to finding out who was stalking me.

Connor and I took Julia to the toy store one night. As we were walking around and Connor was showing Julia all the toys that made noise, my phone beeped with a message. I looked at my phone and read the text message that sat on my screen.

"My hunger for you is getting worse. My love for you is growing stronger, and I'm going crazy not being able to touch you."

Connor was occupied with Julia and a singing toy, so he didn't hear my phone beep. We were having a good night. I didn't want to show him the message and worry him even more than he already was. Julia laughed at the singing bear that Connor held up in front of her. When he went to put it back on the shelf, she screamed.

"Look what you did; now you have to buy it for her," I

said.

"She can't get a new toy every time she screams. She has to learn what 'no' means," he said as he pushed the shopping cart away from the singing bear.

Julia wasn't having it, and I knew he would eventually give in and buy it for her. As we walked down another aisle, Julia threw a temper tantrum. I walked behind Connor, whispering in his ear, "I want that bear, Daddy. Please buy me that bear."

"Ellery, knock it off. That's not fair. She needs to learn she can't have everything she wants."

"Why not? You get everything you want."

"That's different. I'm an adult."

"Are you sure about that?" I smiled as I slapped him on the ass and walked ahead of them.

I could hear Julia from the next aisle over. As I was looking at the dolls, it suddenly became quiet. The sounds of a screaming baby were gone. I rolled my eyes and made my way back to where Connor and Julia were. I saw the singing bear next to her.

"Way to go, Daddy. I knew you'd give in."

"She wouldn't stop screaming. Next time, no means no," he said.

"Yeah, right!" I smiled.

Dinner with Julia was out of the question. She looked really tired, and she was starting to get fussy. Both of us knew that if we took her to a restaurant, we wouldn't be there long, so we headed home and decided to order a pizza. While I fed Julia in her highchair, Connor placed an order for delivery, and I decided to tell him about the text message I received earlier. After I made him promise not to get angry and go off on a tangent, I read him the message. He slammed his fists on the counter so hard, he made me and Julia jump. Julia started screaming and I looked at him, shaking my head.

"I'm so sorry, baby. Daddy didn't mean to scare you," he said as he walked over to her and kissed her head.

"Connor, I warned you. I begged you not to get angry like that," I said as I slammed the spoon down on the table and got up.

"What the hell, Ellery? How do you not expect me to get angry when someone talks to you like that? Damn it. What if this was happening to me by some strange woman? How the fuck would you feel? Huh? Answer me that," he yelled. "We have this same argument all the time. You tell me not to get mad, I do, and then you get pissed off, and it results in me yelling at you."

Anger overtook me as I walked over to him. "Let me make one thing very clear to you. There will never be yelling or fighting in front of Julia. Do you understand me?" I said through gritted teeth as I pushed my finger into his chest.

While he stood there and looked at me, I could see him start to slowly calm down. "You're right, and I apologize to you and Julia," he said as he kissed my forehead and then Julia's. "I'll take her upstairs and get her cleaned up and ready for bed. The pizza should be here shortly," he said.

The doorbell rang and when I answered it, I was shocked to see Phil standing there, holding our pizza.

"Hi, Phil," I said as I gave him a strange look. "What are you doing here and why are you holding our pizzas?"

"Hi, Ellery. I was just down in the lobby and heard the delivery guy say he had pizzas for the Blacks, so I saved him a trip up since I was coming up to see Connor anyway."

"Thanks, Phil." I smiled as I took the pizzas from him.

"Connor will be down in a minute. He's changing Julia. How much do I owe you?" I asked as I reached for my wallet.

"Oh, please, don't worry about it. It's on me."

Connor walked down the stairs and was surprised to see Phil standing in the kitchen.

"Phil, what brings you here, buddy?"

"I have some papers you need to sign," he said.

"It couldn't wait until morning?" Connor asked.

"No, I need to get these faxed over to Japan tonight, and when I went to your office earlier to have you sign them, you'd already left."

"Why don't you sit and have some pizza with us," Connor said.

"Nah, I don't want to interfere with your dinner."

"You're not interfering, Phil. Now sit down and let me get you a drink." Connor insisted.

I took the paper plates and napkins to the living room. Phil followed behind me with the pizza boxes. Connor poured himself a scotch and made Phil a martini. I sat down on the floor, at the coffee table. Connor asked me what I wanted to drink. When I told him a coke, Phil jumped up and said he'd get it. We sat around the coffee table and talked while we ate.

"I'm surprised to see you sitting on the floor, eating pizza, Connor," Phil said.

"Ellery likes things very informal," Connor responded.

"Yep, I don't like all that uppity shit." I laughed.

"Well, Connor has changed quite a bit since he married you," Phil said.

I looked over at Connor and smiled. "He sure has."

"He's a very lucky man to be married to such a beautiful

woman." Phil smiled.

When he said that, I blushed. "Phil, stop it."

"No, I'm serious, Ellery. You are incredibly beautiful, and any man would be lucky to have you."

"Well, thank you. But I'm the lucky one." I smiled.

Connor got up and walked over to the bar to make Phil another drink, while Phil helped me bring the plates and pizza back into the kitchen.

"Thank you for inviting me to stay. It meant a lot to me, Ellery," Phil said as he hugged me tightly.

As I stood there, astounded, I gently patted his back and told him that he was welcome. Connor walked in and handed Phil his drink.

"What's going on in here?" He smiled.

"I was thanking your beautiful wife for having me."

"It was our pleasure, Phil. You know you're always welcome here."

He drank part of his drink, set it on the table, and then announced he had to leave. Connor showed him to the door and gave him the money for the pizza.

"I'll see you tomorrow," Connor said as he shut the door.

He turned around and looked at me as I walked over to him and collapsed in his arms.

"I'm tired. I think I'll go take a hot bath," I said.

"Okay, baby. I'll be up in a while. I have some papers I need to go over and then I'm going to call Detective James."

When I reached the top of the stairs, I stopped in the nursery to check on Julia. She was sound asleep. I started the bath water, poured a capful of bubble bath, and stepped into the tub. As I lay back, I slowly closed my eyes and took in a deep relaxing breath. All I wanted to do was escape into a world where it was only the three of us. As I was dreaming about my alternate world, Connor walked into the bathroom and sat on the edge of the tub.

"Are you enjoying your bath?" he asked.

"Yes, I am. I was dreaming about our alternate world."

Connor looked at me strangely. "What are you talking about?"

"I invented a world where it's only me, you, and Julia. Just the three of us, living happily ever after." I smiled.

"I love your imagination," he said as he lightly ran his finger up and down my arm. "Are you imagining the things I'm doing to you in your alternate world? Are you imagining me making passionate love to you all night long because I can't get enough of you? Are you imagining me whispering 'I love you' in your ear as I'm slowly moving in and out you?"

Whenever Connor talked like that, in that tone, he always put me in a trance. It was like I was frozen by his words and I was unable to move. As he spoke, he fondled my breast. While he stared into my eyes, he ran his thumb over my puckered nipple and leaned over to kiss my lips.

"You need to get out of the bath now," he whispered.

"What if I'm not done yet?" I whispered back.

"You're done, Mrs. Black, because I'm going to take you to your alternate world and do things to you there I've never done before. I'm going to make it so you don't want to come back."

I gasped as he took my hand and stood me up. He grabbed the towel I had sitting next to the tub, wrapped it around me, and helped me out. He dried every part of me in a seductive manner and removed the clip that was holding my hair up, letting it fall over my shoulders. He took in a sharp breath as he placed his hand on the side of my face.

"I'm so in love with you, and I need you. I need you every day. You're my strength and my light and, without you, I'm nothing."

As I smiled at him, he picked me up and carried me to our bed. He gently laid me down as his fingers deftly removed my towel, and he took me to my alternate world. He was right; I didn't want to come back.

Chapter 34

Connor

"You were right, Connor," Paul said as he walked into my office and threw the file on my desk.

I sat there and shook my head as I read the contents inside. "Fuck!" I yelled as I slammed it down.

"I can't believe it either. What are you going to do?"

"I don't know yet," I said as I paced back and forth.

Since I had taken my father's place as CEO of Black Enterprises, I had never needed to ask for his advice, until now. I pulled my phone out of my pocket and dialed him.

"Dad, I need you to come down to the office. I need to talk to you about a situation that's going on."

"All right, Connor, I'll be there as soon as I can."

As I hung up the phone, I walked out to where Valerie sat. "My father will be here shortly. Cancel my meeting for this afternoon and do me a favor and order us some sandwiches from the deli down the street. Nobody, and I mean nobody is to disturb us, not even Phil, do you understand me?"

"What about Mrs. Black?"

"Well, of course her, but she usually just calls my cell phone."

"Very good, Connor. I'll get on those sandwiches now."

She smiled.

I walked back into my office and sat down at my desk. "I want you in on this meeting with my father, Paul."

"I figured as much. Do you want me to call anyone else?"

"No, this is to stay between the three of us."

About an hour later, my father came strolling into my office and Valerie entered with the sandwiches. We took a seat at the table and my father looked at me.

"What's going on, Connor?"

"Take a look at this," I said as I slid the file across the table. "Remember the conversation we had a couple of weeks ago?"

My father opened the file, looked at it, and then looked at me with an expression of shock. "Are you fucking kidding me?"

"I wish I was," I replied.

"I'm at a loss for words, son. I don't know what to think about this."

As I got up from my seat, I walked over to the bar and poured a scotch.

"Connor, I can see the rage in your eyes and the first thing you need to do is to calm down. You won't do anybody any good if you start acting crazy and out of control. Think of the situation and repercussions if you go off the deep end."

He was right. I needed to calm myself and think this through very carefully. I sat back down and the three of us discussed the matter further, trying to formulate a plan of action. Once I was satisfied with what we came up with, my father and Paul left the office, and I made a couple of phone calls. One of the phone calls I made was to Denny to see if he was up for a visit; I hadn't seen him since the first day he was released from the hospital.

* * * *

"You're looking better every day," I said to him as I handed him a bottle of his favorite bourbon.

"Thanks, Connor." He smiled. "How are Ellery and Julia?"

"They're good. I need to talk to you about a situation and something that's going on over at Black Enterprises." I sighed as I sat down in the chair across from him.

Denny had always been like a father to me. He'd done things for me in my younger days that my father would've killed me for if he knew. He'd always had my back and was there when I needed him; a strong-willed man and a person who would give you the shirt off his back if you asked him for it. Nobody in this world, except Ellery, knew how important Denny was to me and that was because he'd become a father figure to her as well. We talked for over an hour, and as I explained the situation to him, he was shocked, just like Paul, my father, and I were.

"You know what you have to do, Connor. You better be careful and, if I was strong enough, I would help you."

"You aren't doing a thing. I can take care of this. I need you to get better because driving in that New York City traffic is killing me."

"Why don't you hire another driver until I can come back?" he asked.

"I don't want another driver, Denny." I smiled. "I need to get home to my wife and daughter. Enjoy the bourbon, and I'll see you soon," I said as I walked out the door.

The drive home was terrible. As I stepped off the elevator and into the penthouse, I heard Ellery's sweet voice singing to Julia. When I walked into the living room, I stood in the archway and watched as Ellery danced around the room with Julia. As I leaned up against the wall, Ellery saw me and smiled.

"Look, Julia, your daddy's home," she said as she turned so Julia could see me.

Julia screeched so loud that it was enough to pierce anyone's eardrums. Ellery danced over to me and I took Julia from her.

"You are awfully loud, little girl." I smiled as I held her up in the air. She continued to screech as drool came from her mouth and onto my face.

Ellery laughed as she handed me a cloth diaper. "You know she drools a lot when she's teething."

I didn't want to ruin the moment, but I had to ask her. "Did you get any more texts today?"

Ellery nodded her head as she walked over to the table and grabbed her phone. I took the phone from her hand and handed Julia back to her. I stood, outraged, as I read the messages.

"Dearest Ellery, I want you on your knees, in front of me, sucking me off until I explode inside your mouth."

"You have no idea what a sexual creature you are to me, Ellery. You don't know what it's like to crave something you can't have."

"I want to tie you up and whip you until you bleed. Then I'll make your wounds better with my tongue as you come from the pleasure you're going to feel."

My skin grew hot and my pulse started racing, but I stayed calm, for Ellery's sake. She looked at me with tears in her eyes as I handed her the phone back. I took Julia from her arms and set her amongst her toys on the floor. When I turned around, I wrapped my arms around her and held her tightly.

"You're a rock. You have more strength over this than I do, and I'm so proud of you, baby."

"You and Julia keep me strong," she whispered.

As I broke our embrace, I told Ellery that I needed to talk to her as we sat down on the couch.

"I need to take a business trip, and I need to leave tomorrow. It's something urgent that came up with the Chicago office and I need to be there to straighten it out."

"I'll go with you."

"As much as I want you to, you'll be safer here. I'll be tied up in meetings and I won't be able to keep an eye on you. I won't be gone long, only a couple of days."

"But I'll miss you," she said.

"I'll miss you too, baby. It's only one night." I hated leaving her, but I had no choice.

Chapter 35

Ellery

As I packed Julia's diaper bag, Connor walked into the nursery, holding her.

"I can't believe you and my baby aren't going to be here tonight." I pouted.

"Just think of the fun you and Peyton will have. You can watch scary movies, make popcorn, and do whatever it is you women do," Connor said.

"I guess," I sighed as I handed him the diaper bag.

Mason was downstairs and eagerly waiting for Connor to hand over Julia. "Come here, princess. We're going to have so much fun! Ellery, don't worry about her. You and Peyton have a fabulous time tonight," he said as he took the diaper bag, kissed me on the cheek, and stepped into the elevator with Julia.

I kissed her goodbye and, as soon as they left, I said my goodbyes to Connor. "Have a safe trip, darling."

"I will. You behave yourself while I'm gone and don't forget that Justin will be outside the door."

"I'll try." I winked.

When the elevator came back up, Connor stepped into it and pushed the button. Just before the doors were about to close, he stopped them.

"I forgot to tell you that Phil is stopping by tonight to drop off some papers."

"Okay. I'll set them in your office."

As Connor let go of the doors and they started to close, he stuck his hand in between them to stop them from closing, stepped out, and hugged me.

"I don't want to go, Ellery."

"Honey, it's only for one night. You said yourself not to worry. What's going on?"

"Nothing. I just hate being away from you," he said as he kissed my head.

"I hate being away from you too, but you have to go. Now come on. Put your big boy pants on and go; you're making things harder," I said as I broke our embrace and patted him on the chest.

"No, Elle, you're the one making things harder." He winked as he looked down at the bulge in his pants.

"Get out of here, Black." I laughed as he stepped onto the elevator.

A couple of hours had passed, and I took a nap. It had been forever since I took a nap without having to worry if Julia was going to wake up. I took the stairs down to the kitchen and opened the refrigerator for a bottle of water. After checking my phone to see if I had any messages, I walked into the living room, turned on the fireplace, and sat down on the couch with a magazine. Being alone and not knowing what to do wasn't sitting right with me, so I grabbed my keys and headed to my studio. When I stepped out the door, I told Justin that I was going down to my art studio. He nodded his head and followed me.

I set a blank canvas on the easel, took out my paints and

brush, and started painting how I saw my alternate world. Each brush stroke helped me escape the dark reality of what was happening in my life. I looked at the clock and I'd been painting for two hours. It suddenly hit me that Phil was coming over to drop off some papers. I put my brush down and stepped outside the apartment. Justin wasn't at the door, and I didn't have time to look for him. I took the elevator up to the penthouse and as I unlocked the door, Phil walked up and startled me.

"I'm sorry, Ellery. Did I startle you?" he asked.

"Just a bit." I laughed. "Come on in. I'm just going to go to the kitchen and wash up. I was painting."

"Oh, that's fine. Please take your time."

I walked into the kitchen and, as I was washing my hands, Phil walked in. "So, do you have the place to yourself tonight?" he asked.

"Yeah. Connor's on that business trip and Julia is spending the night at Mason's. My friend Peyton is coming over and we're having a girl's night," I said as I dried off my hands.

"Sounds like you'll have a great night. When is Peyton coming over?"

A strange look overtook my face, as I couldn't imagine why he'd ask or even care. "She'll be here soon. Do you have those papers for Connor?" I asked.

"Oh, I left—umm—they're in the living room," he said nervously.

"Okay. Well, thank you for dropping them off, Phil. Peyton's going to be here shortly, so I better get ready," I said uneasily.

Something didn't sit right with me. Phil was acting weird. I'd always thought he was strange, but Connor always defended him and said he'd had a bad childhood.

"No problem, Ellery. It's always a pleasure to see you," he said. "Am I making you uncomfortable?"

I stopped, turned around, and looked at him as he slowly walked towards me. "No, of course not. Why would you make me uncomfortable? We've known each other for a long time."

"Yes, we have, and it hasn't been until recently that I've grown quite fond of you," he said as he took a strand of my hair between his fingers.

Something wasn't right, and now wasn't the time to freak out. I needed to remain calm and think clearly. My heart started racing, and I started to sweat. "Peyton is on her way. You really need to go."

"I don't want to go, Ellery. I was hoping that with Connor out of town, we could get to know each other better."

"I think I know you well enough, and it's time you left," I said nervously as I began to walk past him.

He grabbed my arm. His grip was tight as his fingers dug into my arm. "Did you enjoy my text messages and the roses? I wanted to send you more, but I couldn't run the risk of Connor finding out it was me who wanted his wife."

"You—you were the one who sent me all those text messages?" I asked in disbelief and shock.

"Yes, Ellery."

"But, why?"

A sick feeling arose in my stomach, and I needed to sit down because I felt like I was going to pass out. "I need to sit down," I said.

"Of course. I'm sure this is overwhelming for you. You asked me why. The answer is simple; you're beautiful, sensitive, loving, and giving. Do you know how hard it is to find someone like you in this fucked up world we live in? Do you know how I've searched for that special woman my whole life? To think of all the whores I've fucked, trying to find out if there was anything special about them. Then, all of a sudden, there you were. The more I watched your interaction with Connor, the deeper I fell for you."

I began to shake as he walked over and sat down next to me. "Look at you, you're trembling," he said as he tried to pull me into him.

"Don't touch me!" I screamed as I flew off the couch.

"I need to touch you. I want to touch you. I want to know what it feels like to be inside you. I want to feel your come all over my cock and I want to hear you scream when I fuck you."

"You're crazy!" I said as I tried to run to the door.

He followed me and grabbed me from behind, covering my mouth with his hand. "Now be a good girl and do as I say. Connor will never have to know about this, because if you say a word to him or the police, you'll never see that precious baby girl of yours again."

My eyes widened when he said that, and I struggled to get out from his grip. "That's right, Ellery. I know she means the world to you, and your love for her is stronger than any other love on this Earth. Do you promise not to scream?"

I nodded my head as I tried to formulate a plan. He slowly removed his hand from my mouth and ran it down my cheek. Suddenly, I went ballistic.

"You mother fucker! There's one thing you don't do and that's threaten a mother with her child!" I screamed as I rammed my knee into his crotch. He doubled over in pain, and I ran to the door. As I tried to open it, he slammed it shut.

"Please, Ellery, don't make this difficult."

"You're crazy." I started to cry as I slowly backed away from him.

"Not crazy; just in love. You know that it's a proven fact that love can make a person crazy. Look at what it did to Ashlyn. Now, she's one crazy bitch. But I didn't blame her after everything Connor did to her. The way he led her on, took her out, and then fucked her brains out every chance he got. No wonder the girl was messed up."

I could barely swallow. It felt like my throat was closing up. I needed to get to my phone that was in the kitchen. As I turned around and tried to run, Phil grabbed me from behind and threw me on the floor.

"Please stop struggling and enjoy what I'm about to do to you. I promise you'll love it and then all this struggle would've been for nothing."

I lay there, kicking and trying to hit him before he held my wrists above my head with his hand, and he fumbled with the button on my jeans. The tears were falling from my eyes as I looked around the room. While I was struggling, thoughts of Connor and Julia flooded my mind. Suddenly, the door flew open and Connor pulled Phil off of me and punched him as hard as he could. Phil went down and Connor got on top of him. He grabbed Phil's shirt and continuously punched him in the face, again and again as he screamed.

"You son of a bitch! How dare you touch my wife?" he said with each punch.

Detective James ran in and pulled Connor off of him. Justin followed behind and handcuffed Phil.

"You're nothing but a piece of shit, and I'm going to make sure you rot in jail for the rest of your life for what you've done!" Connor yelled.

He turned and looked at me and was instantly by my side, wrapping his arms around me and holding me tightly. "Are you okay, baby? I'm so sorry we weren't here earlier. Did he hurt you?" he asked as he looked me over.

I stood there, shaking, unable to wrap my head around what had happened as I stared at Connor in a daze. The only words I could muster up were, "What are you doing here? I thought you were in Chicago?"

He looked at me and pulled me into him, holding my head against his chest as Justin escorted Phil out of the penthouse. Detective James walked over to me and asked if I was okay. I nodded my head as I looked at him.

"You can relax now, Mrs. Black. He won't be bothering you anymore."

Connor led me over to the couch and continued to hold me. "Baby, I'm so sorry he did this to you," he kept saying as he kissed my head. "Why didn't you tell Justin you left your art studio?"

"I was going to, but he wasn't there," I said, still shaking.

I lifted my head from his chest and looked at him as I began to calm down. "How did you know I was in my studio?" I asked.

Connor stared at me and started to speak with apprehension. "There never was a business trip."

"What?" I said in confusion. "I need a drink."

Connor got up from the couch and walked over to the bar. He took out a glass and poured some whiskey in it. He couldn't hand it to me fast enough as I grabbed the glass from his hands and threw it back, letting the soothing burn take over my body.

"I found out Phil was the one responsible for sending you

the messages. That night he came over to have me sign those papers, he was acting strangely, and I could tell by the way he was looking at you and watching you, something wasn't right. The next morning, I had Paul do some investigating, and he found the phone Phil used to send you the messages. Apparently, he bought it and had it activated in Chicago so it couldn't be traced here to New York. I called Detective James and showed him the evidence. He said it wasn't enough to put him away for a long time, and if he physically tried to harm you, he'd go away for many, many years. So, we came up with this plan to get him here alone with you, knowing he'd try something. But it wasn't supposed to get as far as it did, Ellery, and I'm so sorry."

As I sat there and listened to how Connor and Detective James set this up, tears started pouring from my eyes. "Why didn't you tell me or warn me?" I asked.

"Baby, please, don't cry," he said as he sat down and grabbed my hand.

I pulled away and got up from the couch. "Don't touch me."

"I couldn't tell you because if you knew, you would have acted differently, and we couldn't run the risk of him catching on. It was bad enough he was suspicious of the emergency Chicago trip and that he wasn't going."

"So you were just going to let him rape me?" I screamed.

Connor got up and started to walk towards me. "NO! I wasn't. How the hell could you say that?"

"Because he damn well got close enough! What the fuck, Connor? You didn't think I deserved to know what the hell you and your boys were planning. This is my life, my fucking life, and you should've included me," I screamed as I broke down and fell to my knees.

"Ellery, please try to understand," he said as he kneeled down in front of me.

"Understand what?!" I screamed. "I need time away from you so I can think."

"Don't say that, Ellery. Please, don't say that," he begged as a tear fell from his eye.

I got up from the floor and wiped my eyes. "You keep things from me, even though you promise you won't. I need time away from you because if I don't get it, I *will* hurt you."

"Baby, please!" he yelled as I tore up the stairs.

I slammed the bedroom door shut and locked it. I took a suitcase from the closet and started throwing some clothes in it. When I was packed, I called a cab and took my suitcase downstairs. Connor was sitting on the couch with his face buried in his hands. When he heard me, he looked up.

"I'm going to the beach house, and I'm taking Julia with me. Do not, and I repeat, do not come there. This marriage is hanging by a thread right now and, if you come there, I can promise you that it will be over. I need time."

"How much time do you want?" he asked.

"I don't know. I just don't know," I said as the tears wouldn't stop flowing and I walked out the door.

Chapter 36

Connor

The door shut and, just like that, she was gone. I walked over to the bar to get a drink. I picked up the glass and threw it against the wall. I grabbed the bottle of whiskey and took it upstairs. Whiskey wasn't my drink of choice, but it was right in front of me. I reached the top of the stairs and stepped inside Julia's room. As I looked around, tears started falling from my eyes at the thought that I wouldn't see her for a while. In an instant, my life had unraveled right before my eyes because of my stupidity. I sometimes questioned how the hell I was the CEO of a billion-dollar company. This was not how I planned for things to turn out. Ellery didn't even know that I called Peyton and told her not to come over. She'd find out soon enough after she called her.

I lay down on the bed and replayed the night over and over again as I brought the bottle of whiskey to my mouth. I wasn't going to let Phil hurt Ellery in any way, but Justin slipped up when he let her leave the penthouse. I grabbed my phone and looked at it, hoping she'd left me a message of some sort. But she hadn't. I wanted to know how much time she wanted and needed because I couldn't give her time. She was my wife and the mother of my child, and I wanted them back home. As I drank the last drop of whiskey, I threw the bottle across the room and watched it shatter as it hit the dresser. As the effects of the alcohol clouded my thinking, I felt myself slipping backwards to a time I never wanted to remember.

The nightmare of what happened jolted me awake. I looked over at the time and it was five o'clock in the morning. My head was pounding and my skin was drenched with sweat. I grabbed my phone from the nightstand and prayed Ellery had either called or messaged me. She hadn't. The ache in my heart was back with a vengeance as it screamed in agony. I rolled over and fell back asleep.

* * * *

"What the fuck is going on?!" Peyton's high-pitched voice startled me from an alcohol-induced sleep.

"Jesus Christ, Peyton, this is my bedroom. Get out!"

"I'm not going anywhere, buddy. Are you hung over? You look like shit!"

The last thing I needed right now was Peyton. I stumbled out of bed and walked into the bathroom. "If you don't mind, I need to take a shower."

"Go ahead, but I'll be downstairs making you a pot of coffee, and then we're going to have a little talk."

I stood in the shower and let the hot water beat down on my body. As I put my hands up against the shower wall and closed my eyes, thoughts of Ellery and Julia consumed me. I stepped out, got dressed, and headed downstairs for some much-needed coffee. Peyton had a cup poured and sitting on the table across from her.

"Sit down, now!" Peyton commanded.

"Can I get some aspirin first?" I asked as I shot her a look. "Have you talked to her?"

"Of course I talked to her, and I was with her last night as she was crying her eyes out at Mason's place. "What the fuck were you thinking?"

"It was the only way to trap him and stop this nightmare. I was afraid that if Ellery knew, she would give something away and he would get suspicious. It just wasn't a chance I could take."

"So, to end your nightmare, you created another one for Ellery. Am I right?"

I took two aspirin from the bottle and chased them down with a bottle of water. I sat at the table and glared at Peyton.

"No, you're not right. To end one nightmare, I created two more. My nightmare and Ellery's nightmare. And I have no clue how to end it."

"Leave her alone, that's how you can end it. She'll come to you when she's had time to think about everything. I know you'll go crazy, so I'll text you to let you know how she's doing, even though you don't deserve to know."

"Thank you, Peyton. I owe you big time."

"That's right, you do. In fact, I believe I've done this quite a few times. You owe me, Connor Black." She smiled.

Peyton got up from the chair, walked over to me, and kissed my head. "You seriously need to sit and think about how you're never going to keep anything from Ellery again. Because next time, you may not be so lucky, and she'll leave your dumb ass for good."

As I sat in the chair and finished my coffee, I stared out the window. The clouds were starting to roll in and a storm looked like it was brewing, much like the storm that blew through my life last night. I needed to get to the office and keep my mind off of Ellery, but I missed her and Julia so much. I picked up my phone and sent Ellery a text message.

"I know you said not to contact you, but Julia is my

daughter too, and I want to see her. It's not fair that you took her away and won't let me see her."

About twenty minutes later, she replied.

"You're right. I'll send Julia to the penthouse with Mason tomorrow and then you are to send her back the next day."

I didn't respond because I would've told her that our child wasn't a ping-pong ball, and she didn't deserve to be bounced around like that. At least she was letting me see Julia and that was more than I thought she'd do. I would give her the space she wanted, even if it ended up killing me.

* * * *

The days were long and the nights were longer. I hadn't spoken to Ellery in over a week, and every day, another piece of my soul died. Mason dropped off Julia a couple of times, and Peyton had been keeping me informed about Ellery. I had to keep the rumors at bay about Phil and tell everyone that he decided to leave Black Enterprises for personal reasons. I paid Detective James a great deal of money to keep all this quiet, and I made a huge donation to the New York City Police Department. After working all day and into the evening, I would go home and drink myself to sleep. Peyton told me that Ellery was okay, but that she was sad all the time. It killed me to hear that because I was the cause of her sadness and pain, and I didn't think I'd ever forgive myself for what I'd done to her.

I finished up everything that needed to be done at the office, so I got in the Range Rover and started driving. While I was stopped at a light, I looked to my right and saw a place that I hadn't thought about in a very long time, Club S. I didn't want to go home, so I decided to stop in there and have a drink. The club was hopping, the music was loud, and there were wall-to-wall people. I walked back by the bar and saw there was an open table. I sat down and was immediately greeted by a waitress.

"What can I get you?" she asked.

"Give me a scotch, make it a double, and bring me three."

"You got it, sweetie." She smiled as she walked away.

While I sat in my seat, I looked around at the area that I had frequently visited before I met Ellery. The waitress came back and set the three glasses down in front of me. I drank them and wanted more, so I signaled for her to get me three more. As I was downing the fifth glass of scotch, I heard a familiar voice.

"Well, well, well, if it isn't Connor Black."

I looked over to the side as she sat down next to me. "Hello, Sarah."

"What the hell are you doing here? Where's Ellery?"

"She left me and took Julia with her," I said as I leaned back.

"What? That's crazy. What did you do to make her leave?"

"She thinks I put her life in danger because I didn't tell her something. Fuck, maybe I did. I don't know anymore," I said as I threw back my last glass of scotch. "I thought I was doing the right thing. Maybe I was or I wasn't. The only thing that mattered was Ellery thought otherwise and she left me for it."

Sarah put her hand on top of mine, and I looked at her. "We had some good times, you and I. There was even a moment once when I thought maybe we could become something, even though it would be breaking your rules. Then Ellery walked into your life, and you instantly changed. I'd never seen anyone change as fast as you did. All those years, you were never the person you were meant to be until you met her. You're a good man, Connor, and this is only temporary. I don't know Ellery that well, but from what I do know, and from what I've seen, she's a forgiving person and she'll come around. Just give her some time," she said as she got up and hugged me. "I'm with someone here, so I need to go and find them."

I hoped Sarah was right and that Ellery would be back soon, but until then, I drank my sadness away. I lifted my hand as I saw my waitress walk by. "Bring me three more doubles," I yelled over the loud music.

Chapter 37

Ellery

The house felt empty without Connor. I heard Julia cry, so I walked upstairs to get her from her crib. It had been over a week since I'd seen or talked to Connor. Every second and every minute of each day was killing me slowly. As I took Julia from her crib, she looked at me and smiled. I bundled her up in her jacket and took her down by the water just as the sun was getting ready to set.

"Listen carefully, Julia, and you'll be able to hear the whispers of the ocean."

The soothing sound of the waves lapping against the shoreline made me think of the special times I was with Connor at the beach. My mind traveled back to when Connor proposed to me in California. When I first told him about my past after the autism charity, and when I ran to the beach in the middle of the night before I got the final results of my last treatment. But the most special memory was when Connor asked me to marry him. The ocean held so many memories for me, not only with Connor, but with my mom. The sun was starting to set and, as I pointed to it, I told Julia to look up.

"The sun setting over the ocean will be one of the most beautiful things you'll ever see. Your daddy proposed to me on the beach, just as the sun was setting. He made sure everything was perfect." I smiled.

Julia screeched and then looked at me and put her hand on my face. She knew I was sad, and I could tell how much she missed Connor. I sat down with her and let her run her hands through the sand. The beach, the ocean, and the sunset, would become as special to her as it was to me.

"He misses you, and he's not doing good," I heard a voice say behind me.

I turned around and saw Denny standing a few feet away from us. I smiled and held out my hand for him to sit next to me.

"What are you doing here? Should you even be here?" I asked as I kissed him on the cheek.

"I'm fine. Dana drove. She's in the house, talking to Mason. I don't want to talk about me. How are you doing?"

"I'm okay," I said as I looked out into the ocean water.

"No, you're not. I know you, Ellery, and you miss him just as much as he misses you."

"I'm so mad at him, Denny. How could he do that to me? How many times do I have to tell him not to keep things from me before it sinks into that thick head of his?"

Denny smiled at me and then looked at Julia. "Sometimes, we don't always make the right decisions under pressure and stress. Need I remind you of a few times you didn't make the right decisions where Connor was concerned?"

I laughed and shook my head. "That was different and we weren't married."

"You may not have been married, but you were a couple and you loved him. Listen to me, Connor is Connor, and he always will be. It's how he's wired. His love for you is so powerful that it clouds his judgment sometimes. The only thing he saw when he made the decision not to tell you about

Phil was keeping you safe."

"You're always defending him," I said as I looked over at him.

"Not always. I had a talk with him too. Believe me, I yelled at him and pretty much called him every name in the book. I think he got my point. The two of you can't even be apart for one night, let alone an entire week. Everyone makes mistakes, Ellery."

I glared at him with knitted eyebrows. "Okay, some more than others." He smiled. "Should I remind you about how you lied to Connor and went and saw Ashlyn?"

"Just another thing he didn't tell me," I said as I rolled my eyes.

"And for a good reason. You could have gotten yourself killed. You know that girl is crazy," he said.

It was getting chilly and the winds were starting to pick up. "Let's go inside." I smiled as I picked Julia up and looped my arm around Denny's.

As soon as we walked inside, Dana came over and took Julia from me. "Why don't the two of you stay here tonight and then we can all head back in the morning?" I said.

"You're going back home?" Denny asked.

"Yeah, I think it's about time, and Connor and I need to sit down and have a serious talk."

After I put Julia to bed, the four of us sat around the table and talked. It was eleven o'clock p.m. and my phone started to ring. I looked over and saw it was Connor calling. I wasn't ready to talk to him yet, so I rejected it. A minute later, my phone rang, and it was him again.

"Connor, what do you want?"

"Hi, Ellery, this is Sarah."

I froze as I held the phone up to my ear and my heart started racing with the thought that he was with her.

"I know what you must be thinking right now, and this isn't what it seems. I took Connor's phone to call you because he's here at Club S, a drunken mess, and you need to come get him."

"What the hell is he doing there?" I asked.

"I'm assuming he came in to drink his troubles away. Listen, I'll wait with him until you get here."

"Thank you, Sarah. I'm on my way," I said as I hung up the phone.

Denny looked at me as I got up from my seat. "Now what?"

"Connor is drunk at Club S, and Sarah told me that I need to come get him."

"Do you want me to go and bring his sorry ass home?" Denny said.

"No, I'll go." I picked up the phone and called a cab. "Mason, can you pack up all of Julia's things and bring her home tomorrow? I don't want to wake her up."

"Of course I will," he said as he walked over to me. "Go get your man and spend some time alone. We'll be fine."

* * * *

As I got out of the cab, I stood in front of Club S as the line of people waited impatiently to get into the now famous club. I walked up to the front and stood behind the rope as I called Frankie's name.

"Ellery Black! How are you, girl?" he said.

"I'm good, Frankie. It's nice to see you."

"What are you doing here?"

"Connor's inside and someone called me to come get him."

Frankie lifted the rope. "Go on in, Elle. It was good to see you. If you need my help, come get me."

"Thanks, Frankie. It was good to see you too." I smiled.

The music was loud and people were everywhere. As I pushed my way through the crowd, I headed towards the bar. While I stood there looking around, I felt someone tap me on the shoulder. I turned around and saw Sarah standing there.

"Where is he?" I asked.

"He's over there," Sarah said as she pointed to a table in the corner.

Instantly, I started to have flashbacks of the night when I first saw him. I took in a deep breath and started walking towards him. Sarah grabbed my arm.

"Don't be too hard on him. He's full of regret, and he's sorry."

"So he told you what happened?"

"Not all of it, but I know he messed up. I've never seen love like I do when I see the two of you. It's romantic, and I'm envious of what the two of you have. I didn't think a love like that existed."

"Thank you for keeping an eye on him. I appreciate it." I smiled.

"No problem, Ellery," she said as she walked away.

I stood there and stared at him from across the way. He could barely sit up. After being apart for a week, this wasn't the way I wanted to see him. As I took in another breath, I walked over to him, sat down, and took the glass out of his hand.

"Ellery," he slurred.

"Come on, Connor. It's time to go home," I said as I helped him up.

"Are you coming too," he slurred.

"Yes, I'm coming home. Now let's get out of here."

He put his arm around me as I held him up and helped him to the door. He could barely walk and he was stumbling so badly that he almost took me down. We reached the doors and stepped outside. The cab was parked at the curb. I opened the cab door and tried to help him in.

"Get in the cab, Connor."

"I want to talk first. I don't want to get in the cab."

"Get in the cab, Connor," I said a second time as I pushed him in.

He wouldn't slide over, so I shut the door, got in the other side, and gave the cab driver our address. Connor looked over at me. All I could see was the sadness in his eyes. I was really pissed off that he went to the club, but that was an issue we'd deal with later.

"You're so beautiful," he said as he ran his hand down my cheek.

"You're so drunk," I replied.

He leaned his head on my shoulder, but he kept falling forward. I brought his head down to my lap and softly stroked his hair as he closed his eyes. Shortly after, we arrived in the garage of the penthouse.

"Do you need help getting him out, ma'am?" the cab driver asked.

"I think I can manage," I replied as I handed him a large tip.

"Thank you so much, ma'am!" he said with excitement.

"Thank you for your patience." I smiled.

I sat Connor up and told him to stay there while I walked around to the other side. I opened the door, grabbed his arm and helped him out. He stumbled and it took every bit of strength I had to hold him up and not fall.

"Isn't this a familiar scene?" I said to him as I walked him to the elevator.

I leaned him up against the wall while we waited for the doors to open. His eyes never left mine.

"I want to fuck you so bad," he said.

"Not tonight, baby," I said as the elevator doors opened and I helped him inside.

When we arrived to the penthouse, I helped him off the elevator and tried to get him up the stairs. He kept tripping over the steps and falling.

"Connor, you have to help me out here."

I helped him climb up the stairs on his hands since he was way too drunk to walk up them. As soon as he made it to the top step, I stood him up and helped him to our bedroom. "Are you going to be sick?" I asked.

"Yeah," he said as he nodded his head.

"Hurry and get to the bathroom!" I exclaimed as I pushed him.

He made it to the bathroom just in time, and he started vomiting in the toilet. I left him there, went into the bedroom, and turned down the bed. When I went back into the bathroom, he was lying on the floor. I shook my head and sighed as I ran a washcloth under warm water and put it on his head.

"Come on; you need to get in bed," I said as I sat him up.

"I'm sorry for everything, Ellery. I wouldn't blame you if you left me and never wanted to see me again."

"I'm not going to leave you, Connor. Please give me some help here, so you can go to bed. You need to sleep the alcohol off."

As he was sitting up on the bathroom floor, I lifted his shirt off and helped him up. With my help, he made it to the bed and fell back on it. As I unbuttoned his pants and started to pull them down, he grabbed my hands.

"I love you so much," he slurred.

"I know you do, and I love you too. Now, lift your ass up and help me get your pants off."

Once I had him stripped down to his boxers, I told him to turn around and lie down on his pillow.

"Now, remember to lie on your side," I said as I covered him with the sheet and wiped his forehead with the cloth one last time before he closed his eyes.

As I sighed, I got up from the bed and changed into my pajamas. I washed my face, put my hair in a ponytail, and lay down next to him, watching to make sure he stayed on his side.

* * * *

I opened my eyes and looked at the clock. It was nine o'clock a.m. already, and I couldn't believe I'd slept that late. I rolled over and Connor was still sound asleep. I got out of bed, washed my face, brushed my teeth, and headed to the kitchen to start a pot of coffee. As much as Connor hated my hangover cocktail, he was going to need it desperately when he woke up. I gathered the ingredients and put them in the blender. I was pouring myself a cup of coffee when I heard someone clear his throat from behind me. I slowly turned around and stared at Connor as he leaned up against the wall with his arms folded.

"Didn't I go over the rules with you last night?" he asked.

I couldn't help but smile as I bit down on my bottom lip.

"Come here, baby," he said as he held out his arms.

I walked over to him and wrapped my arms around him as tightly as I could.

"I'm so sorry. Please tell me you forgive me," he begged as he buried his face deep into my neck.

"I forgive you, but we need to talk," I said.

"I know, and I'll do anything to make things right. I love you, and I missed you so much."

I broke our embrace and placed my hands on his face. "I missed you too," I said as I kissed him. "Come sit down and have some coffee and the hangover cocktail I just made."

"You know I hate that stuff, Elle."

"I know you do, but it works and you have to be feeling pretty lousy right now."

"I am," he said as he rubbed his head.

I picked up the glass with the cocktail in it and sat down on his lap. He wrapped his arms around me as I brought the glass to his lips. "Drink." I smiled.

He looked at me, made a face, and took a sip as I tilted the glass. He took it from my hand and chugged it down as fast as he could, then placed the glass on the counter.

"Where's Julia?" he asked.

"She's at the house with Mason. He's going to pack her stuff up and bring her home later."

"Let's go sit on the couch," he said.

We sat on the couch, and I snuggled up against him as he put his arm around me. "Do you remember anything about last night?" I asked.

"Not really. How did you know I was at the club?"

"Sarah used your phone to call me."

"Oh," he said as he looked away.

"It's okay, Connor. She kept an eye on you until I got there. She's a good person. I've misjudged her."

"She is a good person, but don't be going and becoming best friends with her."

I smiled as I stroked his chest. "I wouldn't do that."

When I lifted my head and stared up at him, he brought his mouth down to mine. His kiss was soft and gentle. I've missed his mouth, his kisses, everything, and my body was begging for him. I sat up and straddled him. His small smile grew bigger as he stroked my hair. I brought my lips to his and kissed him with such passion that it made my toes curl. After we made love the second time, Connor called Mason and told him not to bring Julia home because we were coming out to the beach house to stay for a while.

"We're staying at the house? For how long?" I asked.

"I don't know. We can stay for as long as you want."

"What about Black Enterprises? You don't have a VP to help out."

"My dad is going to come out of retirement while I take some time off to spend with my wife and daughter." He smiled.

I smiled back as I kissed him. I wanted nothing more than to have him all to myself for a while. "Thank you," I said.

Connor's hand swept across my cheek. "You're the light in

my life and when you're not around, my world is dark. I will never do anything to jeopardize our relationship again. I make this promise to you, Ellery Black, that from this day forward, I will never keep anything from you. You have my word, baby. I promise forever."

Chapter 38

Connor

It was Julia's first birthday and party today. We'd spent the last two months at the house. I worked from home and occasionally went into the office. My dad had done an excellent job taking over as vice president, but did warn me to find someone quickly because he needed to go back into retirement. Caterers had been in and out of the house all day, preparing for Julia's party. She had just started walking and took her first steps to me. Her first word was "dada" and Ellery was not happy with that.

As I looked around the house at all the balloons that were hanging everywhere, I walked up to Julia's room, where Ellery was getting her ready for the party. The minute she saw me, she said, "Dada" and smiled. As soon as Ellery put her princess dress on her, Julia walked over to me and hugged my legs.

"Can you keep an eye on her while I go and get ready?" she asked.

"Of course I can," I said as I picked up Julia.

I took her out of the room and went downstairs. She smiled and pointed when she saw the balloons.

"Those are for you," I said as I kissed her cheek.

She looked at me and then screamed to hold one. I took one

out of the bunch and gave it to her. She smiled as her hand wrapped around the ribbon that was tied to the balloon. She babbled on as she put her hand in her mouth and looked up at the balloon she was holding. I love my little girl so much. Ellery was my queen and Julia was my princess, and nothing would ever change that.

Guests had started to arrive and the party was underway. We had a total of one hundred people show up to help celebrate Julia's first birthday. It was a day of fun, laughter, and good times with friends and family. Ellery even went to the extreme and invited Sarah. She came with her boyfriend, and they both seemed really happy. Cassidy and Ben were still dating and he confided in me that he was going to ask Cassidy to marry him. Denny had some aggressive chemo treatments for a month and was in remission and doing well.

Julia was exhausted by time the party ended and she was getting cranky. After the last of the guests left, Ellery and I took Julia upstairs and put her in the bathtub. When her bath was finished, Ellery put Julia in her pajamas, we both kissed her cheeks, and then Ellery laid her down in her crib. I held out my hand to Ellery and she took it as we walked out of Julia's room, shutting the door behind us. We both stood outside the door for a moment to make sure she didn't scream. The caterers and cleanup crew were cleaning the house, so I took Ellery outside and down to the beach.

"That was a great party." I said as we sat down in the sand.

"Thanks, honey. It was, wasn't it?" She smiled.

I brought her hand to my lips and kissed it as we looked ahead at the ocean water. "Now that we're alone, there's something I need to tell you," Ellery said.

"What is it, sweetheart?" I asked as I looked at her.

She turned to face me and took my hands in hers. With a

big smile, she placed my hands on her stomach. "We're going to have another baby!"

I sat and looked at her shock. "What? Are you sure? When did you find out?"

"I found out this morning. I wanted to tell you right away, but with all the people in and out, getting the house ready for the party, and then the guests arriving, I figured it would be better to wait until we were alone."

The joy that shot through me was incredible. I was so happy that Ellery was pregnant again and I wanted to shout it from the rooftops. I cupped her face in my hands and I kissed her lips.

"I'm so incredibly happy. Tell me you're happy, baby?"

"I'm so happy. Maybe this one will be a boy." She smiled as she rubbed her tummy.

"It is a boy. Aunt Sadie said so, remember?"

We laughed and hugged each other tight. I got up and held out my hand. Ellery placed her hand in mine as I took her into the house and straight up to our bedroom to celebrate the news.

* * * *

The next eight months passed by so quickly. It seemed like it was only yesterday that Ellery told me she was pregnant. She was scheduled for a C-Section tomorrow morning. We found out through the ultrasound that we were having a baby boy. I was elated at the news that we would have a boy to carry on the Black name and hopefully, someday, take over Black Enterprises. Julia was growing fast and becoming, what Mason liked to call her, a diva. But she was still my little princess and she had me wrapped around her little finger.

After I put Julia to bed, I walked into our bedroom, where

Ellery was sitting sketching on her sketchpad. The Chicago building was finally up and running and the Art Gallery was doing very well. I took off my shirt and pants, put on my pajama bottoms, grabbed my laptop, and sat on the bed next to Ellery. I leaned over and kissed her on the cheek. She turned to me and smiled.

"I need to talk to you."

"About what, baby?" I asked as I opened up my laptop.

"I know we talked about a couple of boys' names, but I've already decided on one for this child."

"Is that so? You decided on a name without consulting me?"

"Yes. Does that really surprise you?" She smiled.

"No, it doesn't. What did you come up with?"

"I want to name our son Collin, after your twin brother."

As I put my hand on her large belly, I smiled at her. "I would love to call my son Collin. Thank you, sweetheart," I said as I kissed her.

"Good, I'm glad you're on board with it. I really wasn't sure how'd you feel about it."

"Collin would be honored to have his nephew named after him."

Ellery smiled and went back to her sketch pad. I answered some emails and read some articles.

"By the way, how's Ben doing?" she asked.

"Ben's doing good. He's settled in his office, and he's buried up to his neck in legal bullshit."

"I think it's great that you hired him, and I know Cassidy is happy."

"He's a great lawyer. He's marrying my sister, and he'll be

at all the family functions. How could I not hire him?" I winked.

"Just think, this time tomorrow, we'll have our second child. I never thought I'd have one child, let alone two," Ellery said.

"Me neither, baby. I never saw kids in my future, until I met you." I smiled as I looked over at her. She looked so tired. I pushed her hair behind her ear and ran the back of my hand across her cheek. "Why don't you put your sketch pad away and get some sleep. You look tired."

"I am tired. It's been a long day," she said as she closed her sketch pad and set it on the nightstand. She leaned over and gave me a kiss on the lips. "I love you."

"I love you too." I smiled.

It hadn't even been five minutes and Ellery was sound asleep. I was thirsty, so I got out of bed and headed downstairs for a bottle of water. On my way back up, I stopped into the spare bedroom that we had turned into a nursery. I flipped the light switch and looked around. The painted ocean blue walls with colorful fish, coral, and seaweed made you feel like you were standing in the bottom of the ocean. The turtles Ellery had painted on the wall were amazing, as were the stars up above on the ceiling. She spent three months painting the room and she just finished putting the final touches on it yesterday. I smiled at the thought that come tomorrow, I'd have a son, and we'd finally be a family of four.

Chapter 39

Ellery

Six years later...

We took the kids out to dinner before heading over to FAO Schwarz. Christmas was in three weeks and the kids were excited to see Santa Claus. We sat in the restaurant, waiting for our food. Julia was sitting next to Connor, and Collin was sitting next to me. Both kids were coloring a picture. Julia kept looking at the group of women who were at the next table. They kept looking over at Connor. I noticed her looking at them, but I didn't say anything. The waitress walked over and set our food down in front of us.

"Julia, eat your chicken fingers," Connor said.

"I will, Daddy, don't worry," she responded as she kept looking at the table next to us.

I knew those women were staring at my husband and, after all these years, I still had a problem with it. But I'd toned it down, and I didn't embarrass Connor as much. Out of the clear blue, Julia looked at Connor.

"Daddy, those women keep staring at you and that's rude."

I almost choked on my salad as I started to laugh. Connor looked at me with wide eyes.

"I know, Julia. Don't worry about it. Just finish your

dinner," he said.

"Mommy, why do they keep staring over here?"

"They keep staring because they think your daddy is very handsome. Now, finish your dinner so we can go see Santa Claus."

Julia smiled as she ate her chicken. Collin was being a good boy and eating his dinner because he was excited to go to the toy store. As we finished eating, the waitress brought our bill and Connor paid. When we got out of the booth, I took Collin's hand and Connor grabbed Julia's. As we were leaving, I instantly froze when I heard Julia speak.

"Hasn't anyone ever told you that staring is rude?" Julia said to the women at the table next to us.

I heard Connor apologizing to them as I smiled and kept walking. When we stepped outside the restaurant, Connor stopped and looked at me.

"Did you hear what your daughter said back there?"

"Yes." I laughed.

"It isn't funny, Ellery. She embarrassed me. Now I have to worry about her too?"

I kissed Connor on the lips. "Yeah, I guess you do," I said as I patted his chest.

"Aren't you going to say anything to her?" he whispered.

"Why don't you?" I asked.

When we were walking down the street to FAO Schwarz, Connor stopped and bent down so he was eye level with Julia. "Julia, what you did back at the restaurant embarrassed Daddy, and I don't want you to do that ever again. Okay?"

"Why, Daddy? Mommy and Aunt Peyton say things to people all the time if they are doing something rude."

Connor shot me a look and I couldn't help but laugh. He stood up, took her hand, and growled at me. "Great, she's just like you."

"Aw, you love it. She's protecting her daddy." I smiled as I hooked my arm around his.

We entered through the doors of FAO Schwarz and the kids were in Heaven. The first thing we did was get in line to see Santa. The line wasn't too long, and all the Christmas decorations and animated people keep the kids occupied. Connor put his arm around me and kissed my head. I smiled as I rested my head on his shoulder. Julia and Collin got along great. She was protective of her brother and stuck up for him, even with us. It was finally our turn and both kids went and sat on Santa's lap.

"What do you want for Christmas?" he asked Collin.

"I want a bike and a train set," he said.

"And what about you, pretty girl?" Santa asked Julia.

"I want an easel and paints, so I can paint beautiful pictures like my mommy. Oh, and I want new Barbies and a baby doll, but it has to be the one that goes potty and comes with diapers and a bottle and really cute clothes. I want jewelry so I can sparkle like a princess. I want this really cool four-story dollhouse with all the furniture and the family of four."

"My, oh my, you sure want a lot of things," Santa said.

"Of course I do, Santa. It's Christmas, and my daddy said I can have anything I want. So I want all that." Julia smiled as she got off his lap. She started walking way, stopped, and turned around. "Oh Santa, I also want an iPad. The 128GB in white with a Hello Kitty case." She smiled.

I looked at Connor. "What?" he asked.

"And you blame me," I said.

He laughed as we walked over and took the kids' hands.

"That's a pretty long list of things, Julia," Connor said.

"Not really, Daddy. There's more. I'll give you my complete Christmas list when we get home. I've been adding to it for months."

Connor shook his head and looked at me. I guess I was going to have to have a little talk with Julia on what Christmas was really about. When we reached the big piano, Collin and Julia ran to it as fast as they could. The piano was their favorite part of the store. Connor and I stood back and watched as our two beautiful children played on it.

"Standing here, like this, I feel like I'm watching me and Cassidy," Connor said.

"It's amazing how fast time flies."

"I bought it," Connor said as he looked at me.

"Bought what?" I asked.

"The big piano. I bought it for them for Christmas. That way we could all play on it, together as a family." He smiled.

I stood there and shook my head. "What?" he asked.

"I bought one too."

Connor pulled me into him and kissed my head. "Great minds think alike, baby. That's okay; we'll keep one at the penthouse and one at the beach house."

* * * *

Christmas had come and gone and, before we knew it, summer had arrived and the kids were out of school. We spent most of our time at the beach house. I was sitting down at the beach with my arms wrapped around my legs, when Julia came up to me.

"Mommy, Daddy's being mean and won't let me have any

ice cream."

"We're going to be eating dinner soon. So I agree with your daddy. No ice cream until after dinner." I smiled as I tapped her on the nose.

"Why are you just sitting here like this? Are you sad?"

"I was just thinking about my mom and how we would spend time at the beach."

"She's dead, right?"

"Yes, Julia. She died when I was a little girl."

"I'm sorry, Mommy," she said as she put her little arm around me. I'm glad you're not dead."

"So am I," a voice said from behind me.

Julia got up and looked at Connor as she put her hands on her hips. "I'm not talking to you right now," she said as she stomped away.

I laughed and Connor sighed as he sat down next to me. "Please tell me it gets better," he said.

"Sorry to break the news to you, but it's only going to get worse."

"Great," he said as he put his arm around me.

Before long, Collin and Julia ran to where Connor and I were sitting. Julia ran up to Connor, threw sand at his back, and then ran away.

"Julia Rose Black, get back here!"

"Sorry, Daddy, but if you want me there, you'll have to catch me." She giggled.

Connor looked at me with a huge smile as he ran after Julia. Collin sat down next me and opened his hand.

"Look what I found." He smiled.

Inside his hand, he held a beautiful pink rock. "It's for you, Mommy, because it's pretty like you."

I took it from his hand and wrapped my arms around him. "You're my sweet boy, and I love you, Collin."

"I love you too, Mommy."

Connor caught Julia and carried her upside down back to where we were sitting. Julia was laughing while begging him to put her down. Connor set her down and kissed her cheek.

"Look, the sun is about to set," I said as I pointed out into the ocean water.

As I held Collin in my lap, Connor pulled Julia onto his and he put his arm around me as we sat there and watched the sunset over the ocean water as a family.

Epilogue

"Look at you," I said as I walked through the door.

"Hi, Dad." Julia smiled as she turned around and looked at me.

I took in a deep breath as I shook my head. "You're so beautiful, Julia. You look just like your mother did on our wedding day. Where did the years go? My little princess is all grown up and getting married," I said as my eyes started to swell with tears.

"Daddy, don't. You're going to make my mascara run and then Uncle Mason will kill you."

"You're right, and we can't have that." I smiled.

"I can't believe I'm getting married. The last year of planning went by so fast."

"Life goes by so fast. Just twenty-three short years ago, I was holding you in my arms for the first time. Now, before you know it, you'll be making me a grandpa."

"Not for a while, Dad." She laughed.

I took in a deep breath and took her hands in mine. "I guess now is as good a time as any to have a little talk with you."

"Dad, if you're going to make me cry, please let's save it until after the wedding."

"You're my little girl and you always will be. No matter how old you are, you'll always be my angel. Today, I'll be giving you away to your husband and as much as I like Jake, it's still hard. Your mother brought light into my dark world and, the day you were born, you made it brighter. I want you to know that."

"Daddy," Julia said as she put one hand on my chest. "You have been the best dad any girl could ask for. You gave me everything I needed to be comfortable, you loved me even when I didn't deserve it, and you taught me about life. You and Mom gave me the best childhood I could ever ask for, and you showed me what love was. The love that the two of you share and give is amazing and, thanks to you, I found that love with Jake."

"I know you did, and I know how much he loves you. I can see it when he looks at you, and I'm proud to call him my son-in law."

"He told me you told him that." She smiled.

"He did?"

"Yes, after you took him out to dinner the other night to have your little talk."

As I smiled at my little girl, the door opened, and Ellery walked in.

"Please tell me your dad isn't making you cry?"

"Nah, we're just having a little father-daughter talk," I said.

"Which results in tears," Ellery said as she looked at Julia.

Julia laughed and turned around and looked in the mirror. Collin walked in and told me he needed help with his tuxedo. As I started to walk out the door, Julia called my name.

"I love you, Dad." She smiled.

"I love you too, baby." I smiled back as I walked out of the room.

* * * *

After I helped Collin with the cufflinks on his tuxedo, I walked into the bedroom and sat down on the bed. A few moments later, Ellery walked in.

"Are you okay, Connor?"

"I'm fine," I said as I got up and fixed my bowtie in the mirror.

"You're really having a hard time with Julia getting married, aren't you?"

"Just a little bit, and it's not like I'm not happy for her, because I am. I love Jake like a son and I know he'll take good care of her, but it's hard to let her go. It seems like it was only yesterday that she was sitting on the floor, playing with her toys."

Ellery wrapped her arms around me and held me tight. "I know it's hard, sweetheart. But you act like you'll never see her again. You bought two apartments one floor down, and had them converted into one big apartment, and she works at Black Enterprises. You'll see her every day."

She was right. I would see her every day. I broke our embrace and looked at my beautiful wife. "Have I told you today how absolutely gorgeous you look?" I smiled.

"You have, but I won't complain if you want to tell me again."

I put my hands on her hips and leaned in closer as my lips brushed against her exposed neck. "You're stunning and elegant, and I want to do very bad things with you," I whispered.

Ellery gasped as she tilted her head and allowed me better access. "As much as I want you to do bad things to me, we have to leave now; the limos are waiting for us." I looked at my watch and saw that she was right. It was time to get our little bride to her groom.

The wedding was taking place in the Conservatory Gardens in Central Park; the exact same spot where Ellery and I got married. No expense was spared for this wedding. It had become the event of the year. We couldn't have asked for a more perfect day. There wasn't a cloud in the sky and the sun was shining brightly. As we pulled up to the Vanderbilt Gates, Ellery kissed me on the cheek and told me she'd see me in a while. I looked out the window at the guests that were already seated and waiting for the ceremony to start.

"Are you ready, sweetheart?" I asked Julia as she sat across from me.

"Yeah, Dad, I'm as ready as I'll ever be." She smiled.

The driver opened the door. I stepped out of the limo and held out my hand, helping Julia from her seat. I led her to the entrance of the gates, and we stood on the edge of the white runner.

"You better not cry," Julia said as she looked at me.

"*You* better not cry." I smiled.

"Mom's going to cry, you know."

"I know she will. She was trying to be strong earlier, but when she sees you walking down the aisle, she'll break down."

"I caught her crying this morning, but she doesn't know that I saw her, so please don't tell her."

The band started to play the "Wedding March" and that was our cue to start walking down the aisle. "Here we go. Are you sure you want to go through with this?" I asked.

"Daddy, stop it. Of course I want to."

With Julia's arm wrapped around mine, I walked my baby

girl down the aisle. Jake was grinning from ear to ear. As I looked over at Ellery, I saw a tear fall from her eye. When we reached the end of the aisle, I placed Julia's hand in Jake's, kissed her on the cheek, and then wiped the single tear that fell from her eye. I took my seat next to Ellery and held her hand. She was trying so hard to hold back the rest of the tears that wanted to fall. I leaned in closer to her and whispered, "Remember your makeup. We have pictures to take after the ceremony."

She nodded her head as we sat there and watched our daughter get married.

* * * *

The reception was held at the Waldorf Astoria Hotel; the same place where Ellery and I had our reception. We arrived before Julia, Jake, and the wedding party did. Peyton and Henry walked in a few moments after us.

"Elle, the ceremony was amazing!" Peyton said.

"Wasn't it? Just think, in a couple of years, we could be doing this again with Collin and Hailey."

I looked at Henry and put my hand on his shoulder. "Good, then it'll be your turn to pay for a wedding like this."

Henry laughed before walking over to the bar to get a drink. I walked over to the table where Denny and Dana were sitting. Both of them were having some health issues, but they wouldn't miss Julia's wedding for anything. Ellery was talking to Cassidy when I walked over and told her that Julia and Jake had arrived. The band introduced the newly married couple and then each person in the bridal party.

After an exceptional dinner, it was time for the bridal dance. Jake took Julia's hand and led her to the dance floor. You could see how much he loved her and adored her. He reminded me of myself. We had been down a bit of a rough road with Julia and a couple of her boyfriends, and Ellery and I were so thankful when she'd met Jake. Ellery stood in front of me, and I wrapped my arms around her as we watched our daughter and son in-law share their first dance as husband and wife.

"Remember our bridal dance?" Ellery asked.

"I sure do. How could I forget? I picked our perfect song."

"I know, and it was perfect. Julia and Jake remind me of us."

Their song had ended, and the song for the bridal party came on. As soon as they introduced Collin and Hailey, everyone cheered.

"Do you think they'll get married?" I asked Ellery.

"Yes. I know he loves her very much, and I wouldn't be surprised if he buys her a ring for her birthday in a few months."

"Poor kids. They don't stand a chance with you and Peyton involved."

Ellery laughed and reached behind me and smacked my ass. "You better watch it, baby. You're getting me hard," I said.

The band had called my name and asked me to step out onto the dance floor, as it was time for our father-daughter dance. I smiled as I walked to Julia and took her hand. The song had started and I began to get a little emotional.

"How are you, Mrs. Jensen?" I asked her.

"I'm great, Dad. How are you?"

"I'm okay." I smiled.

"I know I've told you this a thousand times, but thank you again for the honeymoon." She smiled.

"You're welcome, honey. Did I mention that your mom and I are going too?"

"Dad!" Julia giggled.

"Enjoy yourself, but prepare to work extra hard at the office when you get back." I winked.

"Your dance with Mom is next."

"You didn't tell her I picked out the song, did you?"

"No. I want her to be surprised. It's such a beautiful song, Dad. You're such a romantic."

Our song had ended, and I hugged Julia before taking the hand of my beautiful wife as she stepped out onto the dance floor.

"I would like to introduce to you, the bride's parents, Mr. and Mrs. Connor Black, dancing to 'Close Your Eyes,' handpicked by Mr. Black and dedicated to Mrs. Black," the singer of the band said.

Ellery placed her hand in mine and tears started to form in her eyes as she heard the song that was being sung for her.

"I want you to listen to every word, because this song is exactly how I feel about you. You're the love of my life, the light of my world, and my savior. You'll be those things to me forever," I said as I kissed her lips. "Don't cry. You'll ruin your mascara, and we have one more picture to take."

"I love you, Connor. Even after all these years, you still make my heart race, and you make me incredibly wet." Ellery smiled as she whispered in my ear.

When she said that, I couldn't help but let out a soft moan. "You wait until I get you up to the room later, Mrs. Black. Be prepared to be up all night."

"I'm counting on it, Mr. Black." She grinned from ear to ear.

Our dance had ended, and the night went on perfectly. It was time for Julia and Jake to leave because my plane was waiting to take them to Europe for their honeymoon. As we stood outside the Waldorf Astoria, Ellery, Julia, Collin, and me stood together for one last picture before Julia and Jake climbed into the limo and waved goodbye.

* * * *

The next day, Ellery and I drove to the beach house. I stood at the edge of the shoreline, looking out at the beautiful ocean water and reflected on my life. I'd been nothing but a broken man, and Ellery was nothing but a girl with an illness. Love found and saved both of us and we raised a beautiful family because of it. As I was in deep thought, Ellery walked up and put her arm around me.

"What are you doing out here?" she asked.

"I was just thinking about our life together and how proud I am of us and our children."

She smiled as she placed her hand on my chest. "We've been through a lot over the years, but we made it, and we'll continue to make it. Do you know why?" she asked.

"Why?"

Because infinity is forever, and that's what you are to me. You're my infinity, Mr. Black."

I turned to her and smiled as I traced her lips with my finger before brushing mine against them. "Forever us, baby. It'll always be forever us."

The End

Forever Us Playlist

This Woman's Work

Kate Bush

Little Wonders

Rob Thomas

Demons

Imagine Dragons

I Loved Her First

Heartland

It Won't Be Like This For Long

Darius Rucker

Close Your Eyes

Michael Buble

Butterfly Kisses

Bob Carlisle

Kryptonite

Three Doors Down

Crush

Dave Matthews Band

Hot

Avril Lavigne

Where We Came From

Phillip Phillips

About The Author

Sandi Lynn is a *New York Times* and *USA Today* bestselling author who spends all of her days writing. She published her first novel, *Forever Black* in February 2013 and by time the year ends, she will have a total of five books published. Her addictions are shopping, romance novels, coffee, chocolate, margaritas, and giving readers an escape to another world.

Please come connect with her at:

www.facebook.com/Sandi.Lynn.Author

www.twitter.com/SandilynnWriter

www.authorsandilynn.com

www.pinterest.com/sandilynnWriter

www.instagram.com/sandilynnauthor

https://www.goodreads.com/author/show/6089757.Sandi_Lynn

A Big Thank You

I'm giving a HUGE thank you to all my readers/fans who have given me the courage and strength to keep writing. Your comments and kind words you leave on my facebook fan page and twitter mean the world to me. My journey as a new author has been amazing and I have each and every one of you to thank for it. It's been filled with laughter, tears, and hard work. But most importantly, it's the friendships that have been formed, not only with amazing and wonderful authors and bloggers, but with my readers as well. I would never have made it this far without any of you! You're my inspiration and I thank you from the bottom of my heart! I hope I will get the chance to meet you at the many author events I will be attending in 2014!

xoxo

Sandi Lynn

Made in the USA
San Bernardino, CA
20 November 2013